HEAD GAMEZ

Eugene L. Weems
Timothy R. Richardson

Universal Publishing LLC

HEAD GAMEZ

For information, go to: http://www.UniversalPublishingLLC.com

May be purchased for educational, business, or sales promotional use. For information, please write: Universal Publishing, LLC
Special Markets Department
P.O. Box 99491
Emeryville, California 94662

Cover Design: Stephani Richardson
Cover Art: Eugene Weems
Editor: Terri Harper -- http://www.terristranscripts.net

ISBN: 978-0-9840456-1-7

Library of Congress Cataloguing-in-Publication Data: 2011939314

Universal Publishing, LLC

Printed in the United States of America

This book is dedicated to our mothers,
Aldine Weems and
Yvonne Aubrey-McWoodson,
without whom this book would
not have been possible.

We also dedicate this book to
All you *Ride or Die* females.
We Recognize You.

ACKNOWLEDGEMENTS

Annie Montgomery, Aldine Weems, Larae Weems, Henry Ridley, Sr., Henry Ridley, Jr., Madine Montgomery, Larry Bolden, James Weems, Larry Weems, Bee Johnson, Nicole Hall, Robert Swain, Timothy Blackburn, Tiana & Tiara Blackburn, and Sophia Lim. You are all dearly remembered.

My #1 girl in the world, **Mrs. Betty Sue Ridley.**

My love and respect go out to the following people: Michael Payton, Kisha Gray, Antralisa Shavette Alexander, Elizabeth Hall, Andrea Calloway, Alicia *Black Diamond* Griffin, Gwendolyn James, KeyonJane Whittle, Thelma Adams, Janet A. Berger, Nate J.B. Brown, Marquichea Burns, Theodore *Ted* Cole, Sheila Devereaux, Chi Ali Griffith, Heather Hall, Demond Hammond, Boobie Jacobs, Michael & Yolanda Jacobs, Ray Jacobs, Demetrius McClendon, Lamond Moore, Sean *Frisco* Moran, Threathere Pickett, Terry *T.P.* Prince, Debbie Ridley, Steven Ridley, Stephani Richardson, Curtis Schuler, Ambre Shaw-Sanders, Crystal Shaw, Izana Shaw, Shamar Shaw, Sharel Shaw, Messiah Sims, Charles C.W. Webb, Demarko Weems-Hall, Ebony L. Weems-Mickel, Kishana Weems, Leonard Weems, Sheryl Rene Weems, Nakesha Whittle.

My warmest thanks to my wonderful editor, Terri Harper, for her boundless patience, understanding, sweet personality, and friendship; not to mention all her editorial experience and expertise.

And last, though by no means least, to all my fans.

Eugene L. Weems

ACKNOWLEDGEMENTS

For the women in my life that keep me inspired and encouraged to remain aggressive about success. My mother, **Mrs. Yvonne Aubrey-McWoodson**, and my lovely and remarkably patient wife, **Mrs. Stephani Marie Richardson**. The both of you have become pillars of strength in my weakest moments, and beacons of light on my darkest days. And, for that, my hat is forever removed. Thank you.

To all of my children and the mothers who have raised and protected them in my times of absence, I commend you for your diligent patience and faith in me.

Lastly, but most important in my success as an author, I contribute unequivocally the full magnitude of my appreciation, admiration, and respect to hopefully a future life-long friend, Mr. Eugene L. Weems, for choosing to share his magnificent mind and treasured advice in all things business, and all things funny, and most of all, all dreams that are reachable. To my loyal and good friend, Ronnie "Hassan" Wattley, keep your head. Sky is the limit.

I am truly a blessed man with the people I have in my life.

Thank God, most of all.

Timothy R. Richardson

CHAPTER 1

"Girl, I'll tell you, that mothafucka Suge Knight got nine lives like a kitty cat! I put all them bullets in Tupac, and that fat ass nigga got grazed! Fucked up my perfect record!" Be'oncay was fuming as she took turns between gossiping and sipping on Alize.

"Fuck dat shit! Yo', you can't even shoot straight, bitch! Probably had yo' eyes closed and shit. I sucked dat nigga dick for nothin'. Fat boy still be textin' me all the way in New York, every two minutes, blowin' up my Sidekick. Hate dat nigga with a passion!" Karen was critical of everybody. She could find something negative to say about Heaven.

"Stop it, both of you. It could have happened to anybody, Be'oncay. I should have made you more armor-piercing bullets. Those BMW 700 series are constructed with reinforced alloys. My calculations were off. We'll get him next time." Lisa always looked at the bright side of things.

"Fuck you too, bitch! You ain't suckin' nobody smelly ass dick. Don't be takin' up for dat ho'. Just 'cause you a doctor and stuff, you ain't nobody special. Always takin' up fo' dat bitch, and she can't even sing!" Karen was not about to be double teamed, unless it was in the bedroom.

"I didn't mean to offend you, Karen. I was just..."

"You was just sayin', my ass! Fuck this shit! I shoulda shot Tupac myself and then smoked that Barney lookin' mothafucka like the slob ass bitch he is! Give me y'all money, too, four million dollars. Shittt!"

"Stop it! Stop it right now!" Everybody in the room froze and there was silence. They all knew better than to try and test Meagan. She entered the room and immediately demanded respect.

"Ladies, ladies. We all could have done a little better; the reason for this meeting is because we must start working as a team. Please be seated." Gladiss entered the room shortly after Meagan. She was the supervisor of this organization and the direct link to Yerfwin, the never-seen and seldom heard mastermind behind the existence of the Panhellenic Council. The most omniscient, omnipotent and wealthiest person these women had ever heard of. Gladiss was the only person among them to ever see Yerfwin face to face. "The past is behind us. Suge Knight has increased his personal security team. We must move on. Yerfwin is very disappointed in all of you. Don't worry. I think you ladies did a good job for your first target. We destroyed our primary target. Mr. Knight is nothing without Tupac and Snoop Dogg. Death Row Records is dead." Gladiss eased the tension in the room. "Teamwork. Teamwork. Teamwork." Gladiss preached to the young black women, because she knew they had potential. "You ladies have to help each other. Ms. Stephins, if you still want to go out on your own and kill Suge, you are free to do so. You can leave right now." Gladiss directed a cold stare at a frowning Karen.

"No, Gladiss. I'm fine. Just got a little mad, that's all." Karen was no fool. She wasn't going to make a million dollars for a contract anywhere else in America. How in the fuck did Gladiss know that she was complaining about the hit anyway? The room must have been bugged or something.

"Fine. Let's begin." The phone rang and Gladiss put the call on the speaker phone.

"Good evening, ladies." It was the sound of a slightly digitally modified voice, but everybody knew who it was.

"Good evening, Yerfwin." All the women responded like children in a first grade classroom.

"Your grade for your last assignment was a C minus. I am disappointed with your lack of teamwork. Your next assignment will be to terminate Bad Boy Records. Puff Daddy Combs, Christopher Biggie Wallace, and Mase are the three primary targets. Ms. Gladiss has been provided with all the details of these three individuals, and next month Notorious B.I.G. will be a presenter at the Soul Train Music Awards at the Shrine Auditorium in Los Angeles. Security will be tight, so please be careful. Think, ladies, think. Teamwork. Teamwork. Teamwork. Bye." The line went silent; Yerfwin was gone.

"Okay, ladies. The same compensation applies. One million dollars each. Karen and Be'oncay, you two are assigned to Puff Daddy Combs. Meagan, Notorious B.I.G. is yours. Lisa, you are assigned to Mase. Let's get..."

"No fuckin' way! I'm not gonna work with her." Karen pointed a finger at Be'oncay. Ms. Thang got her ghetto back.

"Yeah, can I work with Meagan or Dr. Lisa?" Be'oncay didn't like the idea of working with Karen either.

"No. You two are together. Yerfwin's orders. Deal or no deal?" Gladiss said in her calm voice.

"Deal," Be'oncay said, not happy at all about the grouping with *Superhead.*

"Shit. I'm cool. Deal." Karen had no choice. She was stuck with *Superweave.*

"Great. Let's begin." Gladiss handed each one of them individual folders with false identification, hangouts, Los Angeles contacts and addresses. "The departure schedules are the same as last time. Good luck."

Gladiss left the Las Vegas Hilton for her mansion in Las Vegas. Ten minutes later, Meagan was on her way back to the Hollywood Hills in California. Ten minutes after that, Dr. Lisa Lesley was leaving for Las Vegas International Airport, on her way back to Detroit, Michigan. After another ten minutes, Be'oncay was headed back to Houston, Texas. Ten minutes later, and mad as fuck for being the last person to leave, again! Karen stormed out of the room with a freshly lit blunt in her mouth and was on her way back to Brooklyn, New York. The ladies of the Panhellenic Council were on the hunt.

"Going, going, back, back, to Cali, Cali."

"Run dat shit again, my nigga! Dat shit dope! 'Nother hit fo' the streets." The music started again and Biggie went into a wicked rhyme flow, just another joint in the line of continuous Bad Boy hits.

Puff Daddy policed the sound engineer and barked out orders like a Marine drill instructor. He made sure that every sound that came from the studio mixing board was recorded to his satisfaction. "Stop! Stop! You fuckin' up. Start over! What is this?" Puff Daddy demanded perfection.

"Yo', kid, what's up? Why you trippin'? You be wildin' out on some stupid shit!" Biggie wanted an explanation. He was the only person in the Bad Boy clique that Puffy respected.

4

"My bad, my nigga. I'm on some other shit. Didn't mean to yell at you." Puff Daddy made a rare apology.

"Fuck it. You know I come from the dome on this shit. My flow is fucked, kid. I'm gonna go fuck wit' Lil Kim. You rap on dis shit yo' self. I'm out." Biggie wobbled out of the studio and headed straight toward the elevator.

"Where you goin'? Where you goin'? Big! Yo', Big! Where you goin'?" Puff had just run away the MVP of Bad Boy Records. He didn't give a fuck because he knew that the black, fat, dead-eyed mothafucka was going to be back eventually, because he was going to need some of Daddy's money. Puffy owned everybody at Bad Boy. He was the HNIC, the Head Nigga in Charge.

"Everybody out! Get the fuck outta here. Get outta my studio!" Puff Daddy was furious and wasn't about to let Biggie Smalls get away with frontin' him off, especially in front of his pawns. The room emptied immediately; niggas and bitches scrambled to get out, like roaches running from a can of RAID. When Sean Puff Daddy Combs spoke, everybody at Bad Boy listened.

Soon Puff was alone in his five million dollar recording studio and his mind was on more important things than another hit single.

"Shit!! Mothafucka!" Puff Daddy cursed out loud. He fucked things up royally by paying five million dollars on the ten million dollar contract for the hit on Suge Knight and Tupac Shakur. They smoked Tupac, but that nigga Suge lived.

"You only get half the money!"

Puff Daddy was no fool and realized that Suge was the gangster, Suge was the money, Suge was the power, Suge Knight was the head of Death Row Records. He had started a fuckin' war and didn't know if he had the money to finish it. To make matters worse, the bitch had threatened to kill everybody signed to Bad Boy Records if

Puffy didn't come up with the rest of her money. She wanted five million dollars by midnight and it was ten minutes after midnight. Puffy didn't have five million dollars cash. He never thought that a woman could carry through on an assassination of Tupac and Suge and get away with it. The bitch pulled it off and now he was stuck. Besides, he was going to need every penny he could get to go into hiding because Suge was definitely going to be coming after him. He had his undercover hideout in Manhattan, and he had no idea how long he was going to need to disappear. Puffy was a dancer, not a gangster. They killed a captain in the Death Row Army but didn't get the general. He started a war with the whole West Coast, and he had no idea what he was going to fight it with.

CHAPTER 2

One year earlier in Las Vegas, Nevada

"Tupac involved in shootout on movie set of *Above the Rim*. Assault and battery charges filed against Tupac Shakur by Hughes Brothers on movie set of *Menace to Society*. Tupac involved in shooting of off-duty New York police officer. Tupac sexually assaults Janet Jackson on set of *Poetic Justice*. Rape charges filed against Tupac Shakur in Maryland. Tupac sentenced to eight years in prison for sexual assault. Record bail posted by Death Row C.E.O. Suge Knight for Tupac Shakur's release from prison."

Gladiss Night read the journeys of Tupac Shakur and came to the conclusion that he was out of control and something had to be done about it.

"Fuck Delores Tucker! Fuck Arsenio Hall! Fuck Bill Clinton! Fuck Oprah! Fuck Biggie! Fuck Mase! Fuck Puffy! Fuck New York! Die mothafuckas, die!"

Gladiss pressed stop on the remote control of her CD player. She heard enough of Tupac's latest release on Death Row Records, *Machiavelli*.

She opened the thick file on Suge Knight, and it wasn't any better.

7

"Los Angeles Rams cheerleader arrested at airport transporting twenty kilos of cocaine. Darryl Henley chased from L.A. Rams practice facilities by armed gunmen; Suge Knight involved. Darryl Henley of L.A. Rams sentenced to prison for drug-trafficking. Suge Knight sued by Eric 'Eazy-E' Wright for extortion. Dr. Dre, Snoop Dogg, D.O.C., and Michell'e leave Ruthless Records for Death Row. Vanilla Ice hung out of hotel window and extorted by Suge Knight. Superstar R & B artists held at gunpoint and forced to perform on Tupac's debut album on Death Row Records. Dr. Dre's longtime girlfriend, Michell'e pregnant by Suge Knight. Dr. Dre walks away from a two hundred -million dollar stake in Death Row Records. Eazy-E dies of AIDS. Death Row Records CEO Marion 'Suge' Knight insults Puff Daddy at Source Music Awards in New York. Death Row Records declares war on Bad Boy Records. Death Row and Luke Records exchange gunfire at Jack the Rapper Convention in Atlanta. Suge opens Club 662 (M.O.B.) in Las Vegas."

Gladiss was not a big fan of the local newspapers as a source of information, but she got a slap in the face that woke her up to reality when her daughter was raped at a Death Row Records music video shoot. She had been in the music industry as a legendary performer for years and had never seen anything like Death Row Records. They were thugs with microphones and were holding the music industry hostage. Gladiss planned to put an end to the madness but she needed a little financial backing to put everything together. There was only one person that she knew with that kind of money, whom she met many years ago as a young undergraduate of Alpha Kappa Alpha Sorority, Inc. She needed a team that was just as ruthless as the thugs at Death Row and she already had four women in mind: Meagan Goodwin, Alpha Kappa Alpha; Dr. Lisa Lesley, Sigma Gamma Rho; Be'oncay Knolls, Zeta Phi Beta; and possibly

Karen Stephins, Delta Sigma Theta. Now she had to come up with the money to put her team together, and it was time to call Chicago and make things happen. The beef between Death Row and Bad Boy was out of control, and Gladiss had a question for Puff Daddy. How much money was he willing to spend to make his problems with Death Row disappear forever?

Gladiss called her personal assistant, Deborah Short, to get the answer to that question.

Los Angeles, California

"Stop, nigga! Keep yo' hands offa me!" Meagan Goodwin slapped away the feisty hand that groped her round booty. The little girl had grown up to become big and strong since her motion picture debut in the movie *Friday* as the frustrated kid in line at Big Worm's ice cream truck. A quick one-liner of, "Dang! I hate him...," fueled an ambition for a pretty little face to become a movie star. Meagan managed to find enough work in commercials, modeling and performing in rap music videos to pay her tuition at UCLA. Her minor role in *Friday* paved the way for Meagan through many doors in Hollywood, but after she pledged Alpha Kappa sorority, several magazine spreads, music videos, and a few minor roles in a few movies, Meagan was ready for the big time. So when she was called to appear in Tupac's video as the main love interest, she jumped at the opportunity. But Pac turned out to be a fuckin' pervert. He seemed to have more arms than a damn octopus. As soon as Meagan slapped one hand away from her ass, another hand was feeling on her tits. The nigga was already out on bail for a rape charge.

"Mothafucka!" Meagan was fed with up with the molestations. She connected with a stiff jab to Tupac's nose.

9

"Fuckin' bitch! You bitch…"

Pac grabbed his nose in pain. Two guerilla-looking bodyguards dressed in all red jumped on Meagan and started beating her like a remake of the Rodney King video. Meagan gathered herself and managed to put together a kick-punch combination that swiftly floored one of the bodyguards. The second flunkie soon joined him, the victim of a vicious elbow to his throat. Meagan was a first degree black-belt in Tae Kwon Do. A gun exploded and Meagan collapsed to the ground.

"Karate dat, bitch!"

Suge Knight appeared from the shadows.

Detroit, Michigan

"He's bleeding internally! You're losing him doctor!" Nurse Adler yelled in the operating room.

"Increase his oxygen flow! More IV to his bloodstream. Hurry! Hurry!" Dr. Lesley was the top brain surgeon at Detroit Memorial Hospital.

Flat line.

"He's dead! You killed him! I can't fucking believe it!" Nurse Adler barked at Dr. Lesley, clearly disrespecting her authority.

"What?! I didn't kill anybody! What are you talking about, nurse?!" Lesley questioned.

"You killed him! You….you should have stopped the internal bleeding." Nurse Adler refused to back down.

"It was brain surgery! Nobody told me anything about internal bleeding. Let me see that x-ray chart." Dr. Lesley grabbed the chart from her assistant. "Some…somebody switched the charts. This chart is for a replacement aortic valve, heart surgery. Oh my God!"

Two days later.

"Dr. Lesley, your license is officially revoked until the review committee investigates this case. The Robinson family has filed a one hundred million dollar lawsuit against this hospital. Your incompetence may have put us out of business. Get the fuck out of my office!" John Furhman, the hospital administrator, was irate.

"Sir, I…."

"Get the fuck out!"

Dr. Lesley left the office in tears. It seemed like the world was against her.

"Great job, Nurse Adler. We finally got that nigger bitch. That was an excellent idea of yours to switch the medical charts. I am impressed." Furhman engaged in pillow talk with his head nurse.

"I learned from the best. I couldn't stand taking orders from that jigaboo! I'm glad she's gone, fuckin' nigger brain surgeons. What's next, president?!" The registered nurse responded.

"You should have seen the look on her face. Coulda bought that coon for a wooden nickel," Furhman said with a smirk on his face. "Enough about her, let's celebrate!"

The two hospital employees engaged in another two-minute sex session.

"My God! I can't believe this shit!" Dr. Lesley reflected back on her week. She could not understand why she was fired from the hospital, and her license to practice medicine was stripped away from her. It was worse than her experiences during Hell Week when she pledged Sigma Gamma Rho. What was she going to do now?

Lisa Lesley worked her ass off to get through college and then medical school at John Hopkins University, and now it was all gone in an instant. The whole situation was not even her fault. Nurse Adler gave her the wrong chart.

"How am I going to live without a job?" Dr. Lesley asked herself a serious question as she surfed through the channels on her big screen plasma television in her penthouse apartment. She stopped at a commercial promoting the Los Angeles Sparks of the new professional basketball league for women, the WNBA. "Well, I better start working on my jump shot!" A light bulb came on inside the head of a genius.

Houston, Texas:

"Let me hear y'all hit dat shit again." Tupac said to the lovely trio of Houston talent, known as Destiny's Child. They sang as if their lives depended on it. Pac eyed the very sexy honey blond sister in the middle lustfully. "Y'all bitches can sing. Sounds like En Vogue and shit, but can you rap? Death Row already got Michell'e."

Be'oncay, the honey blond, began a nursery school-type rap. "Nah...that's cool! Just gimme the demo. Maybe I can hook y'all up with Shock G. You, you stay! I wanna talk to you about some thangs!" He chose Be'oncay and the other women were ushered from the room, disappointed.

"I like you, but the rest of 'dem other two bitches don't sound too hot. I want you to sing da hook on my next cut. How 'bout that?"

Tupac moved in, too close for comfort.

"I don't...I dunno. Me and my friends are a group. I ain't gon' leave 'em hangin' like dat." Be'oncay chose her words carefully because she knew that she was in the presence of a rap legend. She still couldn't believe that she was alone in a hotel room with Tupac Shakur!

"Leave dem bitches! I got big plans fo' ya. Come here!" Pac grabbed her by both arms roughly and put his face to hers. Then he shoved his tongue down her throat.

"Ahhh! Shit, bitch! You bit my shit!"

Be'oncay tried to bite out a chunk of his tongue. She kneed him in the nuts.

"Crazzzy bitch! Crazy mothafucka! I don't care who da fuck you is! Fuck you Tupac, sing on yo' own shit!" A vicious kick to the head followed and Be'oncay fled the room.

"Napo...Napolean, Kato, git dat bitch!!" Pac yelled out demands to his homies.

Be'oncay managed to make it to her Honda Accord in the parking garage of the hotel. The bucket came to life and she burned rubber by pressing pedal to the metal. She desperately wanted to put as much distance between her and Tupac as possible.

"Mothafucka!" She noticed the two flunkies in her rear-view mirror, giving chase in a black BMW. Be'oncay didn't worry too much because she knew how to shake their asses. Houston was her hometown. A right, a sharp left, then a fast right and she lost them like a bad habit. Her heart pounded in her throat because she heard about all the rumors about Death Row, especially Tupac and Suge. The rapes and gangbangin' sex sessions of ten niggas fuckin' one woman. Well, Tupac had fucked with the wrong bitch. Be'oncay Knolls was nobody's victim. One day she was going to make it big-time, and she was going to take her home girls with her. The world was going to say her name.

Brooklyn, New York:

"Bitch, I don't give a fuck! You gon' sell that pussy!" Another crushing blow connected to Karen's already bloodied face.

"Fuck you! Nigga, I ain't doin' shit!" Karen was stubborn and fought back as much as she could.

"Bitch, I'ma kill yo' ass!"

A lamp crashed against Kool G.'s head.

"My baby! My baby!" He kicked her in the stomach.

"Fuck dat baby shit. Probably ain't even mine!" Kool G. stopped his assault and battery for a second.

"Git up bitch. Clean yo' self up. Pun expectin' you at nine! Here!" Kool G. tossed Karen a dingy face rag. He breathed heavily and talked in spurts.

She unballed herself from the human knot that had become a familiar position for the past several months. Karen's body hurt from the top of her head to the bottom of her feet. She didn't care about the physical pain because she was more focused on the words that were spoken.

"Fuck you G! You nothin' mothafucka! Fuckin has-been, ass nigga!" Karen may have lost the fist-fight, but she wasn't going to lose the argument.

"Shit! Look at my face! I shoulda killed dat nigga!" She looked at the reflection of herself in the bathroom mirror. The sight was a fraction of the beauty that Karen was accustomed to seeing look back at her. "How can I be in that fuckin' Craig Mack video lookin' like this?"

Karen started the process of applying heavy layers of makeup to her face. She regretted the day she ever met Kool G. Rapp on the set of the *Symphony* music video. Karen actually had her eyes set on Big Daddy Kane, but he chose a light-skinned Puerto Rican bitch over her. Now she was stuck with this wood rat lookin' nigga who had teeth that looked like he was chewing on rocks. Life was fucked-up like that, and Karen had been tossed around between New York rappers more than stolen rap lyrics. Karen didn't believe in doing anything half-assed. She strived for perfection; nothing but the best. Her oral copulation skills earned her the name "Superhead", the best blow-job in the business.

"Knock! Knock! Knock!" The bathroom door caved in.

"Bitch. Git that money! Go get that money!"

Karen stormed out of the apartment and walked toward the subway.

"Fuck you, rat mouth mothafucka!"

New York attitude to the fullest, because nobody could out-talk Karen Stephins. She was the best hooker in the state of New York, and one day the world was going to read about her.

Eugene L. Weems, Timothy R. Richardson

CHAPTER 3

Las Vegas, Nevada. Eight months earlier

"The contract on Death Row has been secured. Five million dollars was deposited into our Tobago account."

Deborah passed the details along to Gladiss in the bathroom stall of the women's restroom at the MGM Grand Hotel.

"Fine."

No more words were spoken between the women, and Gladiss exited the restroom. She finally had all the pieces to the puzzle, and it was time for the next phase of her plan. Death Row Records and Bad Boy Records brought the beef between them to a worldwide audience. They brought a new definition to the term "banging" on wax, and now everybody was being held hostage to the antics of these ignorant niggas. They degraded black women in their music videos and demoralized them in their songs. Rap was taking over the nation and this garbage sold millions of albums. And the owners of Gangsta Rap made millions of dollars. A fool and his money will always part, and these heathens were fools to the highest degree. Eventually the words would have to be followed up by actions because those were the rules of the streets. Gladiss didn't care about Death Row or Bad Boy. Actually, she hated what they stood for and wanted both companies destroyed. The easiest way to destroy a

17

people is to divide and conquer. So while these enemies were busy threatening and destroying each other's reputation, Gladiss was going to move in for the kill.

She put the finishing touches on the invitations, about one step closer to making her vision turn into a reality. Yerfwin was all in, and anything Gladiss needed was readily available. Now she needed to gather her troops together. An organization is only as strong as the members who make up that organization. Black women were under attack by these hoodlums, and she was not going to sit back idle and do nothing about it. The time had come for serious action, and Gladiss couldn't believe how stupid hatred made people. She was going to destroy Death Row and Bad Boy Records, and Puff Daddy was going to pay the money to make it happen. She got on her computer and entered her password, 1-9-0-8, and initiated the next phase of her plan.

Los Angeles, California

"Sorry, don't call us, we'll call you." Another audition, another rejection. It seemed like the only bitches getting work in Hollywood these days were the ho's who spread their legs open. The wider they opened their legs, the bigger the movie role they received. Meagan Goodwin wasn't going to play that silly game. Maybe she was just being paranoid, or maybe this particular role just wasn't the right role for her, but ever since her incident with Tupac, Meagan couldn't find a gig anywhere in Hollywood. Not even as a movie extra. Death Row put out the word that she was shot because she was a thief and stole some jewelry. Suge shot her in the ass because she was hard to work with and an out of control, conceited karate chick. The damage was done to her physically and professionally. Meagan recovered well from the physical, but the damage done to her career was making it hard for her to make a living.

Meagan pulled up to her apartment in Westwood, parked her Honda Accord, and climbed the stairs to her humble home. She was still a beautiful black woman, full pouting lips, long creamy legs, and a heart-shaped ass. Ms. Goodwin was very sexy, but sexy couldn't pay her bills anymore. Rent was three weeks late, the light bill was a month behind, her fall tuition at UCLA film school was overdue, and a repossession was put out for her car. Meagan needed something to happen soon or she was going to lose everything. She looked through the tall stack of bills and her depression grew with each envelope she read and tossed away.

"What da fuck!"

She opened a letter addressed to her from a sender in Las Vegas.

"Lucky winner! You have been selected as a finalist with a chance to make one million dollars!"

On a normal day Meagan would have tossed the junk mail in the trash with the rest of the garbage, but she was in a desperate situation. "Looks like somebody's headed to Las Vegas." Desperate times called for desperate measures.

Detroit, Michigan:

Life in the WNBA was not all that it was cut out to be. Dr. Lesley not only made the team, but was the leading scorer for the L.A. Sparks and a rising star. However, her starting salary as a professional basketball player in the league was 50 thousand dollars – the maximum contract. It was chump change compared to the one hundred million dollar contracts of her NBA counterparts that were given out to men like free government cheese. To make matters worse, it was only half of what she made working as a brain surgeon at Detroit Memorial Hospital.

Her bills piled up like wrecked cars at the Indy 500; student loans, mortgage payments, car note, gas, electric, credit cards, and Macy's. Dr. Lesley's future as a doctor didn't look bright at all. John Furhman was not even close to reinstating her license anytime soon. In fact, it would be a miracle if he didn't press criminal charges against her. Dr. Lesley was kind of slow to figure people out and now she realized that it was Nurse Adler who switched the medical charts, and she did it on purpose. The truth of the situation was that Lisa Lesley was a sweet, compassionate and nice lady but if you fucked her over, she became a ruthless killer. Dr. Lisa had no respect for life anymore. She had seen death too many times to fear it.

"YOU ARE A WINNER! Dr. Lisa Lesley you have been selected as a finalist, with a chance to win one million dollars!" Lisa looked at the letter and smiled. Her prayers were answered. She had never been to Las Vegas and a million dollars sounded like a fortune right now. An ankle sprain or a knee injury should do the trick and get her coach off her back. "One million dollars!" Dr. Lisa made up her mind and was going to do whatever it took to get to Vegas. In the meantime, she had some important business to tend to. She had to pay that white bitch, Nurse Adler, a little visit.

"Nurse Barbara Adler Dies in Drug Overdose!" Dr. Lesley looked at the headlines of the *Detroit Tribune* feeling satisfied. A few well-placed injections of PCP always did the trick. Another fool who made the mistake of taking kindness for weakness, and it was time for better things. Bye-bye WNBA, hello Las Vegas. Dr. Lesley hated leaving her teammates during the thick of her rookie season, but she could think of a million reasons why going to Las Vegas was a better decision.

Houston, Texas

"We don't need no female groups! You can sing back-up on my single, though," Willie D. said with a gold-toothed smile.

"Nah, I'm cool honey. We a group. Destiny's Child. I gotta go."

Be'oncay scooped up her demo and left the offices of Rap-A-Lot records. She already heard the same lame-ass conversation from H-town rappers for years. "Sing my hook for me. We don't need a female singin' group. Wanna be in my video? Can you rap?" The rejections came more and more. All these rap mothafuckas wanted the same thing when it came to Be'oncay. One look at her honey brown thighs, apple-shaped bottom, and melon-sized breasts, and they forgot about everything else. The only thing Be'oncay wanted in her life was a chance to sing her music. Making rap videos wasn't her thing. No more beauty pageants. No more dating to get her demo listened to. She wanted to break the stereotypes and prove to the world that a black woman could be sexy and intelligent. Be'oncay even went to college at Texas Southern University for three years, pledged Zeta Phi Beta, and graduated with a 3.8 GPA in economics. The only thing that stopped her from going for her Master's Degree at the University of Houston was her music. Be'oncay loved her music! So when she hooked with Kelly and Veronica to form the group, Destiny's Child and won four talent shows in a row, she knew that it was time to make the decision of her young life - the life of a diva, or an office job in corporate America as a CPA. Be'oncay chose the glamorous life of music.

Mama told her that there would be days like this, another demo tape rejection, another offer to be a video ho. She thought back to her days running crack from Fifth Ward to New Orleans for five thousand dollars a trip, and setting up high roller out-of-towners to get jacked. The money came in boatloads, and she was only sixteen years old. Today was a different day, and her life of luxury seemed a million years in the past. Paying for her college education and hours and hours of studio time left a hole in her pockets the size of the Astrodome. What was she going to do? Rap-a-Lot Records and Suave House Records were the biggest record companies in Houston and they only signed rappers. Be'oncay couldn't rap a lick; she was born to sing. She was down to her last ten thousand dollars.

"Bills, bills, bills! Damn that would make a good song! Hey, what's this?" Be'oncay went through the mail at her southwest Houston home.

"Lucky Winner! You have been selected as a finalist, and will have a chance to make one million dollars!" Be'oncay immediately thought of it as junk mail, but the first-class airline ticket and hotel reservation at the Las Vegas Hilton were very official.

"Yeah! Yes, somebody goin' to Vegas, sugar!" Her luck finally took a turn for the better. A million dollars was more than enough money to start her own label. Be'oncay was crazy in love. "Las Vegas, here I come!" Be'oncay did the booty bounce then started packing her bags, and she made sure she took her demo tape with her.

Brooklyn, New York

"Yo bitch! Get da fuck outta my house!" Kool G. Rapp was on another drunken rampage. New York was a big city but rap rumors traveled in very small circles. The word had spread around town about Karen sleeping with Big Pun and giving him Superhead. Now Kool G was the laughing stock of the neighborhood because Big Pun was a fat, nasty-looking and disgusting blob of a man, and putting out a song that the woman who sucked his dick was Kool G's main squeeze was very bad news. Kool G couldn't live with that reputation, and being a rapper was all about image.

"Fuck you! You made me do it!" Karen argued in her defense.

"Fuck dat! Take yo' shit!" He grabbed a handful of Karen's hair and drug her outside of the raggedy Brooklyn apartment. She was on the floor of the hallway, then he started throwing out her shit with very little respect for her personal property.

"Stop it! Stop! I can get my own shit! I'll go, mothafucka, I'll go! Karen yelled from the hallway, and now there was a full audience gathered watching with great interest and enjoying the neighborhood drama.

"Fuck dat! You fuckin skeezer! Suckin' dat fat nigga dick. Kick rocks bitch!" Kool G was out of control with anger.

"My notes, my book! What about my mail?" Karen didn't care about anything but getting her book, and she was expecting a response from a publisher.

"Here bitch! You and yo' shit can go! You ain't gon' be shit anyway!" Kool G threw a thick notepad at Karen that hit her in the face, then threw her a thick stack of letters with her name on them.

"Fuck you, G! Rot in hell nigga! You rat mouth mothafucka! You ain't nothin but a sorry nigga! I'm pregnant wit' yo' baby!" Karen argued to mute ears, but nobody was going to get in the last word on Karen Stephins.

Later on at a cheesy motel room in Queens, Karen could not believe how bad her luck was going for the past twenty-four hours.

She was homeless, broke, and four months pregnant. The future looked fucked up for Ms. Stephins. She was relieved to finally be free from the mental, emotional, physical and sexual abuse that Kool G. Rapp inflicted on her, but she didn't have enough money to live on. She was four months pregnant and eating for two people. The only thing she had going for her was her book manuscript, a blow-by-blow diary of the adventures of a video vixen. Kool G was her ticket into the world of rappers, professional athletes, singers and actors. He was her high-class pimp and Karen figured that if she was going to be sucking, she might as well make a little money out of the deal. Everything was cool until that fool Big Pun started running his mouth. To make matters worse, he wasn't even that good. One of those big body, rice dick mothafuckas who talked too much. Big Pun was definitely going to pay for blowing up her spot, and putting her out there like that on a fuckin' record was a major violation of the code. Life with Kool G was bad, but at least she had a life.

Through the chaos and confusion at least she managed to get the manuscript and most of her mail.

"Congratulations! You've been selected as a finalist, with a chance to make one million dollars." Karen couldn't believe it. She looked through the envelope and found a first-class airplane ticket to Las Vegas and a hotel room reservation for the Las Vegas Hilton. She knew the shit was real because a plane ticket to Las Vegas from New York was higher than a mothafucka; it cost a fortune.

She pushed her luck and continued her search through her mail for an acceptance letter from a publisher. But instead of more good news, she only found more bills. It still didn't rain on her parade because with a million dollars, she could publish the book herself. If the contest turned out to be a scam, Karen had a back-up plan. She could become an escort at one of those high-class brothels, like the

24

Mustang Ranch. Anything was better than staying in New York and returning to a life of living in dirty motels and hustlin' on the ghetto streets.

It was an easy decision for Karen to make. A chance to make a million dollars in Las Vegas was better than becoming a guaranteed statistic in New York.

"Viva, Las Vegas!" Karen couldn't wait to get away from New York and everybody who lived there.

Eugene L. Weems, Timothy R. Richardson

CHAPTER 4

Las Vegas, Nevada

"Welcome! My name is Gladiss Nyte." The room was silent; everybody knew who Gladiss was. "You have been selected to become a member of our secret society, the Panhellenic Council. We organized a very important mission. I want to offer you one million dollars for your involvement in this mission.

We know everything about you Meagan. You pledged AKA at UCLA, your movie role in *Friday,* your evening job as a stripper at the Barbary Coast, the commercials and small bit parts in movies. We know where your parents live, your sister and your grandmother. Deborah, bring in the money!"

Deborah Short entered the room like Jerome from The Time would respond to Morris Day, holding a large silver-plated suitcase. Gladiss cracked it open. Meagan couldn't resist looking inside at the contents, and was blessed with the site of several tall stacks of one hundred dollar bills.

"One million dollars cash! Very few people will ever see this amount of money in their lifetime. Your signature on this contract makes you the owner of this money and a respected member of our organization." Gladiss was finished with her sales presentation.

"What's the catch?" It seemed like a deal that was too good to be true. Nobody had ever given Meagan anything for free.

"You must complete an intense training in weapons, demolitions, and martial arts. We know about your black belt. After training you will be given an assignment. Are you in?" Gladiss responded.

Meagan didn't hesitate anymore. She wasn't going to pass up on this type of money. If she didn't like what was going on, she could just return the money later. One million dollars was a fortune and could set her up for life in Hollywood. "Yes! Yes, Ms. Nyte. I'm in." She signed the contract.

"Dr. Lesley, this is a once in a lifetime opportunity to get paid for services you have been rendering for free. We know about your recent murder of Barbara Adler. Nice piece of work. We know about your present financial situation, and it looks like you'll never get your medical license back. We need you on our team. Your expertise is desperately needed by our excellent organization. We need you Dr. Lesley. Let's make history together."

Dr. Lesley was dumfounded and surprised that somebody knew about her Dr. Jekyl and Ms. Hyde bi-polar disorder, and was upset. Lisa was a six-foot two-inch black goddess with a beautiful face, long silky muscular legs, and generally fit the tall, dumb, naïve runway model image. On the other hand, she had a dark side that was a ruthless killer. When pushed past her limit, Dr. Lesley would become as vicious as a tiger trapped in a corner.

"One million dollars! All you have to do is complete our training, and you can never discuss this meeting or any other activities from this organization with anyone. Remember, the

Panhellenic Council has eyes everywhere." Gladiss opened the suitcase piled high with tall stacks of one hundred dollar bills. Lisa had never seen so much money in her life! It was a fortune.

"So what's it gonna be, Doc?" A very rare moment of informality from Gladiss, but she knew how angry it made Dr. Lesley when people called her "Doc". Ms. Nyte had done her research. In fact, Gladiss knew everything about Lisa Lesley and hired the top investigators and computer minds in the world to get that information. She was challenging Dr. Lesley, backing her into that corner.

"What if I say no!" Lisa responded in a defiant tone of desperation.

"You lose your license to practice medicine, dribble a basketball up and down a long piece of wood, making a fraction of what your male counterparts make in the NBA, and die a dumb black bimbo who had a wicked jumpshot!" Gladiss hit a nerve. Dr. Lesley's eyes turned red from the heat of anger, she transformed. "However, my lovely Dr. Lisa, if you join us, if you say yes, you will be making yourself a part of a team that has the potential to change the world. You can make enough money with us to start your own private medical practice and help the children of America. Help the children, Lisa!" Gladiss knew how much Lisa loved the kids.

Dr. Lesley sat in silence for a moment, staring in the eyes of Gladiss, then looking at the shining silver suitcase and the greenbacks in tall money stacks. It seemed like the chance of a lifetime, an offer too good to be true, and Lisa looked for the catch. A million dollars was a lot of money and Gladiss was right, she could open a children's clinic and save the lives of a lot of little people. For Dr. Lesley, it wasn't about the money; it was about what she could do with the money. She thought about the murder of

Nurse Adler and wondered how Gladiss knew about the crime committed. Lisa also knew that these people were not a police organization because if they were, she would have been in handcuffs. Gladiss Nyte was a star and if it was all right with Gladiss, maybe it was cool with her. Dr. Lisa wanted to change the world and help the children.

"Yes! I will sign the contract with your organization. I would be honored to be a member of your team." Lisa signed.

"One million dollars cash! We just want you as a member of our secret organization. We also need you to complete an intense training and carry out an important mission." Be'oncay eyed the suitcase full of money. She had seen a couple hundred thousand in cash before, back in her drug runnin' days, but that shit wasn't her money. One million dollars looked like a gold mine. She could work wonders with that type of money. It was enough to finance her own record company and buy her group some new outfits. For young Be'oncay it was the chance of a lifetime, but what was the trick? Because nothing came to Be'oncay Knolls without a problem attached, this shit was too good to be true.

"So what's it gonna be, Be'oncay? Do you want to do your music and be a star like me?" Gladiss pointed at the suitcase for effect. "Or do you want to be just another big booty, hoochie mama from Houston that could have made it big?" Gladiss closed the suitcase.

"Hold it right there, honey! Don't go nowhere wit' dat money. I'm signin' and, Ms. Gladiss, my booty ain't big, it's phatt, p-h-a-t-t! Pretty, Hot And Texas Temptin'!" Be'oncay managed to get a smile out of Gladiss.

"Ms. Stephins, we have one million dollars to offer you for membership in our secret organization. You will..."

"Is that shit real?!" Karen stared at all the tall stacks of Benjamins in the suitcase in disbelief.

"Yes Karen, it's very real. Please don't interrupt me again." Gladiss gave her a cold stare.

"O...okay, okay, I'm cool Gladiss. I like yo' records. Take it easy." Karen responded as nervous as a contestant opening the last suitcase on *Deal or No Deal*."

"Okay. You were selected as a finalist to become a member of our secret organization. You will have to finish training and sign a contract of commitment. Would you like to be a part of our organization?"

"Hellmothafuckin yeah!" Karen only had one word to say about that, the answer was simple. She snatched the contract, signed it, accepted the private cell phone, grabbed the suitcase, said her goodbyes, and was on her way to the airport. Karen Stephins was all about the money, and would have sucked the devil's dick for a million dollars cash. Karen finally had the money to publish her book and start a new life, anywhere she wanted.

Gladiss sat in the study and reviewed the progress notes on Meagan, Dr. Lesley, Be'oncay and Karen from their three-month training in Phoenix, Arizona. Commander Eugene Weems was their drill instructor, a heavily-decorated Navy Seal, retired Lieutenant Commander, and former kickboxing champion. He was a true success story, a man who beat the odds of the street life, and was a billionaire business tycoon.

Everybody showed up on time, except for Karen who tried to run off to Jamaica with her million dollars but was quickly found, and reminded of her contractual commitment.

Each woman was unique and an asset to the organization in a different way.

Meagan was a third-degree black belt, had very strong connections in the movie industry, and knew the culture of Hollywood movers and shakers.

Dr. Lisa Lesley was a certified genius with an I.Q. of 198. She was an expert in pharmaceuticals, explosives and concoctions. Dr. Lesley had a dark side that was a mad scientist just waiting to be released. Lisa was a welcome asset to the Panhellenic Council.

Be'oncay Knolls was an excellent marksman and sharpshooter. She began her love affair with firearms at the tender age of seven, and perfected her skills going deer hunting with her father. Shooting was her specialty. Nobody could make a gun holler like Be'oncay Knolls.

Last, but definitely not least, was Karen Stephins. She was good at everything she did but was a master at male manipulation. She was going to be a valuable asset at gaining access to places that women never seen before. New York was her stomping grounds, and Karen was the queen of the streets of New York. She knew everything there was to know about the streets and the niggas that ran them. Her pregnancy rescued her from some of the physical aspects of the trainings, but she more than made up for it with her valuable input in planning things. Ms. Stephins was a walking encyclopedia of knowledge and knew every intricate detail about every rapper in America, and every rapper knew about "Superhead."

CHAPTER 5

Las Vegas, Nevada

"Congratulations ladies! You have been successful in completing all trainings for membership in the Panhellenic Council. Now comes the next phase of your commitment. I am impressed with your efforts so far, and I believe that time will prove me right for selecting you. At this time I would like to introduce you to Yerfwin!" Gladiss pressed the intercom button and the phone came to life.

"Good evening ladies. I am Yerfwin. Your assignment is to terminate Suge Knight, Tupac Shakur, and Snoop Dogg. We want Death Row Records destroyed. Good luck ladies. Good-bye." The line went dead.

"What da fuck?! What you mean?! Kill Tupac and Suge? Them niggas larger than life. I bought Pac album!" Karen spoke at the empty phone.

"He ain't all dat! Nigga shot me in the ass! He a mothafuckin' rapist, that's why he went to prison anyway!" Meagan spoke from experience and had the bullet wound to show for it.

"Yeah! I can't stand dem fools either. Met Tupac in H-town and he bad news! Let's smoke dem fools!" Be'oncay was ready to try out her new trainings.

"He did make the song *Dear Mama*. I wonder, can we talk things over with him?" Dr. Lesley suggested the therapeutical route. Her mind swiftly shifted back to her personal thoughts of the handsome, sexy and intelligent drill instructor, who her body was craving. Dr. Lisa admired Commander Weems' gentlemanly ways and swagger, and saw rare qualities within him that clearly spelled out husband material. She had plans on winning his heart because he had unknowingly won hers. Dr. Lesley also knew she would have to mobilize her efforts fast, because Meagan had her eyes on the prize as well.

"Enough!" Gladiss spoke loud and clear, and demanded order like a nun in a Catholic school. "The decision is non-negotiable! You ladies have four million dollars of my money! I am the boss! We are in the real world! You don't get something for nothing. Either you are in or you are out! Each of you signed a contract. You are legally responsible, but I am offering you the chance to walk away, right now. No questions asked but, of course, we want our money back!" Gladiss now had everybody's attention in the room. Was it a deal with the devil?

"Meagan?"

"Of course I'm in Gladiss. Time for some pay back!" Meagan had a mean mug on her face.

"Be'oncay?"

"Fuck Death Row. Dem niggas wouldn't sign me and my girls anyway! Pop go da weasel!" Be'oncay could still feel Pac's hands molesting her body from the hotel incident in Houston. Nothing could compare to the anger of a woman scorned.

"Doctor?"

34

"Of course! I'm in. I read all about these thugs in the papers; a very negative influence on the children, degrades black women. I've killed for less." Ms. Hyde was speaking.

"Karen, if you don't like the assignment, you can give the money back and..."

"Fuck you Gladiss! I said I bought da nigga album; don't mean I love him dat much!" I ain't going nowhere!"

Gladiss' open palm was introduced to Karen's face with a violent force. The sound of the sharp blow echoed like thunder struck the room. "No! Fuck you, Karen! You need to respect your elders. You got a very dirty mouth for a young lady!" Gladiss gathered herself and returned to her seat. Karen had that effect on people.

"Hey! What you do dat for?" Karen charged toward Gladiss, but Be'oncay, Meagan and Lisa held her back.

"Let her go! You are free to leave. Get out! In your pregnant state, you won't be any help to us on this assignment anyway. Go have your baby! We'll be in contact with you. You are dismissed!"

She stormed out of the room. Nobody got in the last word on Karen Stephins. "Cool wit' me! Your loss. Thanks for the money!" She yelled on her way to the elevator.

"Okay ladies. Teamwork! We are a team and we need to work together if we are going to be successful. The target date for operation Death Row is September 1996 at the MGM Grand Hotel. Mike Tyson will fight Bruce Seldon for the heavyweight championship. Tupac is going to perform a song for Mike Tyson when he enters the ring. There will also be a concert at Suge Knight's Club 662. Both targets must be terminated. Meagan, you are assigned to Suge Knight. Be'oncay, Tupac is yours and, Dr. Lisa, you will be responsible for Snoop Dogg. Lisa, we will also need your expertise in preparing the necessary ammunitions, explosives, and armor-piercing bullets for the mission. Teamwork, teamwork, teamwork! Eugene will coordinate all your moves, and make sure that you have the necessary tools to be successful. Be sure to use your trainings. I believe in you, so believe in yourself. Meeting adjourned. The same departure rules apply. Good luck ladies." Gladiss handed each of them a folder then left the room. Ten minutes passed by then Meagan departed without a word. After another ten minutes Dr. Lesley was gone, and ten minutes later Be'oncay shook the spot. It was time for war.

Gladiss relaxed in the back seat of her Rolls Royce limo and was deep in thought. She reflected back on the meeting and the events that took place. She hated losing her composure and slapping the shit out of Karen, but she learned from her days growing up in the projects that when you are placed in a situation of chaos and confusion in a group setting, you must silence the loudest source of hostility. Karen was the biggest source of opposition, and Gladiss knew from the beginning that Ms. Stephins was going to be the toughest cookie to crumble. Alpha Kappa Alpha and Delta Sigma Theta sororities held a historic rivalry that dated all the way back to the 1910's and continues on to this day. Karen most definitely had the Delta attitude and street persona to add to it, but Gladiss was not going to let that get in the way of her plans. She had to keep her eye on the big picture because she needed Karen's help to make victory possible.

Compton, California:

Meagan cruised the streets of Compton, heading toward Rosecrans and Atlantic Boulevard, following a couple Death Row flunkies named Le-Bo and Stone. They parked their Mercedes Benz 500 at the meet-up spot at Leuders Park. They were pawns in the Leuders Park Pirus, M.O.B.s. Suge Knight was the king of this Compton gang, and used it to recruit foot soldiers for his Death Row army. Meagan was an excellent chess player; in fact, she believed that the game of chess was a lot like the game of life. You had to kill a few pawns in order to get within striking distance of the king.

"Hey good lookin'. Where could a sista get a ounce of dat sticky?" Stone took one look at Meagan and got an instant woody. They didn't make bodies like hers in the ghetto anymore. Her tight apple bottom jeans formed a fat camel toe in the center of her crotch.

"Blood! Baby girl, I got ya. But I need to get that phone number." Stone continued the transaction in broad daylight. He didn't give a fuck if she was an undercover cop because Death Row had strong connections at the Compton Sheriff's, L.A. Sheriff's and L.A.P.D. The fat platinum chain with the diamond Death Row emblem was his guaranteed "get out of jail free" card. Even the mayor of Compton, Omar Bradley, was bowing down to Death Row.

"Two seventy-five!" He showed Meagan a fat baggie of lime green buds that smelled like the funky sweet, sticky icky.

"Cool, good lookin' out." Meagan handed Stone three crisp new Benjamins. Stone handed her the baggie and she put it away.

"What's up wit' dem digits?" Stone wasn't going to be denied.

"Oh yeah. Here." Meagan wrote down her number and handed him the folded piece of paper. "I'm Meagan. Call me." She sounded like a 900 commercial and shit.

"Fo' sho' I'ma holla at ya. Damn you look good in dem jeans." Stone struck the jackpot and watched Meagan walk away, sheer poetry in motion as she hopped in her bright yellow Hummer 3. He got the strange feeling that he saw her somewhere before. "Blood!

That's that bitch from King magazine!" Le-Bo finally realized who she was. "Wait until I tell Suge about dis shit. Dat bitch a model and shit!" Stone was smiling from ear to ear.

Meagan puffed on the Chronic blunt and navigated her way through traffic on the 110 freeway. She was satisfied, with her mind on her money, and her money on her mind. The first move was made and the game of chess was started. She knew that a pawn's only purpose in life was to impress the king, and men gossiped just as much as women. Meagan's ears were already burning from the conversation she knew was going on about her. She knew from her trainings with Commander Weems that you entered an organization the same way you entered a building. You entered it from the bottom and worked your way up to the top. Suge Knight had more security around him than the Pope. He was as tall as an oak tree, a permanent structure, solid and strong in the City of Compton. Meagan knew a lot about smokin' trees and she understood that in order to kill an oak tree, you had to cut off the roots.

New York, New York

Dr. Lesley focused on the task at hand, Dogg Pound Gangsta Crips were scheduled to do their video shoot for their single, *New York, New York*, and time was perfect. An anonymous caller had basically made a terrorist threat against Snoop Dogg during a radio interview on HOTT 97.7. The Death Row entourage was gathered in the movie trailer. There was so much Chronic smoke, you could smell it a mile away. Lisa was dressed in black on black. The only indication of her presence on this New York night was the glistening shine of the steel of her AK-47 assault rifle that was loaded with a long banana clip of armor-piercing bullets. The ammo was Dr.

Lesley's brainchild, a little something she learned in training. She was close enough to reach out and touch the trailer. Now was the time. She backed up a bit.

Tak! Tak! Tak! Tak! Tak! Tak! Tak! Tak! Tak! Tak! The deadly rounds spit out like popcorn kernels responding to heat. She emptied one clip, then inserted another.

"Tak! Tak! Tak! Tak, tak, tak, tak! Tak! Tak!" The bullets spit out like chewing tobacco at a redneck convention. Ms. Hyde smiled, then fled the scene like a thief in the night.

"Two dead in shootout, Snoop Dogg emerges unscathed. New York versus California Rap War to blame." Dr. Lisa Lesley read the headlines of the New York times.

"Shit! I can't believe it!" She read about the bodyguard who sacrificed his life by laying on top of Snoop Dogg and absorbing the bullets for him. Dr. Lesley underestimated the loyalty that Snoop's flunkies had for him, and vowed to never make the same mistake again. Maybe the rumors about paying Crips twenty dollar bags of Chronic and a few forty ounces of malt liquor were untrue. Mistakes, mistakes, mistakes, and Dr. Lisa hated making mistakes. She was a perfectionist and wished that she stayed with her first thought and used the C4 explosives Commander Weems suggested. Now she had to chalk it up as a waste of time and energy. The doctor had lost a battle, but she refused to lose the war. Failure was not an option. She was going to kill Snoop Dogg.

Eugene L. Weems, Timothy R. Richardson

CHAPTER 6

Back at an upper Manhattan hospital

"Damn, Cuzz! I can't believe that the l'il homie Half Dead took a bullet to the throat. I lost two homies behind dis shit. These New York Niggas ain't playin, and dat nigga Suge don't do nuthin' for the blue side of Death Row. Fuck dat slob ass nigga, we makin' mo' money than Pac!" Snoop hollered at Daz and Korrupt, then he stepped into his white Cadillac with his trusted homie, Tray Dee.

"I'm hungry as a mothafucka, paid all dat money fo' the Millennium Broadway Hotel, and dat food nasty as fuck! Let's go get some pizza, Cuzz." The tires screamed as they peeled away from the curb and headed to Sal's Pizza in Brooklyn. Snoop was still shook by the previous day's activities, high as fuck, and as paranoid as Rodney King at an L.A.P.D. policeman's ball. They parked the car, and the smoke from the Chronic was as thick as London smog because Snoop chain smoked blunts of the California sticky like Newports.

"Hey! Yo! You, Snoop Dogg, nigga?" Two New Yorkers approached the smoke-filled Caddy.

"No autographs! Move back, fool!" Tray Dee didn't trust nobody, especially after what happened earlier.

"Fuck dat shit! We don't want no autograph! We 'bout business! I got somethin' else for ya!" The New York nigga reached his hands into his jacket.

"Pop! Pop! Pop! Pop!" Tray let off four rounds from his 9 mm handgun. The New York thug fell to the ground, leaking like a used condom.

"It's a demo, fool! Kid, you shot my nigga! He Rap son! You shot him fo' a fuckin' demo!" The tires of the white Caddy burned as Tray Dee put the pedal to the metal.

"Cuzz! We gotta get the fuck out of New York. Shit been all bad since that radio interview. Go to the airport nigga! Now!" Snoop was ready to get ghost. They could add him to the DPG video later. He couldn't believe Tray Dee blasted that fool in the parking lot, but his homie was always a trigger happy nigga. Ever since he went triple platinum on Death Row Records, the police had been on his ass, harassing him about smokin' Chronic, and his gang affiliations. Now that shit was on a whole different level. Murder was a different case. Murder was twenty five to life. He realized that he should have never listened to Suge Knight.

"Why in the fuck did I come to New York!?" So what if his albums didn't sell there, he had fans in other places all over the world.

"Fuck New York! Let's shake da spot!" Tray Dee agreed with Snoop on that one. They parked the Cadillac in the long term parking terminal and strolled to the entrance of the airport at JFK International. They approached the United Airlines ticket counter.

"Two first class tickets to LAX "Cuzz, I'm outta here." Snoop received the same look of surprise that his presence attracted like a magnet. The young white chick stared at him for a moment, then, "Y...You look like..."

42

"Snoop D-O double gezzle!" He completed the sentence for her. "What's crackalackin', my white nizzle?"

"Sorry, Mr. um...Mr. Dogg. Two tickets coming right up, sir!" The lady at the ticket counter molested the computer keyboard with her fingers, and a ticket started printing. "That'll be one thousand, nine hundred and fifty-seven dollars each. The total is three thousand nine hundred and fourteen dollars, please." Snoop Dogg pulled out a large bank roll of crisp big face Franklins and Snoop counted them off faster than a money counting machine.

"Flight 1906 departs in one hour, gate 27, sir," the attendant announced as she handed Snoop the two tickets and his change with a groupie lookin' smile. "Pl...Please, Mr. Dogg. Can I have your autograph?" The lady knew that she was in the presence of rap royalty.

"Fo' snizzel, my white nizzel." Snoop signed the piece of paper, then handed it back to the cashier. Snoop loved the fans.

"Fuck! A whole hour in dis bitch! Let's go to da bar, Cuzz!" Snoop said to Tray Dee.

"Hold up, O.G. I can't make it past the metal detectors. I'm still packin." Tray Dee made a quick move into the bathroom, then exited a 9 mm lighter. The two gangsters walked through the metal detectors of the airport and headed toward the waiting area by gate 27.

"Let's hit dat spot over there, Cuzz, get some hot wangs and thangs. I still ain't ate shit!" They dipped into a sports bar.

"Damn, Cuzz! Pass the ball Kobe!" Snoop Dogg yelled at the big screen and chomped on hot wings and fries. Tray Dee sipped on gin and juice, and the two gangsters anxiously waited for their flight.

"Five mo' minutes to go!" Tray Dee announced, glancing at his Rolex watch.

"Man, I'm 'bout to shake Death Row and start my own shit! Dre gone. Michell'e pregnant. That nigga Suge is foul! Damn, pass the fuckin' ball, Kobe! Fuck it, let's bounce. This game over anyway! Let's shake the spot, Cuzz." Snoop paid the bill, left a hefty tip, and they left the sports bar. Dr. Lesley was close behind and looking for a chance to make her move.

"Excuse me, sir. Are you Calvin Broadus? Are you Snoop Dogg?" the neatly dressed white nigga in the suit asked.

"Yeah, my nizzle. See, Tray Dee? I got all kinds of fans, Cuzz. They love me in New York..."

"N.Y.P.D. home chicken! You under arrest! You murdered Tyrone Edwards. An APB was put out for you an hour ago!" He grabbed Snoop by his skinny arms and applied the cold steel of the handcuffs with ease. Three other N.Y.P.D. cops emerged from the shadows and quickly gaffled Tray Dee. The two Death Row Records affiliates were then patted down and placed in the waiting patrol cars.

"Snoop Dogg Arrested on Murder Charges in New York!!" Dr. Lesley read the front page headlines of the New York Times.

"Shit!! Shit! Shit!!" Now there was no way to complete her assignment, because not even Dr. Lisa could figure out a plan to get to Snoop in a men's prison. Her mistake cost her a bundle. She lost the war but how could she have predicted that those niggas would blast an innocent kid. Lisa made a call to Eugene in Las Vegas, then followed his orders and caught the first thing smoking, home to Detroit. Although she failed in her mission, Dr. Lesley was still in it to win it. There was no doubt she was now totally addicted to the thrill of the hunt. She was hooked from this moment on and Snoop Dogg was lucky he went to jail, or his ass would have been the past.

Los Angeles, California

"I changed my mind, sugar. I'll sing in yo' song. I'll do whatever it takes!" Be'oncay gave Pac some groupie love.

"Fo' sho', 'bout time you came over to the west side. Money Over Bitches, MOB. Yo' homegirls almost cost you a shot at gettin' paid. Death Row don't wait fo' nobody! Turn around, let me take a look at dat ass again."

"Bossy, huh. You know, I like that. I love a man who know what he want." Be'oncay made a glamorous spin, then made her butt cheeks do a booty bounce.

"Damn, girl! Do dat shit again. You got skills and you fine as fuck." Tupac approached her, hands at the ready.

"Slow down! I ain't no hit it and quit it type bitch! I know how you get around. You gotta take me out!" Be'oncay said, slappin' at Mr. Octopus' hands.

"You one a dem snooty type bitches. You gotta be gettin' paid to get wit' a nigga!" The whites of Tupac's eyes turned red with anger, and the transformation took place right before Be'oncay's eyes. Tupac was spoiled and used to getting whatever he wanted. Nobody said no to the M.V.P. of Death Row Records. He was a Rap superstar.

"No. No, baby. I'm just sayin', let's take it slow. AIDs and stuff is out there. I'm worth the wait, honey. I promise." Be'oncay gave Pac a seductive stare.

"Knock! Knock! Knock!"

The pounding sound at the door of the suite startled them. Be'oncay thanked God for the interruption.

"Who dat? Who dat?" Tupac barked, successfully distracted.

"It's me. Capone! Suge want you in da studio, blood!" Even the M.V.P. had to listen to the C.E.O.

"Tell dat nigga I'll be there!" Pac responded, trying to keep his swagger and salvage his role as a superstar.

"Aight, blood. I'll 'B' you there!" Capone was gone.

"Now back to you. You come in here lookin' all good and shit! Shakin' yo ass like dat and ain't givin' up no ass? Okay, baby, I'll play yo' game. I like yo' attitude. You one a dem librarian type, square bitches. I'ma take you to the studio wit' me, and maybe to da Tyson fight in Vegas. You a dime piece. Let's ride!" Pac had a role for Be'oncay because he knew that a female that fly could definitely be good for his image.

Be'oncay felt relieved that she didn't have to kick Tupac's little ass again. She was in, and rode toward Death Row Records headquarters in the passenger seat of Tupac's Jaguar, satisfied to be inside the private circle. Completing a hit on Tupac was going to be risky business, because that nigga had more people around him than Osama Bin Laden. Getting close enough to him to deaden him was the easy part, but getting away unnoticed was going to take a miracle.

Be'oncay glanced in the rearview mirror, playing it off like she was applying lipstick to her full lips. She couldn't help but notice the three D-Bo types dressed in red stuffed in the back seats, and the Death Row pendants around their necks sparkling with diamonds. Be'oncay wondered what was the big deal about Tupac anyway. He was disrespectful to women, and looked at them as mere sex objects. He was arrogant, sexist, and cursed like a New York taxi driver. The invite to the Tyson fight was all the opportunity she needed, and Be'oncay decided to chill for now and perfect her plan. She was a million miles away from Houston, so she knew about miracles, and a slim chance at killing this fool was better than no chance at all.

"Mmoooothafuuukaa! AAAaaahh!! Ummph!" Karen felt the walls of her vagina stretch further than any of her numerous sexual episodes combined. "Dis shit hurt! Gimme some drugs! Knock my ass out! Gimme a enema!" Karen abandoned her decision to have natural childbirth because she thought she was a lot tougher than the white bitches on Oprah who bragged about their natural deliveries.

"I see the crown of the head. One more push, Karen. You can do it!" the doctor said, ignoring Karen's request for drugs, because everybody in the hospital knew about Ms. Stephins and her mouth. She was driving the medical staff crazy with her requests and gave out more orders that the Queen of England.

"Fuuuuck Yoooo! Uuuuump! AAaaah!" Karen released a loud scream like that bitch on *The Exorcist*.

"Wwaaaaah! Waaaaah! Waaaaah!" It was a bouncing baby boy. Karen Stephins was a mother, and father.

"Give him here. He so handsome! Look just like he mama!" Karen showed a rare sign of compassion. "Li'l nigga, almost killed my black ass! Made my pussy hurt like a mothafucka!" Well, almost.

Later on that night, Karen was alone in her Manhattan penthouse breastfeeding her son. She looked around at her plush surroundings, and she liked what she saw. The million dollars came in handy and at the perfect time. If it wasn't for that bitch Gladiss in Las Vegas, she would probably be living with her homegirl, Kiesha, in the projects and living off welfare. Now she had a chance to self-publish her book, and provide a life for her son. Karen hated to

47

admit it, but she owed Gladiss and Superhead always paid her debts. Even though she had an exterior as tough as nails, her heart was as soft as a baby's bottom.

Karen was a very loyal person, and she stayed down with the few people who helped her in life. Now that the burden of baby delivery was finally over, she could set the record straight with the fools in Las Vegas. If they gave away a million dollars just like that, there had to be more money where that came from, and Karen wanted in on the hog killing.

"Yeah, Kiesha. I need you to watch my baby for a couple weeks. Yeah, I know the little nigga bad, but I'll pay you good, girl. Get over here, bitch. I'm going to California!"

CHAPTER 7

Las Vegas, Nevada - Fight Night.
Mike Tyson versus Bruce Seldon

Tupac rambled off a rhyme flow about the invincibility of his pahtnah, Iron Mike Tyson. The crowd went wild and joined in on the worship of this boxing god, fresh from the Indiana prison system. Be'oncay sat and witnessed the whole thing, and noticed Meagan in attendance with one of Suge Knight's flunkies. Be'oncay almost fell over in her seat when she saw Karen Stephins enter the MGM Arena, on the arm of Suge Knight! Damn that bitch moved fast, didn't she just have a baby? Ms. Knolls didn't give a fuck about what was going on during the fight because she and Meagan had already agreed that it was going to be a better opportunity to take care of business after the fight was over. Tupac was the biggest star in the arena and Death Row gangsters seemed to be everywhere. The bright red jackets, black brim hats, and distinctive diamond pendants were omnipresent. As expected, Tyson made a quick job out of Bruce Seldon and the fight was over almost before it began.

"I'm goin' back stage to holla at my boy. Suge takin' me to da club. Go back to da room. Get that pussy ready! Meet me at da club! We fuckin' later on tonight! Iron Mike Tyson, baby!"

Tupac left the scene and Be'oncay went upstairs, but not to the hotel room she and Tupac shared. Instead, she met with Dr. Lesley, Meagan and Karen in a room registered to an anonymous guest.

"Here are your weapons, bullets are in the cartridges. Be careful. I didn't have enough materials to make too many. Good luck." Dr. Lesley handed Meagan and Be'oncay the straps.

"They takin' the BMW 740i, Suge already told me! It's in the parking garage in V.I.P." Karen had become a very good friend of Suge's. Superhead tended to have that effect on niggas.

"Cool. The car is out back. Let's go, Be'oncay." Meagan was dressed in all black, and started making her way out of the room.

"Hey! Where my gun at!?" Karen wanted to get in on the action.

"We out!" Be'oncay said, as she and Meagan exited the hotel room carrying big backpacks, then the door slammed behind them.

"Where my gun at!?" Karen repeated, staring at Dr. Lesley.

"You don't get a gun, sorry. Direct orders from Gladiss. Sorry again," Lisa Lesley said with a sincere teacher-like look on her face.

"Y'all bitches fuckin' up. Y'all need me! Fuck it then. I'm gone!" Karen went into a fit of anger, then stormed out the room, headed downstairs to the blackjack table. Nobody was going to get in the last word on Karen Stephins.

Downstairs, after stompin' out a fool from Compton's South Side Crips, the Death row gangsters left the hotel to a long line of luxury vehicles parked at the curb. Meagan and Be'oncay followed them, and the hunt was on. The BMW maneuvered through Las Vegas traffic with the greatest of ease, because Death Row owned the streets no matter where they touched down. Meagan was an excellent driver and controlled the Honda Accord with the expertise of a NASCAR driver. The years of dealing with Los Angeles traffic made her a road warrior. The opportunity came when the BMW 740i stopped at a traffic light a couple blocks away from Club 662.

"Now, B! Get 'em now!" Meagan yelled. Be'oncay jumped out of the car and the 9 mm screamed, "Pop! Pop! Pop! Pop! Pop! Pop! Pop! The deadly bullets found their targets. Nobody could shoot like Be'oncay.

"Time! Let's move!" Meagan said, glancing at her stop watch. Be'oncay jumped into the Honda, and the tires roared as the car jetted away from the crime scene.

"Tupac Shakur and Suge Knight Involved in Las Vegas Shootout!" Gladiss read the headlines of the Las Vegas Review Journal. The news of the shooting was everywhere and even made worldwide headlines. Tupac was said to be in critical condition but Suge only suffered a small graze to the head. Be'oncay explained how, when the bullets started flying, Suge ducked behind Tupac and she couldn't get a decent shot at him. Gladiss was interrupted by the sound of the ringing of her private phone.

"Gladiss!" She answered the line knowing that it could only be one person calling her.

"Puff Daddy refused to pay the other half of the agreed upon figure. I tried to argue our position, but..."

"Don't worry about it! Organize a meeting with the girls. All of them! Now! I have plans for Mr. Puffy Combs." Gladiss didn't care about the money. It was all about the integrity.

"Yes, ma'am. I'm on it. Anything else?" Deborah responded.

"No, not at this time." Gladiss hung up the phone.

"Yerfwin, we have a problem. The element in New York has reneged on his agreement. I recommend immediate termination of his organization." Gladiss spoke on the closed circuit radio.

"Affirmative. We must silence the threat. Mr. Knight is a formidable foe. We cannot allow word to get out." Yerfwin responded.

"Yes. The meeting is already scheduled. I am requesting permission to initiate the plan." Gladiss said.

"Permission granted, Ms. Nyte. Failure is not an option. Understand?" Yerfwin sounded disappointed.

"Yes...yes, boss. I understand." Gladiss said with a hint of fear in her voice.

"Goodbye, Gladiss." The call ended with a click.

Gladiss could not believe that the Panhellenic Council was almost doomed after only one mission. Her brain child was now standing on its last leg. She was relieved that she was able to buy valuable time to prove to Yerfwin that she could make something out of the young women and salvage the mission. The only way that she could make it happen was to make the young women work as a team. Teamwork was going to be the key to success.

"Tupac Shukar pronounced dead at a Las Vegas hospital!" Gladiss was interrupted from her thoughts by the announcement on CNN. A slight smile of satisfaction came to her face. Part of the west coast problem was taken care of, but she knew that it was going to be impossible to get to Suge Knight now. He was probably being guarded with more protection than the gold in Fort Knox. However, Puff Daddy and Biggie were a different situation. She immediately thought about the upcoming Soul Train Music Awards show coming to Los Angeles. Gladiss picked up the phone.

"Yeah, Jimmy. I want you to book Biggie as a presenter at the awards show. I like his music," Gladiss lied.

"Sure...sure, Ms. Nyte. Anything you want. I'll keep this between me and you. Money is not an object." Jimmy was speaking to a legend.

"Thanks, Jimmy." The line went dead. Now it was time to reorganize the troops and get the females back together for an important mission. They had a little over a month to work out all the kinks and force them to work as a team. Gladiss soon realized that she had her work cut out for her, especially when it came to Karen Stephins. However, Gladiss was an expert when it came to shaping young black women, and she had a very successful daughter to show for it. She put together her master plan, because there was no way that she was going to allow Puff Daddy and Biggie to get away with murder and not pay her for it.

Eugene L. Weems, Timothy R. Richardson

CHAPTER 8

Los Angeles, California

The Tupac Shakur murder created a gang war between the Bloods and the Crips. It was like World War III in Compton, and there were casualties on both sides. Many people died on the city streets.

Meagan had no idea that Tupac was loved and admired by so many people. "If they only knew," Meagan exclaimed as another show paid tribute to Pac's legacy on television. A laundry list of stars gave teary eyed memories of their encounters with Tupac. Suge Knight blamed the South Side Crips and Bad Boy Records, and the word on the street was there was a two million dollar hit on Sean "Puffy" Combs and Christopher "Biggie" Wallace. The streets of Southcentral Los Angeles were in Chaos.

"How could Tupac be murdered in Las Vegas with all them motherfuckin' cameras and nobody saw nothing?" The rumors circulated everywhere and the theories were in the thousands. Meagan was a culprit and participant in the ultimate hip hop crime of the century.

Meagan was interrupted by the ringing of the phone that Gladiss gave her years ago. "Yes, this is Meagan speaking. Meagan Goodwin," she answered, being very professional.

"Las Vegas Hilton, room 777. Friday. 8:00 p.m."

The line went dead but there was no mistaking who it was. Meagan was stunned as she hung up the phone. She pulled out her stash of Chronic, poured herself a tall glass of Hypnotiq and started her private celebration. Meagan lived life to the fullest because getting shot made her realize that life could never be taken for granted. Today was a rare moment to rest, and Friday was going to be back to business. Meagan loved taking care of business.

Houston, Texas

Be'oncay was still fuming and hated that she made the mistake of not killing Suge Knight. She wished that she'd had a least one more clip of ammo that night in Vegas. Be'oncay wished for one more chance to do the whole night over again. The entire episode replayed over and over again in her mind. The only thing that she wanted in life was perfection in everything she did, that was how her daddy raised her, the best and nothing less.

The ifs, shouldas, couldas, and wouldas came rambling through her brain. "Why?" she said to herself as she looked at another interview with Suge Knight on television. The failed assassination attempt made him an overnight celebrity, a superstar. It seemed like the media portrayed him as a fuckin' martyr or something, like he had a mission or world-changing purpose. They treated Suge Knight like a victim!

"Riing! Riing!" Be'oncay was interrupted from her critical thinking by the sound of a telephone ringing. She answered it, "Hey, honey. Be'oncay Knolls speaking," she said into the receiver.

"Friday, Las Vegas Hilton, Room 777. 8:00 p.m. Be there."

The line went dead.

"Well, excuse me! That was ugly. How rude." Be'oncay began her mental preparations. She had to cancel rehearsal with the girls on Friday. Be'oncay was going back to Las Vegas. She loved show business.

Detroit, Michigan

Dr. Lisa Lesley was disappointed by her failure at the airport, and now her inability to prepare enough ammo for Be'oncay and Meagan to get the job done in Las Vegas. The life of an assassin was not going very well for her, and Dr. Lisa hated failure. On a scale of one to ten, she rated her performance a three, an F minus, a failure, not even close to a passing score.

She hoped for another chance to prove her worth but, if not, the million dollars would go a long way in starting her children's clinic.

Dr. Lesley could also complete her very important research on her miracle drug, Formula 7, a bacteria and virus killing concoction that destroyed 98 percent of the viruses that caused AIDS, syphilis, tuberculosis, sickle cell and even cancer.

Dr. Lesley had the power to change the world with her discovery, but America was not interested in cures because there was more money in keeping people highly medicated. The multi-billion dollar pharmaceuticals industry didn't see much profit in one-time customers. The real money was made on repeat customers. They existed on lifetime commitments. Dr. Lesley knew the politics of medications in this country and, thus, decided to take her idea to a foreign land with less restrictions.

She hated that her career as an assassin was so short-lived because she enjoyed the adrenaline rush of killing rappers. The hit records, strip clubs and bragging and boasting were all messages that

Dr. Lisa wanted to silence before they corrupted the children forever. She was a fan of Motown.

"Riing! Riing!" Dr. Lesley was disrupted from her thoughts of saving the world by the sound of a phone ringing. "Yes, Dr. Lisa Lesley speaking. May I help you?" Lisa answered the phone.

"Friday, Hilton Hotel, Las Vegas, room 777, 8:00 p.m.

The line went dead. Lisa knew all about Las Vegas and the meeting months ago that changed her life. Maybe she had given up too soon and she couldn't wait to find out. She started packing her bags for the weekend, the excitement of the kill was back. Dr. Lesley was ready for action, and she loved Las Vegas.

Brooklyn, New York

The news about the death of Tupac Shukar spread around the streets of New York like bootleg CDs. Everybody had their theory on who took out Tupac, and most rumors pointed straight at Puff Daddy and Biggie, the Bad Boy camp shot callers. The murder raised up the street credibility of their crew as high as gas prices.

Karen looked at the situation and thought about how funny the whole thing was, and that the idiots in the Rap world never once suspected a woman of being capable of pulling off the crime. What a shame! The world will never know the truth because Karen told a lot of shit, but she would never tell anyone about the Panhellenic Council. Gladiss had actually put together a pretty good thing, but too bad she was too blind to see that Karen was the best woman for the job.

"That skeezer Be'oncay couldn't shoot a bullet and hit the ocean if she was standing on the beach!" Karen hated those Zeta Phi Beta bitches. "That pussy lipped ho' Meagan bitch can't even act. Shit, she can't drive either." Karen really, really, hated those Alpha Kappa Alpha bitches. She blamed Gladiss for the failure of the entire mission, for not allowing her to kill Suge when she had the chance.

"I'm gone be all right!" Karen said out loud, not doing a good job of lying to herself. She wanted desperately to become a part of something besides her sorority, and liked the idea of the Panhellenic Council. The best thing she could do was be a good provider for her son. Karen was interrupted from her thoughts by the ringing of the private phone provided to her by Gladiss.

"Who the fuck is this?" Karen had a special way of answering the phone.

"Las Vegas Hilton, Friday at 8:00 p.m. Reservation is under your name."

The line went dead.

"Motherfucka!" Karen wanted some answers because she was tired of getting the runaround. Either she was in or she was out. These bitches were as wishy-washy as some of the niggas she fucked with on the streets of New York. However, a deal was a deal, and those mothafuckas had found her once before, but this time Karen was going to put it all on the line. She had a bone to pick with those bitches in Las Vegas, and you know that Karen always got the last word.

Eugene L. Weems, Timothy R. Richardson

CHAPTER 9

Los Angeles, California - Soul Train Music Awards
Shrine Auditorium, March 7, 1997

The chorus of boos rained down from the nose bleed seats section of the auditorium. The California hate toward Biggie was predictable because Tupac Shukar was murdered just six short months earlier in Las Vegas. The truth was clear that everybody knew that Puffy and Biggie had something to do with it. The ongoing beef between Biggie and Pac fueled a nationwide beef of epic proportions.

Tupac released *California Love, Hit 'Em Up* and *21 Gun Salute* and *Hail Mary*. "Nigga lookin' like Larry Holmes, flabby and sick, tryin' to playa hate on my shit, can eat a fat dick." Nobody could debate that. There was no mistaking who Pac was talking about.

Biggie had a powerful pen and responded with, *Warning, Get Money, Going Back To Cali* and the horrible ballsy, *Who Shot Ya*. To push the knife further into Tupac's legacy, the song, *Going Back To Cali* was released a few weeks after Tupac's death. Biggie was the young street hypocrite battling back and forth with tracks from Bad Boy studios, spittin' venom at Pac and Death Row. But playin' the "We not paper studio gangsters" role in magazines and

61

interviews on television. The Rap public wasn't stupid. Everybody knew that Biggie hated Tupac for fuckin' Faith Evans back in the day. He could hide the truth from the media but that nigga couldn't lie to the streets. Wars have been fought because of women, and the battle between the East Coast and the West Coast was no different.

Biggie exited the stage with a big "fuck you" sign from his middle finger, pointed toward the heavens. The gesture just added fuel to the fire and the boo birds got louder and the insults more severe. Biggie should have known better than to come to Cali, and it was only six months since Pac was put six feet under. He might as well have pulled down his big draw's and took a shit on Tupac's grave. His west coast appearance was the ultimate show of disrespect and he never made a positive comment about Tupac. The evidence of his mistake was popping up like popcorn. Biggie was in denial, but the signs were everywhere.

There was the car that rolled up next to his rental on Sunset Boulevard, with that fool talking shit to him about Tupac's murder, and then throwing up the "W" sign, fingers twisted in the middle. The insults shouted their way when he and his crew were at the Beverly Center, out looking for fresh gear. The members of Puffy's security detail who got earloads of warnings from almost, anonymous sources, about death around the corner and possible hits, while they were out partying at the Century club and House of Blues. The warnings came from mere pawns in the game, but the Bad Boy nobodies still had associates who had their ears to the streets. The crown prince of Bad Boy Records didn't give a fuck. Biggie ignored all the signs and blew them off as "playa haters, hatin' a nigga."

Meagan couldn't believe her luck! "Shit! That fat ass nigga, crazy ass fuck!" She was fuming with anger as she stormed out of the Four Seasons Hotel. "A week's worth of planning thrown down the fuckin' drain!" Meagan stuffed another blunt full with Chronic and quickly lit up. The research was done perfectly, she had the hotel manager in the palm of her hands. The room service uniform was starched and pressed and hugged her flawless curves perfectly. Meagan had the room key and also Biggie's schedule was memorized to the exact second.

It was the perfect plan until Big Poppa decided to go Grape Ape and give Charli Baltimore an Ike Turner type beatdown. You can take the nigga out the hood, but you can never take the hood out the nigga. The powers that be were so upset that not even Biggie and Puffy Combs could come up with enough money to stop their eviction from the Four Seasons Hotel. Apparently there were still some things that money couldn't buy, and these white folks weren't selling. So Biggie and his crew had to take their circus on the road to a new location, minus a bruised and battered Charli Baltimore of course.

Meagan followed the caravan to the Westwood Marquis Hotel and hoped that the rumors of Biggie's trip to London were false. A Bad Boy trip to Europe would have ruined everything. Meagan only had connections in California. Once Biggie left the West Coast, all bets were off. She swiftly blended in with the tail end of the entourage and approached the front desk.

"My cousin with Biggie 'n dem. I got lost in traffic. What room dey in?" Meagan performed her best booty bouncer at a strip club persona.

"Room 112," the clerk responded, eyeing lustfully at the tempting cleavage of Meagan's hooters. Eventually his eyes travelled up a bit and rested on the sight of her full, pouting lips and he looked like he wanted to taste them.

Meagan managed to escape, then dipped in the service pantry and, just as she suspected, Biggie and his crew had already ordered. "Extra large sausage pizza, room 112! Extra special saliva sauce, if you know what I mean! West siiide!" The cook said as he spit a big loogy on the finished pizza. He was obviously a Tupac fan. Everybody in the hotel knew about the arrival of the notorious B.I.G. and his crew from New York. Shit, they had enough niggas with them to start an African village. Meagan quickly got the attention of the Mexican bellhop.

"Cincuenta dolares if you let me deliver that pizza amigo!" The bellhop looked at the big faced image of Grant and handed over the silver platter in a millisecond.

"Knock! Knock! Knock! Room service!" Meagan was forced to yell because of the loud music and even louder conversations that leaked from room 112.

"Yo, Shorty! Damn, you fine! Wanna room wit' us?" Lil Cease said, eyes as yellow as a fake gold chain. The official blunt roller of the crew and groupie go-getter was always on the prowl for fowl.

"No, thanks. I got a delivery. Order a pizza?" Meagan showed him the large tray.

"Ah shit, come in," Cease responded, upset with the rejection. Most California bitches were stuck up, and not even cash money could change their attitude.

Meagan entered the room and saw about thirty people crammed into the master suite. It was worse than a scene from a pad in the projects. Black folks were everywhere, in chairs, on couches, sitting on the floor, standing up, and a few walked around stalking like hungry vultures waiting for a fool to slip and make the mistake of leaving their seat.

Meagan discreetly checked the small of her back for the Glock 9 mm and realized that taking out Biggie in this room would be nothing short of suicide. She knew all about Biggie's crew from the files and her briefings from Commander Weems. They purchased heat from the Crips in Compton and she had no idea who was packin'. Meagan was a bad bitch, but even she knew that the *Kill Bill* type shit that the white bitch did in the movies wasn't possible in real life.

"Twenty five, ninety five, please!" Meagan said, still surveying the room, yet to see Biggie.

"Damn you right, homie. Dis bitch is fine! Here, Shorty. Keep da change." D-Roc handed Meagan a crispy clean big-face Franklin and scooped up the pizza. "You sure ya don't wanna sit and take a load off? We need some mo' females for da video. How 'bout it?" D-Roc wasn't going to give up on this West Coast dime piece.

"No...no, thank you. Gotta work, big boy." Meagan was getting a contact high from the heavy fog of weed smoke that consumed the room. It smelled like a Marijuana factory and she couldn't even see five feet in front of her. Meagan made her exit.

In the comfort of her Lexus bubble, Meagan contemplated her next move. Biggie was confident, secure and arrogant. The East Coast gangster believed that he was untouchable. He was also very naïve if he thought that nobody could touch him in California. The combination of weed and alcohol was eating away at the core of his security team. Add the females and the natural beauty of his surroundings, and Meagan knew that eventually Biggie Smalls and his crew would get caught with their pants down. With every passing second in Cali, Big became more and more comfortable that there would be no retaliation for the Tupac shooting.

Meagan had other plans because she knew, eventually, Christopher was going to go to one of his spots, like Rochester Big and Tall, or the beach, or on a mission to re-up on his supply of the sticky green aromatic buds of the Chronic. How could Biggie resist Cali? It was only a matter of time before he went steppin' out on the town. Nobody could resist the beauty of California, and when Biggie gave in to the temptation of the streets, Meagan was going to be right there waiting for him.

Biggie lounged near the pool of the Westwood Marquis Hotel, chillin' like a villain, smoking on a fat Bob Marley-like blunt, in full view of a no-smoking sign, watching the white kids play in the pool, splashing water on each other like a Baywatch commercial. Biggie was on top of the world, and the world was his for the taking. Now that Tupac was out of the way and Snoop Dogg was in prison on murder charges, there was no competition for Big Poppa. He was the best Rapper in the world. Biggie was going to do his thing. He was preparing to follow up his album, *Life After Death*, with a triple album to speed up fulfilling his contractual obligations to Puff and get the fuck away from Bad Boy Records. Biggie wanted to be free to do his own shit.

"Fuck Puffy! Can't even keep me in a hotel!" Biggie grunted to himself, starting to hate the "High Roller" persona created. The hasty hotel move had cost him half of his entourage and now he was stuck with an undermanned and unprepared security team of mostly New York niggas, unfamiliar with the streets of Cali. A lot of the South Side Crip niggas that he had already paid out of his own pockets shook the spot when the Beverly Hills Police showed up at the other spot. The Beverly Hills Cop type shit that Eddie Murphy put in his movies was real stuff. A nigga was just a nigga with money in Beverly Hills. Biggie might as well have been offering those crackers Monopoly money. His cash wasn't worth a damn in this part of California. He got a real taste of how it felt to be black in Cali, real NWA type shit.

Some funny shit had been happening since he left New York and touched down in Cali. Charli Baltimore cheating on him with a nigga from the Death Row clique. That's a no-no! He got boos from the crowd at the Soul Train Music Awards. The constant mean mugs and rejections he got from bitches when he went out in public. Shit, a call girl even turned down his money because of Tupac's murder. Biggie couldn't even buy a piece of pussy in Cal anymore. It was a Pussy Strike against Bad Boy Records and anybody who associated with them. Biggie saw the storm coming and was smart enough to know that he had to rise above the East versus West Coast shit. That's why he want to jet to London and get far away from the trenches in this war. Death had that type of effect on a nigga and Biggie had two kids that he want to see grow up. However, Puffy put an end to his international escape with stiff demands that he do the Soul Train Music Awards appearance to promote his album in California. Biggie didn't give a fuck about sellin' records in Cali or the fact that he wasn't a Rap star on the West Coast. He was the king of New York! "I shouldn't have ta take no orders from a fuckin' dancer!" Biggie puffed on his Chronic blunt, stressed out of his wits.

Christopher Wallace had big plans. There was so much shit he wanted to accomplish, that was going to blow him up in the game, bigger than Bad Boy and even Puffy. He was making major paper moves right in front of Puff's eyes. His record label, Undeas

Entertainment, that he co-owned with Lance "Un" Rivera. The launching of his restaurant, Big Poppa's Chicken and Waffles in Harlem. His own clothing line, Brooklyn Mint, for his gangsters in New York. A specialty clothing boutique named, Big and Heavy's was also in the works. Rapper, Heavy D, was going to partner up with Biggie on this venture, to give the big and tall customers a chance to be fitted in the latest fashions. Biggie had other dreams of starting a movie studio, making films, commercials, and even television sitcoms. He was a visionary and the more weed he smoked, the more creative shit he came up with.

Biggie thought back to his first visit to California, back in 1994, before Death Row blew up like the World Trade. He came to Los Angeles for eight weeks during the summer and he brought his entire Brooklyn crew with him. California love was in great abundance. He was a star. The perfect big, black, ugly, and broke nigga from the ghetto who made it large with a hit record. Big brothers finally had a star to look up to and he proved that a nigga didn't have to be light-skinned and a skinny mothafucka to fuck models and R & B singers and actresses. He put big, black, and ugly niggas on the map.

His West Coast itinerary was jam-packed with record signings, promotional gigs at Summer Jam, college mix shows, Saturday night proms, mom and pop store appearances, and dropping by local radio stations. There was no hating, and he invaded every club in Southcentral L.A. and Compton. Biggie Smalls was doing real big thangs.

What a difference three years could make. He went from being in the lime light to being in the dark. Who would have thought that his road dog of yesterday, Tupac Shakur, would survive prison and blow up after his small role in the movie, *Juice*. Tupac took that Bishop role with him to the street and his dealings with the niggas from Queens just made it worse. Why did he have to get shot at the studio where Biggie invited him to bust a few verses on his album?

He found out later that Puff Daddy had set up the whole thing because Biggie said some shit about wanting to smoke Tupac for runnin' up in Faith Evans. Shit! He was just high and mad about trying to turn a ho' into a housewife. Biggie didn't give a fuck about Tupac back then, but who would have thought that a little ass thug nigga, with a big mouth, would blow up like a nuclear bomb. He lived through the five bullets, and now he had the strength of the Death Row army behind him. To top things off, Tupac blamed the whole shooting on Biggie and now it was all out war. Tupac got smoked and now everybody pointed the finger at the notorious B.I.G. The motharfuckas in California treated Tupac's death like the crucifixion of Jesus Christ. The whole world mourned when Pac got shot.

Biggie thought about the titles Puffy put on his albums; *Ready to Die*, and now, *Life After Death*. "How could a nigga have a life after death if he ain't even dead yet?" Only Puff Daddy had the answer to that question.

Eugene L. Weems, Timothy R. Richardson

CHAPTER 10

Westwood, California

Meagan followed the green Suburban and she finally got the opening to make her move. She knew that time was running out and that she had to smoke Biggie before he took off for London. Meagan didn't have any connections in Europe yet, so a successful assassination in a foreign land was out of the question. California was Meagan's stomping grounds, the Cali streets were her domain. It was now or never.

The big green Chevy Suburban turned on Wilshire Boulevard. There were only a few people in the vehicle, but Meagan didn't care. The only person she was worried about being in the Suburban was Biggie Smalls. She knew exactly where he was seated and he wasn't going to be hard to miss.

Eugene Weems taught her how to perfect her shooting skills and she thought back to the intense training. Meagan had learned from the best how to make her weapon an extension of her arm. The proper breathing techniques to use when taking aim, and how to target vital areas of the body to cause instant death. Meagan only learned one way to shoot, and that was to shoot to kill.

She positioned her yellow Hummer directly behind the green Suburban. Meagan allowed her foot to ease up off the accelerator and soon dropped back about four car lengths and watched as the bright red brake lights of the Chevy illuminated when the driver stopped at a red light across from the Peterson Automotive Museum. It was time for some action! Meagan put the pedal to the floor and the yellow Hummer rocketed toward the stable Chevy Suburban.

CRAASSH! The indestructible combat vehicle rammed into the commercial Suburban and the alloyed steel of the Hummer won the battle of metal colliding with metal.

"What...what the fuck!?" Biggie was thrown from his seat on impact. He spilled his drink all over his Versace suit, it seemed like an earthquake. D-Roc hit his head on the steering wheel and was knocked out cold. Suddenly, the rear passenger side door was opened, and a female figure dressed in black appeared, a lovely angel of death.

"Pop! Pop! Pop! Pop! Pop! The bullets from the Glock 9 mm swiftly found their target. Biggie screamed as he felt the burning sensation of hot lead penetrate his flesh. He leaked blood like a runny faucet and Meagan watched the life slowly leave his body. Biggie was gone.

Meagan disappeared to her yellow Hummer like a thief in the night. The reinforced steel of her war chariot was barely damaged and her Hummer was still running. She pushed the joystick to the drive position and headed straight to her hideout. She pulled off her red bandana, blended into the freeway traffic, sprayed on a little perfume and navigated her way home. The transformation was complete. Meagan was back to looking like a fine, sexy, young, black woman and smelling good. Nobody would have ever suspected a woman of taking out one of the baddest gangsters ever to pick up a microphone. Nobody would have ever thought that a black woman was smart enough, or had the guts to smoke the killer Bad Boy.

"You just keep thinking, a nigga making so much money, their lifestyle should be more protected," Biggie once said, talking indirectly about Tupac, but was he really thinking about himself?" "Their lives should be more protected where things like a drive-by shooting ain't supposed to happen. He's supposed to have lots of security. He ain't even supposed to be sittin' by no window." The notorious B.I.G. learned the hard way, at the intersection of Wilshire and Fairfax, that what goes around comes around. Biggie learned that anybody could get caught slippin' in the darkness.

Manhattan, New York

"Christopher 'Notorious B.I.G.' Wallace Dead! Victim of Drive-By Shooting in Los Angeles!"

Puffy Combs looked at the headlines of the New York Times and feared for his life. He never never thought, in a million years, that somebody would be able to scare him. He was the man who put the "Bad" in Bad Boy Records. Who would have thought that Deborah Short would come back blasting like that! The cold thing about it was that everybody and they mama thought it was Suge Knight who blasted Biggie, but Puff knew better than that. Puff Daddy was shaking in his Sean John boots because he didn't know who was going to be next. He was going to lay low for awhile because he wasn't about to get capped. Nobody knew about his secret hideout.

Puffy didn't care about anybody else on his label. He was selfish like that. In fact, the shooting was making his pockets fat. The album, *Life After Death*, was selling off the racks. His manufacturer couldn't print copies fast enough to keep up with the orders. Puffy was going to lay real low, stay out of sight, and try to think of a way to get that bitch, Deborah, off his back.

Sean Combs puffed on the freshly rolled blunt, nervous as a black man sitting in a Mormon Church. He blew a lot of money trying to take out Tupac. His enemies were piling up like tooth decay between his double teeth. Suge Knight, niggas in Queens, baby mamas wanting child support, Biggie's moms, Tupac's moms, Andre Warrell, Steve Stout, the whole state of California, and now everybody in Brooklyn. Out of all these people, Puffy feared Deborah Short the most, and this bitch really made him paranoid.

"What am I gonna do now?" Puff asked himself a serious question. He couldn't go to the police for protection because Deborah had five million dollars of his money in a Tobago bank account as proof of a partial payment for a hit on Tupac.

Sean John was blessed with too much money and too little to do with it. He thought back to his early days and realized that he should have kept his black ass R & B. Puffy should have stayed fuckin' with Jodeci, Father iC, Mary J. Blige, 112, and Total type shit. He was a club dancer and promoter, not a fuckin' gangster. Biggie and his crew changed all that shit with one hit album. Gangster Rap money came too fast and easy and Puffy loved fast and easy money. Money meant everything to Sean John Combs. The more money he made, the more money he wanted. More money, more enemies, and more fuckin' problems.

Harlem, New York

"Whyyy" Why are you doin' this to meee? Please don't! I'll do anything!" Mase was on his knees, pleading for his life. Puffy had abandoned him and disappeared after Biggie's death. The boulder-sized barrel of the 44 Magnum was just inches away from his dome. Mase was no gangster, it was the closest he had ever been to death. The tall, tan, leggy sister with the pretty, young face turned out to be a cold-blooded killer when they were alone in his penthouse. Mase wanted to get a blow job, not get his head blown off.

"Well, sir. What are you going to say in twenty seconds that will stop me from killing you?" Dr. Jekyll was talking. Mase was at the mercy of a bi-polar bitch.

"I...I'll do anything! Want me to rap? I...I can sing..." WHAP! The butt end of the hard cannon came down hard of Mase's skull and blood squirted out like oil in a fresh oil strike.

"Shut the fuck up! I'm in charge. You talk when I say so!" Mr. Hyde was talking now. The prettiest bitches were always the craziest. Mase pissed on himself and whimpered like a hurt puppy. He didn't dare want to upset this crazy bitch again. She was too handy with a handgun. Mase nodded in approval then looked at her with a sad, submissive look in his teary eyes. "Okay. Sir, you have twenty seconds beginning now." Dr. Jekyll was talking again.

"I don't wanna die because I ain't no gangsta. I ain't had nothin' to do wit' Pac gettin' shot. Fuck Puffy! He don't pay me shit anyway. He just buy me clothes and jewelry for the videos. My jewelry ain't even real! I drive a Chevy Geo. I ain't got no money. I ain't no gangster. I used to go to church!" Mase talked faster than any rap he said before.

"Ten seconds! Eight seconds!" Lisa barked.

"I'm sooorrry! I didn't doooo nothin' to you. I got a sister. I'll stop rappin' right now. I'll go to work at McDonald's. I'll go back to church. Pleaaasssee! Please!" Mase pleaded for his life.

75

"Five seconds! Three seconds!" Dr. Lesley looked Mase dead in his eyes and it was a look that made him have another bowel movement. He was sweating like a piece of cake sitting in front of Charles Barkley. Mase saw death in her eyes and knew that this beautiful angel was capable of the ugly act.

"Please! My kids! Who gone raise them!!?" Mase closed his eyes.

"One!!" Lisa heard the magic words, "my kids." Dr. Lesley came out of her homicidal trance and thought about the kids. "Damn, what's that smell?" She looked at Mase and the embarrassing look he had on his face. He looked like a kindergarten kid who ate too much chili.

"I'm sorry. Nigga ain't used to dyin' like this."

"I'm not going to kill you today. Okay. I want you to go to church, become a preacher or deacon and help the kids. If I ever hear anything about you rapping again, I'll be back. I promise. Understand, Mase?" Dr. Lisa looked like a parent scolding a child.

"Yes! Anything! I'll do it! No mo' rappin' and I'ma goin' to church. Mase love the kids!" Mase was relieved.

"Go home to your family."

Mase ran out of the suite of the hotel and leaked a trail of doo-doo behind him.

"You what?" What da fuck you talkin' about? You need me! You under contract!" Puffy didn't take the news that he was losing his top artist too well.

"I'm gone, Puff! Make yo' own records! I'm retired! No mo' raps, goin' to church. I'ma preach. Bye, Puffy!"

Puffy Combs heard a loud click. Mase had called him out of the blue, shook up like a pair of Las Vegas dice, and retired from the Rap game without an explanation. "Punk mothafucka!!" Puffy threw the bottle of Cristal at the mirror on his dresser. The glass shattered into a million pieces. Mase was supposed to be his meal ticket. He was shaping Mase to be the star to keep Bad Boy Records on top, but all of a sudden he quits without an explanation. Puff had never heard his flunky so spooked. Something was definitely wrong. He knew instantly that it was Deborah's doing. Puffy had to do something before he lost everything.

"Deborah. Ms. Short. I'm sorry. I quit. You win. I wired ten million dollars to your account. It's all I got! Please leave me alone. I give up. "I'ma start makin' some clothes. No mo' music for me. Please forgive me." Puff made sure that everything was covered in the message and realized that he had fucked with the wrong bitch. It wasn't about the money anymore. The money was rolling in from sales of Biggie's album. Ten million dollars wasn't worth dying for. He just hoped that it was enough to keep the angels of death from appearing at his door.

Eugene L. Weems, Timothy R. Richardson

CHAPTER 11

Las Vegas, Nevada

Gladiss played the message over and over again, then absorbed the words Puffy spoke. It was funny what a little death could do to an arrogant, demanding, and pig-headed music tycoon. Puff Daddy was begging and pleading for his life like O.J. Simpson at another murder trial. After a brief conversation with Deborah Short, the receipt of the ten million dollar deposit into the Tobago account was confirmed. The money was not the main issue, the problem was the blatant disrespect. The entire situation was always about the disrespect of black women, and the poor influence that they had on children. The ball was back in Gladiss' court and she knew how to throw down a slam dunk.

"Yerfwin, Gladiss speaking." Gladiss had to talk things over with a higher power.

"Yes, Gladiss, I heard the news. Biggie is dead, Mase went religious, and Sean Combs is in hiding." Yerfwin knew everything.

"I await your course of action, Yerfwin." Gladiss wouldn't dare make a move without a directive from her superior.

"The commitment Mr. Combs made is acceptable. Bad Boy Records is safe for now. Our primary opposition was from Death Row. I will be waiting and watching Mr. Combs very closely. Abort the mission." Yerfwin hung up the telephone.

Gladiss knew she had to act fast because Be'oncay and Karen were on the case and, if her recollection proved correct, Sean John was on the verge of being cooked meat. Karen knew every crack and crevice of the state of New York like the pimples of her behind. Puff Daddy was definitely going to be found and then smoked like a Michael Jackson jehri curl on fire.

Brooklyn, New York

"Shut up, bitch! Before I drop you off in the projects and tell the homies to hold you hostage." Karen and Be'oncay argued every second of their time together since the start of their assignment.

"Fuck you! Fuck you, Karen! I'll kill every nigga in New York if I hafta! Ya'll projects ain't got shit on Fifth Ward, bitch! I'm only gon' be so many bitches! My name is Be'oncay! Where alligator mouth at? I can't wait to leave this shit hole!" Be'oncay was ready to shake New York and Karen Stephins. Karen was getting on her last nerve.

"Shut up, bitch! Bitch, I'm tryin' to drive!" Karen responded with another verbal assault using the B word. She made a quick turn onto the bridge and continued toward Manhattan.

"That's it, mothafucka. I'm gone give you a M-town ass whoopin." Be'oncay connected a vicious left jab. The black BMW screeched to a halt in the middle of the bridge. Karen retaliated with a stiff right jab to the nose. "Bitch!" Be'oncay responded with a swift combination of fist blows to Karen's dome, then slapped her with an open palm to the ear. Karen's bell was rung. The close combat continued and Be'oncay was winning the battle.

"Okay, freeze!" Karen held a razor sharp baby machete to Be'oncay's neck and Be'oncay held a snub-nosed .38 to Karen's stomach. Neither woman would budge an inch.

"Honk! Honk! HONK! Move da fuck outta da way!" The standoff was interrupted by the sound of an impatient New Yorker and a horn blowing competition soon followed on the bridge.

"Okay, okay, Be'oncay. Let's make a deal. Let's go make this million. Truce?" Karen knew a real gangster bitch when she saw one.

"Okay, Karen. I just want my proper respects. I ain't no punk bitch! If not you can keep this motha right here and we can end this shit right now. I ain't scared a dyin'!" Be'oncay had an angry look in her eyes.

"I said, cool, homegirl. Chill." Karen retreated.

"Okay, Karen. I'm cool, honey." Be'oncay came back to reality. "Y'all southern black women, crazy than a mothafucka!"

They laughed together, Karen got in the last word, but she made a mental note to never call Be'oncay a bitch again, at least not to her face.

Manhattan, New York. Later on that night

"My homegirl, Kim Porter, told me where he at. I promised her that I was gonna get her a ounce of dat California Chronic," Karen said after she hung up her cell phone.

"Damn, honey. Puffy girl gave him up for a ounce of weed! Where's the loyalty?" Be'oncay responded, liking Karen a little more, now that they had an understanding.

"Yeah, girl. You must not smoke weed. California got the best shit in the world. That Chronic shit, OOOH wee! It's the bomb! It makes me wanna fuck all night! Gives me the munchies like a mothafucka. I get so horny off that shit, my pussy gotta get fed." Karen's vagina got wet just thinking about the last time she had the Chronic.

"Well, that's some stuff you can keep fo' yoself, sugar. I can barely handle ses," Be'oncay confessed.

"Don't knock it till you try it. Hey, we here." Karen pulled the BMW to the curb. "Ready?" Karen asked her new crime partner.

"Ready like Freddy, honey! Let's do this." Be'oncay gave Karen a pound and they exited the black car.

"Apartment 227." Karen announced their destination. The two women made it past security with ease and headed upstairs to the second floor. The guard at the front desk eyed the pair of apple bottoms as they entered the elevator.

"Some fools have all the luck!" He knew exactly where they were headed because Puff Daddy kept a steady flow of women coming back and forth to his penthouse. He even remembered Jennifer Lopez making the trek to room 227. Money could buy anything, because with Puffy, it wasn't about his personality and definitely not his looks.

"Bam! Bam! Bam!" Be'oncay kicked in the door. Karen blasted the bodyguard. He didn't have a chance. Puffy made a run for it and ran for the window. Be'oncay pounced on him like a lioness in heat, then grabbed him. Puff Daddy was taped with the thick, gray duct tape quicker than a calf at a rodeo.

"Mmmmm! Mmmmm! Mmmmm!" Puffy couldn't talk and he hated it. The two women had their faces concealed, one with a red bandana, the other with a blue bandanna. He didn't know who in the fuck they were. The only thing Puff knew for sure was that they were women and they were deadly. They took out his high paid bodyguard like he was nothing and Damian was the top security man in New York. Puff glanced at his former protector and pussy magnet as he laid on the floor, motionless, and leaking blood like a heavy period.

He sat in the leather chair while one of the women went around his large penthouse with a couple duffle bags collecting anything of value. The other woman emptied out about an ounce of powder cocaine on the coffee table and then, "POP! POP! POP! POP!" She then place the empty gun in Puff's sweating hand. The loud sound of the music disguised the noise of the gunshots. Everybody in the building knew about Puffy's parties.

"Okay, Puff Daddy. Cocaine, a shootout, looks like a drug deal gone bad. Everybody know you like to party, honey." Be'oncay aimed her weapon at Sean John's head and was just about to pull the trigger.

"Wait! Shit! Wait! I need the combination to the safe first," Karen said, walking in the room with two big bags of shit, looking like a black female Santa Claus. "Remember what Commander Weems said." She whispered the words in Be'oncay's ear. "It ain't a robbery unless you hit the safe."

"Okay, ask him," Be'oncay replied, still pointing the gun at Puffy's thick skull.

"What's the combination, Diddy?" Karen said as she snatched the thick strip of gray tape from crocodile mouth.

"Please! Pleeeease! Don't kill me! I paid the money! I ain't no gangster! It was Biggie's idea! You can have anything you want! I don't wanna diiiie!" And you thought Mase was bad. This nigga was worse than Tammy Faye Baker. The tears that fell formed a puddle at his feet and the words poured out faster than a rhyme flow by Twista.

"Shut up, bitch!" Karen hit Puff Daddy with a manicured back hand, a precise Pimp Slap. She had experienced it many times before, but it felt good to be on the other end of the action. Puffy felt a stinging sensation and soon it felt like his face was on fire.

"Okay, okay! Please don't hit me again! Dat shit hurt! I ain't got nothin'. Biggie dead! Mase preachin' and shit! 112, Total, they left me!" Puffy pleaded for forgiveness.

"Combination?" Karen showed him the beginnings of another pimp slap.

"O...Okay! 7 left, 7 right, 7 left. It's behind the picture of J-Lo. Take it! Take it all! Just don't kill me! I paid the money! I paid it!" Puff was giving up hope.

"Watch him. Don't let him outta yo' sight. Don't kill him yet, I'ma make sure he gave us the right combination first. If he lyin', I got somma that mercenary torture shit we learned in training for possum mouth!"

Karen headed for the master bedroom. She entered the bedroom, tossed away the J-Lo portrait, and attacked the wall safe. Faster than it took her painted nails to dry at the Korean nail salon, Karen had a third bag filled with cash, jewelry, a whip, a wig, and a garter belt. Apparently Sean Combs had been keeping in touch with his feminine side.

"Time to puff, Puffy!" Karen adjusted the three duffel bags, then handed one to Be'oncay, but she made sure it wasn't the one with the money and the whip. "Pop go the Weas..."

"Riiing! Riiing! Riiing!" The private phone tucked in Be'oncay's bra rang out loud, disrupting Puffy's send off.

"Yeah, who is it?" Be'oncay questioned, clearly mad at the interruption.

84

"Yes, Be'oncay. Abort the mission, Ms. Knolls. Abort the mission immediately!" The line went dead.

"Okay, Puffy. Today is your lucky day, honey. We ain't gonna kill you today, but we need you to do us a favor." Be'oncay removed the tape from his mouth again.

"Thank you!!!! Thank you! Anything you want!!" Puff was relieved.

"Okay, okay. No more gangster shit. Puff Daddy is dead, D-E-A-D. Change your name..." Be'oncay began.

"Shitty Ditty? Shitty Diddy? P. Diddy? From now on you Diddy, understand?" Karen suggested, because his breath smelled like shit.

"Yeah, Diddy sounds cool." Be'oncay made a game out of it. "Let's bounce!"

P. Diddy breathed a sigh of relief as the two masked women exited the room. Damn, it was a close call. It was even closer than his role in that movie, *Monster's Ball*, but getting executed in real life was no joke. "Thank you, Jesus. I ain't trippin' on bitches no mo'. Heeelllp! Heeelllp! Somebody help me!!" Puffy screamed at the top of his lungs but nobody heard him because of the music.

Eugene L. Weems, Timothy R. Richardson

CHAPTER 12

Las Vegas, Nevada - One Year later

Gladiss was satisfied with the mission. Rap music was placed back in the proper hands. Will Smith was at the top of the charts again with the hit single, *Summertime*, and Gladiss liked Will Smith. Cash Money and No Limit Records were blowing up on the streets, smoking weed and bling, blinging was the subject of their raps. Smoking blunts was far better than smokin' niggas. Scarface was large in the south, but he was socially aware. Keith Sweat, Toni Braxton, Babyface, Boys II Men, and even New Edition balanced out any rap music with images of making love or treating women with respect. Music was back to normal. Well, almost.

"Aftermath Entertainment presents Eminem!" Gladiss looked at the crazy blond white boy with the wicked rhyme flow bust lyrics about his mother. Well, it was white-on-white crime, so it wasn't any of her business to get involved. Gladiss never understood white people anyway, and they never understood her either. However, this new blond, blue-eyed sensation, a reincarnation of Vanilla Ice, with a talent for rap and a mouth almost as dirty as Karen's, grabbed her attention. She was most definitely going to keep an eye on this Dr. Dre protégé because wherever Dre went, success always followed. The World Class Wreckin' Crew, platinum. N.W.A., Eazy-E, D.O.C., all platinum or gold plaques. It wasn't a secret that Dr. Dre was the brains behind Death Row Records. The release of his Chronic 2000 album on Aftermath Entertainment changed the Rap game. Gladiss was most definitely watching Andre Young and Eminem because she knew that Dre still had a lot of thug left in him.

Suge had more problems than a college entry exam. He was being sued by Harry O's wife for the hundreds of millions he promised in return for lending Suge the start-up money to open the doors of Death Row Records. The entire roster of his label abandoned him, and Jimmy Iovine no longer distributed his products on Interscope Records. Korrupt was the only fool who remained on the sinking ship, so Suge made him president. The Feds and the L.A.P.D. were watching him like Barry Bond's taking a piss test for steroids and hoped that he made one false move. Mr. Knight was still on parole. His world was crumbling and it was only going to be a matter of time before he had nothing but crumbs left.

On the East Coast, "P-Diddy" and Bad Boy Records took a similar blow. Mase became an ordained minister and devoted his talents to gospel rap. He planned to donate the proceeds to the kids in New York. The entire Bad Boy camp had albums ready, but P. Diddy couldn't afford to finance their releases. The absence of ten million dollars cash and everything of value he owned left a hole in his pocket the size of the Statue of Liberty. Instead of music, Shitty-Diddy focused his attentions on breaking into the fashion industry. He stole Biggie's idea and introduced the world to Sean John and apparently learned a lot from his experience. Everything worked out perfectly and life was back to how Gladiss once knew it.

Hollywood, California

What a difference a year made. Meagan Goodwin was living large and in charge. She owned a nice condo in Hollywood Hills and her phone was ringing off the hook. Her appearance in the movie, *Biker Boys*, made her the new up and coming black actress. The risk she took of putting up two hundred and fifty thousand dollars to help finance the production of the movie paid big dividends. She was an executive producer and a Hollywood sex symbol. A young black version of Pamela Anderson with better acting skills. Her full, pouting lips and flawless figure were the object of every man's desire. The movie scripts rained down at her doorstep like water in a Seattle rainy season. They came in non-stop and some of the roles were in quality movies. Meagan was the new Halle Berry, before Halle sold out.

The acting roles were only the cream on top. The model shoots and magazine articles made her the fast and easy money. Ms. Goodwin was living life on all cylinders, full speed ahead! She was finally living out her dreams and she owed it all to Gladiss Nyte and the Panhellenic Council.

Houston, Texas

"Destiny's Child Certified Platinum! *Say My Name* number one on the Billboard Hot 200 Chart. *Bills, Bills, Bills*, number three on the R & B charts. Destiny's Child launches worldwide tour. Destiny's Child inks recording contract with Sony Urban Music."

Be'oncay was excited and happy about her career and was finally in control of her life. The fools who hated her vocals and didn't give her a chance to make it were now begging her to do favors for them. Be'oncay was an R & B sensation and H-Town female singers were finally on the map for the entire world to see. She had used most of her money to start Be'oncay Records, and soon afterwards, Sony came running to her with a swift but large offer to buy her out, and signed Destiny's Child to a multimillion dollar, four album deal. Be'oncay was in the money and living out her dreams on stage.

She had it all, the glitz, the glamour, the bling, the cars. Be'oncay hired her father to become her personal manager and her days were filled with activities from sun up to sun down. She thanked God and the Panhellenic Council that now somebody could make and sell an album about more than packin' gats or going to prison. America was making love to her music and young black women had a new attitude of self-respect. The world was finally saying her name.

Detroit, Michigan

"Ladies and Gentlemen. I would like to introduce the owner, founder and senior medical doctor of Children's World 24 Medical Clinic, Dr. Lesley!"

A thunderous round of applause erupted from the mostly black, Latino, and poor white audience. Dr. Lesley approached the podium.

"Friends, family and fellow doctors. We did it! We finally made a place to heal our children and extinguish the presence of pain and suffering in our communities. We must understand that every time we treat a child it makes the world a little better. Our mission is to change the world, one child at a time. I want to thank each and every one of you for supporting this worthy cause. The children are the future."

Dr. Lesley saluted the audience. "Okay, let her rip!"

The rope and large tarp fell to the ground revealing a large one story building with a large globe and the words, "Children's World Medical Clinic," in fancy lettering. Dr. Lesley's dream was made a reality with the help of a federal grant and a bank loan, but none of it would have been possible without the money from the two hits. Dr. Lesley went from having no future to having a chance to change the world.

Dr. Lesley hired an excellent staff of doctors, four black doctors, two Hispanics, two Asians and two whites. It was a rainbow coalition of doctors and they each passed intense background checks for community service. They also were trained for cultural sensitivity and child behavioral sciences. The entire staff was made well aware of Dr. Lesley's reputation of being as cute and cuddly as a teddy bear, but if you made the mistake of upsetting her, she was as deadly as a grizzly.

There was no denying it was Dr. Lesley's world. She kept her job in the WNBA and was going to use her role as a professional athlete and superstar in the league to promote her clinic and fight for higher salaries for women in pro sports. Lisa thought about the little girls who were going to one day become women and wanted to make things better for them.

Sometimes she would think about her life and how badly she wanted children, and one person came to mind; Commander Eugene Weems. Dr. Lesley had finally found a man that was worthy of her love but for now she would keep it a secret.

Life was excellent for Lisa, the negative of being fired from the hospital had been changed into a wonderful positive and a life that she never imagined being possible. She had her children's clinic, a promising basketball career, and had met the man of her dreams. Dr.

Lesley was finally living a gratifying life and she owed it all to the Panhellenic Council and she always paid her debts.

Manhattan, New York

"Yeah, B. I hooked the whole shit up girl! Jay-Z been dyin' to meet you for the longest. Dat nigga scared of me because of dat Big Pun bullshit, but I'm cool. That nigga got big paper, doin' big thangs since Biggie died. You game?" Karen took a break from reading *Prison Secrets* and made her daily phone call to her sister, Be'oncay.

"Honey, I don't know. He way in New York and I'm in Houston. I start tour next week with my group. Gotta do a video shoot. I'm swamped, sugar." Be'oncay thought about her schedule.

"Girl, you betta stop trippin'. Give up that juicy booty sometime! You know he got them big ass lips. I hear he reeeeaal good at kissin' dat clit, girl! Have yo little sexy ass shakin' and shiverin'. You need some dick in yo' life. You work too hard, Be'oncay! You gone pass out like that bitch, Mariah Carey."

"Okay! Okay! Karen, I'll go out wit' the nigga. Just quit fuckin' wit' me, shit! You always thinkin' 'bout sex, with your horny ass!" Be'oncay knew that she couldn't out talk Karen Stephins.

"Yeah, yeah, yeah! You just think about me when you bustin' a nut on them big ass lips!" The two sisters started laughing. Karen always kept it real.

"You crazy bitch! Hook it up. Call you tomorrow," Be'oncay' responded.

"Fuck you, ho'. You know you like that shit, everybody love sex. Keep it real, B. When you bust that nut, oooh! Shit, girl!"

"Shut up! I'm laughing so hard, my stomach hurt! Quit trippin' Karen." Be'oncay was out of breath with laughter.

92

"Okay, girl. I gotta finish by book anyway. Holla back, B."
The two ladies hung up their phones. Karen felt good to finally be appreciated and accepted.

Karen fired up a blunt of Orange Haze and poured herself a tall glass of Grand Marnier. She was on the final pages of *Prison Secrets* by Eugene Weems. In fact, she had been reading a lot lately. "*Carol Cummings*" by Delbert Smith, *Death Around the Corner* by C-Murder, and *Other Side of the Mirror* by Eugene Weems and Tim Richardson. Karen didn't fuck with nothing but the best in street lit.

She loved reading but she had an even bigger passion for writing books. She was finally finished writing her book, *Confessions of a Video Vixen*. The manuscript was finished and at the typesetter. The only thing she was waiting for was the graphic artist to finish her book cover. Karen couldn't wait to see her finished book and share her story with the world.

At first she was hesitant about putting celebrities on blast, fuckin' up happy homes and shit, but after a relationship with Kool G. Rapp, Karen didn't give a fuck. It was all about the money. She didn't care about hurting rich mothafucka's feelings. In her view, if they loved their families so much, they would have kept they dicks in their pants. She didn't put all the blame on the men though, because if the wives were doing their jobs the right way, the line wouldn't have been so long with fools wanting Superhead.

Karen was tired of the whole scene, who fuckin' who, and he say, she say. She wanted to get some of that book money, bless a few bitches with some game, get rich, and raise up her young son. Things were moving fast and she had no doubt that her book was going to be her ticket to a good life for her family. She wanted to leave New York, the fast life, and all the horrible memories of her past.

After reading *Death Around the Corner*, she was reminded about her visit to New Orleans. Karen had respect for those Cash Money and Tru niggas and the things that they were doing in the hood.

"Umm!" She glanced at the cover of *XXL Magazine* and saw Li'l Wayne, tattoos everywhere, standing on a pile of money. "Yeah, round trip ticket, first class to New Orleans!" Karen only traveled one way, and it was time for a little vacation.

CHAPTER 13

Las Vegas, Nevada - Six Years Later

"50 Cent Certified Diamond, *Get Rich or Die Tryin'* reaches ten million albums sold. 50 Cent Assaults Ja Rule at KJIS Summer Jam. G-Unit declares War on Murder, Inc. 50 Cent dumps Vivica Fox in Heated Argument. 50 Cent Declares War on Fat Joe. Compton Rapper, The Game, Inks Contract With G-Unit Records. 50 Cent Arrested on Gun Charges. Rap Lyrics in 50 Cent's Song Links New York Drug Lord, Supreme, to Murder Inc. G-Unit Clothing Line Surpasses 100 Million Dollars in Annual Sales. Harlem Rapper, Mase, Un-Retires and Signs Contract with G-Unit Records."

Gladiss looked at the news about the biggest New York rapper since Biggie.

Dr. Dre didn't fail at his ability to create another urban legend. First there was Ice Cube, then D.O.C., then Eazy-E, then Snoop Dogg, then Xibit, then Tupac, then Eminem, and now Curtis "50 Cent" Jackson. It must have been something in the water that Andre Young drank at Centennial High School in Compton, or maybe it was the 40 ounces he guzzled as a DJ for the Wreckin' Crew.

Most of these rappers had potential and were already stars, but one visit with the good doctor and they came out the studio superstars. Once upon a time, Andre Young was at the top of

Gladiss' list with NWA, especially when he slapped Dee Barnes, and when NWA had beef with Ice Cube.

He became an even greater target when he abandoned Ruthless Records and joined Death Row and Suge Knight. Either it was a stroke of luck or Dr. Dre was the smartest nigga in the world. He managed to start having problems with Suge and never got too deeply involved in the industry bullying to remain a target. In fact, the opposite thing happened. Suge Knight attacked Dre for stepping away from Death Row and Tupac even slandered his sexuality on a song. The incident that really victimized him was when the CEO of Death Row refused to give Dre his portion of the multimillion dollar empire that he helped create, but everybody knew that Suge was very good at fuckin' people out of their money.

Dr. Dre left the Wreckin' Crew and the Wreckin' Crew wrecked. Andre Young left NWA and nobody even noticed Ruthless Records anymore. Dre left Death Row Records and now they could barely keep the electricity on. Enter Dr. Dre's own label, Aftermath Entertainment. Chronic 2000, Eminem, Snoop Dogg, and now 50 Cent, gangster rap had a new home.

Personally, Gladiss liked Dr. Dre, a once poor black man from Compton who overcame the odds. He was married, treated his wife decent, and he took care of his homies. Dre was a businessman. He had also worked his way up from the bottom, and Gladiss couldn't do anything but respect that.

Now, 50 Cent was an entirely different story. His first single before being signed to Shady Records was *How to Rob*! He had a positive role model in Dr. Dre but his checkered past in New York was starting to take over. His hateful attitude toward Ja Rule and Murder Inc. was eating away at his success and the gangster began to take over.

Eminem signed 50 to a million dollar contract and now he was a member of the Aftermath pyramid. Every time 50 Cent got paid, Slim Shady made money, and every time Eminem made money, Dr. Dre made money. It was the old pyramid game and Andre Young was finally on top this time.

50 Cent was everywhere, the new king of New York. He was a brilliant businessman and diversified his investments. G-Unit Records, G-Unit Clothing and Shoes, vitamin water, watches, books, video games, movies and even a limited edition Dodge in his name. The magazines loved him and his trademark. G-Unit was recognized all over the world. "Curtis Jackson" was a mega mogul, and music was what got his foot in the door. But now he owned the whole house. The more he branched out on his own, the bigger his empire became. On the wave of the 10 million albums he sold off *Get Rich or Die Tryin'*, 50 Cent formed the G-Unit clique. 50 Cent, Young Buck and Lloyd Banks served as the foundation. The trio did the G-Unit album that went double platinum, then Lloyd Banks' album sold 1.5 million, then Young Buck's solo album sold over a million albums. 50 Cent could do no wrong, and with all the success and becoming a major player in the rap game, out came the player haters. The future of 50 Cent and G-Unit was in Gladiss' hands.

New York, New York

The bad publicity that 50 Cent was giving Murder Inc. was ruining Ja Rule's career. "Yo, Gotti! I can't take dis shit no mo'! He killin' me man! Can't sell no records wit' that nigga saltin' up Murder Inc.!" Ja Rule had a pretty good run of hits with his Louis Armstrong vocals and not quite Tupac rap style. His latest release didn't even go aluminum. 50 Cent was killing his street credibility.

"Yo, son. I'm doin' all I can. I wish we woulda collapsed that nigga when we scarfaced his ass. Shit! Why did he hafta sign wit' that nigga, Dr. Dre and that white boy. They down wit' Jimmy Iovine now!

We can't fuck wit' them, they got mad backup, that nigga big time Mafia!" Irv Gotti had cheese, but Jimmy Iovine had a cheese factory.

"I'm a kill dat nigga myself! Fuck it! He survived nine slugs, but that nigga ain't bulletproof!" Ja Rule was all talk, he feared 50 cent.

"Chill, little nigga, you just concentrate on makin' me a hit record wit' Ashanti. I can handle G-Unit. Let me holla at Fat Joe and put some money together. I'ma holla at dis broad, Deborah. I got it unda control." Irv responded to his little Teenaged Mutant Ninja Turtle looking friend.

"I'ma chill, make some records, smoke weed, calm my nerves, my nigga. I'm outa here, Gotti!" Ja Rule knew his place, the real power brokers were going to deal with the situation.

"Holla back later, Rule!"

Irv Gotti was alone in the studio. Irv couldn't believe it. Who would have thought that a nothin', low life, dope peddlin' nigga like 50 Cent would blow up like nitroglycerine. He was just a two-bit hustler in Jamaica Queens, a nobody who jacked Ja Rule for a platinum chain. His biggest claim to fame was stealing a fuckin' chain! Irv made the order to smoke the fool who took Rule's chain, and that led to 50 Cent getting' hot lead. Nine bullets and a nigga didn't die! Not only did Curtis Jackson live, the bullet to his jaw made him talk with a slur, and that fuckin' slur is what kicked his rap style up to another level. Nobody sounded like 50, and that slow, slurish type, almost mumble, was the hook that pushed his album over the edge, all the way to over ten million sold and counting. The same nigga that Gotti laughed at when he heard his demo years ago was now a megastar, and 50 Cent wasn't going to let bygones be bygones. As soon as Curtis got a microphone in his hands, he declared war on Ja Rule and Murder Inc., and now he had an audience of at least ten million people who believed every word he said. Ja Rule's career was sinking, Murder Inc. was sinking. Irv had a lotta money saved up and he was going to need to form an alliance to tackle this problem once and for all. 50 had over ten million fans, but he also had about ten million enemies, and most of them were in New York. Irv was going to bring them together and try to change 50 Cent into loose change.

Hollywood Hills, California

Meagan was a certified diva, the new young black female face in Hollywood. She was in the top five most desired black actresses in Hollywood. *Biker Boys* was a classic film and made a lot of money, and now she worked on *Stomp Da Yard*. The modeling, commercials, and product endorsements flooded her agent's office with contract offers. Everybody wanted a piece of this dime. Meagan finished her business degree in finance and had a multimillion dollar investment portfolio. A couple lucky professional athletes were blessed with her presence and the tabloids connected her intimately to Reggie Bush, but everybody in the hood knew that a UCLA Bruin would never fuck with a USC Trojan. It was like trying to mix oil with water.

Sugarland, Texas

Fuckin' Karen was right, Jay-Z's fat ass lips did feel real nice and soft on Be'oncay's clit. They felt so good that she put them there over and over again. But don't get it twisted, Be'oncay did her share of giving Jay so much brain he could have been a brain surgeon. She and Jay-Z were the royal couple of hip hop and pop music. Jay-Z had finally shook those suckas, Damon Dash and Cam'ron, and took over Rockafella Records, and was president of Def-Jam. Be'oncay decided to leave her two friends behind and was a solo superstar. Meagan had even hooked her up with a couple movie roles, and she had a very successful acting career as well. Be'oncay Knolls was the finest woman in the music industry and Jay was one of the richest rappers in the world. Bonnie and Clyde were the hottest couple in show business.

Detroit, Michigan

The secret relationship between Dr. Lisa Lesley and Commander Eugene Weems was torrid. Lisa never imagined that her young body was capable of such earth shattering climaxes. Commander Weems didn't just know what to do to a body to make it meet swift and timely death; he had mastered the knowledge of what places to touch to bring her body back to life. Dr. Lisa was in love, but she had to stay patient. Love was a new emotion for her and she had a full plate of other activities to keep her occupied, and so did her man.

Children's World Medical Clinic was off and running, and she opened clinics in Flint, Michigan and Chicago. The LA Sparks won two NBA Championships and Lisa received the first million dollar contract in women's professional basketball history. There was still a lot of work to do, but Dr. Lesley was well on her way to changing the world.

"Who's number one? Who's number fuckin' one on the New York Times Bestseller List? It's me, Be'oncay! I can't believe this shit!" Karen was a bestselling author, but she still had a dirty mouth.

"I knew it! I knew you could do it, girl. I'm so proud of you, honey. Shit, I bought about a thousand copies myself. I'm just glad Jay wasn't in that shit, girl. A lot of niggas mad at you!" Be'oncay was her number one fan.

"Fuck 'em, girl! They wasn't thinkin' about me when I was broke, pregnant, and homeless! Them muthafuckas shoulda thought about that when they unzipped they pants. I didn't even put everything in the book! I coulda really been dirty, girl!" Karen was satisfied with her decision. It was all about the money.

"You crazy, but you right about that shit. I got yo' back. Let me know if we gotta smoke a nigga. You know you my girl, right," Be'oncay said with a serious tone in her voice.

"I got you, B. Don't trip, girl, everything is cool. Ain't nobody fuckin' wit' me too bad, nothing I can't handle. Niggas just bumpin' they gums, but I do want to ask you a favor, though." Karen got serious for a moment.

"What's up, girl? What is it?" Be'oncay asked, concerned.

"Could you ask yo' man, can I borrow them juicy ass lips for a couple nights, my pussy lonely! I need to rub 'em down there and keep em company!" They both busted up laughing.

"Fuck you, bitch! My man lips ain't that big. I love dat nigga, Jay. Get a life ho! Love ya, but I gotta go," Be'oncay responded.

"Just fuckin' wit ya B. Have a nice day!" The two women hung up their phones.

Karen still couldn't believe it. She self-published her book and now everybody wanted a piece of Superhead. All of the physical, mental and sexual abuse she suffered at the hands of arrogant men were taken and twisted to be used to make her pockets fat.

"Who the real pimp now, niggas!" Karen asked herself the question and it felt good to be able to answer it truthfully, "Karen Stephins!"

It felt nice to be a success after all the years of being a victim. She picked up her phone and called New Orleans. It was time to do a little celebrating.

"Wayne! Baby, what's up!" Karen knew exactly who to call, the fireman, to put out her fire.

"Hey, shorty, I was jus' thinkin' about you. I wrote a song for you. Check dis' out..." Karen listened to the self-proclaimed greatest rapper alive and thought to herself, Life doesn't get any better than this!

CHAPTER 14

Las Vegas, Nevada

"Compton gangster rapper The Game is signing to G-Unit Records."

"Tony Yayo released from prison, signed to G-Unit Records. 50 Cent stars in movie *Get Rich or Die Tryin.* Mobb Deep joins G-Unit family. Dr. Dre assaulted at BET Music Awards show. Young Buck arrested in stabbing assault of a fool who bombed on Dre at BET Awards show. Rapper, The Game, goes triple platinum. G-Unit involved in shootout with members of Murder Inc. 50 Cent declares war on Terror Squad and Fat Joe."

Gladiss read the headlines about the activities of G-Unit Records and 50 Cent and didn't like what she was reading one bit. Curtis Jackson was getting closer and closer to becoming another Death Row. Yeah, the rapes and degradation of black women were not an issue, but the street battles with Murder Inc. and Terror Squad were getting very gangster. 50 was a more sophisticated thug than Suge Knight ever was. He didn't physically intimidate his enemies that dared to go against him. He just shut them down financially and destroyed their ability to make money. Gladiss decided that she would accept the $5 million contract that was put out on G-Unit Records and put an end to the madness, but first she needed approval from her superior.

"Yerfwin, I hope that all is well. I hate to trouble you, but.."

"So, Ms. Gladiss, you decided to partake in the offer on G-Unit from the powers that be in New York." Gladiss wondered how Yerfwin managed to know everything.

"Yes, Yerfwin, I want your approval in this matter. We don't need another Death Row, Bad Boy type war. We've come too far for that crap to happen again." Gladiss pleaded her case.

"Yes, Gladiss, I understand. Curtis did a lot of bad to a lot of people in New York while he was growing up. We cannot underestimate 50 Cent. I approve of the mission. Goodbye." Yerfwin was gone. Gladiss released a sigh of relief, then went into action.

"Deborah, yes, the mission is a go! All monies are to be deposited in our Tobago Bank Account. Arrange the meeting for one week from today. You may begin. Goodbye." Gladiss hung up the phone, the Panhellenic Council was back in action.

Brooklyn, New York

Curtis '50 Cent' Jackson sat in the plush headquarters of G-Unit Records sipping on an $8,000 bottle of Louis XIII Remy Black Pearl. He was a million miles form his Jamaica Queens beginnings and the life of a two-bit crack dealer and stick-up kid. Fuckin' with Dr. Dre had that type of effect on niggas. 50 Cent learned the hard way that sometimes you have to be careful what you ask for when you're rapping on CDs. In his megasuperdynamic hit, *In Da Club* that blew him up in the rap game like Hiroshima, 50 said, "I just want them to love me like they loved Pac." Well, the rap game loved Tupac so much that they shot him five times, sent him to prison, and got him murdered in Las Vegas. Now 50 Cent was loved about as much as Pac. Eleven million albums sold don't lie, but with all the love came the haters. The jealousy, envy, and the beefs with fools who spit on him when he was, "the underground king, but I ain't been crowned, I'm the diamond in the dirt, but I can't been found..." 50 said it best, "Many men wish death upon me..."

The haters piled up like dollars in 50's bank account, more money, more niggas hating. The jealous muthafuckas in New York, Fat Joe, Cam'ron and Ja Rule and Murder Inc. He destroyed them in record sales. Their albums went double lead, his went diamond. The only way for niggas to shine in their careers was by slinging salt at 50 Cent and G-Unit. Fat Joe was just a broke ass Ms. Piggy lookin' muthafucka, a fat lightweight who couldn't make a platinum album in a platinum factory. Irv Gotti was a different story. Murder Inc. was built off drug money and had strong mob connections. Those niggas meant serious business. 50 had the nine bullet holes in his body to show for it. The battle with Murder Inc. was definitely going to be settled in the streets.

The hate had even infiltrated his record company. He still had his loyal homies, Lloyd Banks and Young Buck. They were battle-tested rooks and were down with 50 from the start, but Curtis wanted to expand his empire. He couldn't take over the world with three muthafuckas. 50 Cent expanded his kingdom by signing Spyder Loc from Cali, Olivia from New York, and a couple other young artists. They fit on the G-Unit team well and patiently waited for their time to shine. The worrying actually began when he signed his second wave of artists and ignored the advice of other people around him, because fools on the streets were saying 50 went soft and Hollywood, so he lost his fuckin' mind and signed Tony Yayo fresh out of prison, who couldn't rap a lick but was quick to slap a critic. He signed Mobb Deep, whose biggest claim to fame was starting a rap war with Tupac and ended up Pac's personal punching bag. The war with Tupac almost destroyed their career. He gave the has-been, wannabe gangster nobody who signed to G-Unit for top dollars Porsches, platinum and diamond jewelry, and a million dollar promotions campaign. The fools were treated like stars and they had never released an album that went platinum.

Lloyd Banks and Young Buck felt slighted. The major, super, bi-color, catastrophic straw that broke the camel's back with stupidity was when 50 Cent signed Mase. Yes, that Mase! The same doo-doo droppin', go be a preacher, and I got kids, Mase. The cold part about it was that Mase didn't have any fuckin' kids! He lied to Lisa about the whole thing. To make matters worse, Mase turned in his Bible for a notepad and was back to callin' women bitches and whores. P-Diddy actually saved Mase from embarrassing himself by filing a lawsuit against G-Unit and 50 Cent, blocking the release of any material by Mase on G-Unit Records. The good reverend Mase was still under contract with Bad Boy Records for life and Puffy wasn't accepting any buyouts. It wasn't about the money for 'Shitty-Diddy.' Sean John had hundreds of millions from his clothing line, cologne and catalog from Biggie's music. It was about the principle. Mase left Puffy when he was down and out and had nothing, but now he was coming out of retirement and joined with the 'new' king of New York rap. There was no way that Diddy was going to take that shit sitting down, even if it took every penny he had in his bank account to keep Mase from rapping again. 50 Cent had managed to create himself another enemy in New York.

The mistake 50 made that added fuel to the fire was when he signed the Compton California MC named The Game. The Game was like a horrible gangrene that ate way deep at the foundation of G-Unit Records. 50 Cent had built his empire on unity, trust and loyalty. The Game was a loner, didn't trust a muthafucka, and he had no loyalty to anyone but himself. The fact that his debut album, *The Documentary*, sold over four million copies but was powered with beats from Dr. Dre and a lot of hooks and rhyme features from 50 Cent, didn't mean shit to The Game. Jayson Taylor believed that it was his super dynamic rhyme flow that was responsible for the sell of every unit, at least it was what his manager, Jimmy Henchman, wanted him to believe. Yeah, that Jimmy Henchman, the same muthafucka that was managing Tupac and who scheduled his recording session with Biggie at that New York studio where Tupac got shot five times. The same nigga that got Pac the role in the movie, *Juice* as Bishop, and recommended that Pac sell the thug image. The Game was being brainwashed into thinking that he was a superstar and didn't need anybody but Jimmy Henchman.

The Game's head blew up bigger than Jupiter. He didn't listen to anybody, especially 50 Cent. He got a tattoo of Eazy-E, a Compton crip from Nutty Block, blasted on his body and he was supposed to be a Blood from Cedar Block. The fool then went and got another tattoo of a butterfly pasted on his face, and claimed to be an OG Gangsta. After tons of criticism, the nigga covered up the butterfly with a big LA, and the clown was supposed to be from Compton. Anybody whoever banged a blue or red rag in Southern California knew that there was a big difference between representing Los Angeles and claiming Compton. A Compton Piru with LA tattoo was a super duper no-no. The Game was alone in his gangster philosophies and was also put on blast by Mya.

She was a pretty female, but only a semi-successful R and B singer. Her rejections of his many advances were all over the pages of *King Magazine*, but he didn't stop there. He basically harassed Vida Guerra, a fucking video booty ho, and she made her rejections of his advances known to the public. The bitch even dropped an album and dissed him in a rap song. The Game had lost his fuckin' mind and stooped down to a lower level than Prince without his high heels. The nigga was battle rappin' with video bitches. 50 was fed up.

"Yo, kid, you gone! You ain't part of G-Unit no mo'! Take yo' shit and leave. Don't come back!" 50 yelled at the Game.

"Come on, 50, We need you man. We'll change up. Can't we work things out!" Jimmy Henchman did all the talking. Being booted off G-Unit was going to put a stop to Game's cash flow, and when Game lost money, Jimmy lost money.

"Fuck dat Blood! I got Dre, I got Compton, and I got Black Wall Street!" The Game interjected.

"Oh, yeah! You ain't got Dre no more fool, I'm a holla at Jimmy Iovine! We'll see about that!" 50 put his foot down.

"What? Wait, come on 50, baby. The album *Doctor's Advocate* is already finished. Dre got songs on there. Let's settle this like gentlemen. This album is big!" Jimmy was thinking about the money.

"Fuck dat, Blood! The album is finished. 50 ain't nobody, he jealous of me! Dre gon' fuck wit' us!" The Game was overconfident. He knew who the real hit maker was.

"Oh, yeah! Well, I got the master, nigga! You signed to my record label. I paid for the tracks and it was recorded in my studio. I pay the light bills in this bitch! Ain't nonna that shit Dre produced gone see daylight! *Doctor's Advocate*, ha, ha, ha! Get the fuck outta my sight!" 50 gave them both a mean mug, and the Game and his manager left the office.

"Yo, Jim! I just dropped the Game from my label! I'm gon' send you the album, minus Dr. Dre tracks. You promote the shit! My people ain't pushin' it to the streets!" 50 hung up the phone in the CEO of Interscope Records face. You can get away with a stunt like that when you sold over 22 million albums in less than four years for his company.

One of his problems were solved. Curtis Jackson was going to cut his losses and move on. After his birthday, he was going to drop Mobb Deep from the label, put back the release of Tony Yayo's album, and definitely get rid of Mase. Niggas were gonna be running for cover because 50 ruled G-Unit with an iron fist. When the smoke cleared, he was going to be left with Lloyd Banks, Young Buck, Olivia, and Spider Loc. 50 contemplated dumping Spider Loc, but he couldn't do it. The Los Angeles Crips from Rollin 60s were the first ones to show him love when he touched down in Cali. Spider was also his California weed connect, the Crips had the bomb Chronic, and 50 Cent was crazy, but he was no fool. He also decided to keep Tony Yayo around for sentimental reasons. The nigga couldn't rap that good, but he was a loyal muthafucka and had been down with 50 since the 1980s.

Another problem was solved. Drastic times called for drastic measures. He thought about the haters in New York. He wasn't worried about Fat Joe. He was a nobody, wannabe, and now rendered insignificant. Joe was just a fat nigga with a fat mouth, a studio gangster. Cam'ron was a nothing ass clown, a wannabe. And now that Jay-Z owned Rocafella and Cam sided with Damon Dash, Cam'ron was garbage. Besides, how could 50 take a nigga that dressed in pink serouisly?

The only person who had the money and power to touch him was Irv Gotti and Murder Inc. He thought back to the nightmare of being filled with hot lead and how they tried to smoke him for a fuckin' gold chain. He had almost died for crumbs! It was time for payback. 50 dialed 1-800-WE-TIP, "Hello, dis' call is anonymous. Supreme used drug money to start Murder Inc. with' Irv Gotti. Listen to song five on 50 Cent album. It's all there!" He hung up the phone and smiled. All of his problems were solved, or were they just beginning?

CHAPTER 15

Hollywood, California

Meagan was on the set of *Stomp Da Yard*, a movie about fraternity and sorority life at a black college. Meagan was the star, executive producer, and co-writer.

"Cut! Ms. Goodwin, you have a call." Meagan was in the middle of a love scene with Omar Epps.

"What? Who? I'm on the set! You wastin' my money! You wastin' my film on a phone call! Gimme that phone!" Meagan was on a rampage.

"Meagan, Deborah Short. Friday, 8 o'clock, Las Vegas Hilton, be there." The line went dead.

'Oh, okay." Meagan slowly came back to reality.

"Okay, people, let's finish this movie! I got big business this weekend. Come on, makeup, let's do this." Meagan was back in action.

Houston, Texas

"How y'all feelin' out there! I wrote this song for my real good friend. It goes something like this…"

The music blasted from the giant speakers at the Astrodome, the final stop in Be'oncays worldwide tour. The system at the Astrodome screamed. 75 cities in three months, and she started it where she ended it, in H-Town before her hometown fans. She went into her song, *Crazy in Love*, and gyrated her shapley hips like only Be'oncay could. Her dad appeared and approached her in the middle of her performance.

"Telephone, Be'oncay!" He handed her the cellular phone.

"Wha...What?!" Be'oncay stopped, stunned, midperformance. The fans in the audience roared. They thought it was part of the act.

"8 o'clock, Las Vegas Hilton, check in at the front desk." The line went dead. Be'oncay handed her father back the phone.

"Hey, DJ, kick dat beat! From the top, one, two, three!" The music kicked in and the show went on like nothing ever happened.

Be'oncay was a performer. She lived for the music. Too bad she had to cancel her lip therapy session with Jay-Z in the Bahamas, but business waited for nobody.

Detroit, Michigan

"Roooar! Yeeeaaah!" The sold-out crowd at the Palace in Auburn Hills, Michigan went crazy. Dr. L had just thrown down a slam dunk. The player/coach of the LA Sparks was on a roll and her fans loved her. The stat sheet was overflowing, 53 points, 15 assists, and 18 rebounds, another triple double. To make things even more impressive, she had 9 blocked shots and was only one block away form her fourth triple double of the season. The WNBA was taking over the nation and had surpassed the NHL and major league baseball in television ratings. Dr. L was the hands-down MVP of the league and the first player to earn a $10 million contract with the

WNBA. There were even talks of a tryout for the Los Angeles Lakers, but Dr. Lesley was all woman. She did it for the women and children.

"Timeout, time!" The assistant coach barked at the referee. The players headed toward the bench. The LA Sparks were ahead by 11 points and clearly had the momentum.

"What, timeout?!" The talented player/coach didn't take too kindly to Bill Lambdier stopping the action.

"Sorry, coach. Here, it's for you." Bill handed Dr. Lesley the cell phone.

"Yes! Who is it??! This better be good!" Lisa was irate, Mr. Hyde came out.

"Friday, 8 p.m., Las Vegas Hilton." The phone went dead.

"Okay, very well." Lisa returned to the bench with the rest of the team.

"Candice Parker, buckle down on Number 32. Joy, quit camping out in the key. Watch the petty fouls, Felicia. And Rhonda, you gotta box out. We getting' killed on the boards! We can do this! Keep your mind in the game. Sparks on three, Sparks on three. One, two, three, Sparks!" Lisa knew how to bring out the best in everybody around her on the basketball court, or in the operating room. She was a natural born leader and she always paid her debts.

New York, New York

"OOOh! Ooooh! Baby! Just like that! I'm, I'm cumin ..."

"Cut!" Mr. Marcus was on the verge of a major eruption. The action was interrupted at the peak of Karen's performance.

"What da fuck?!" The black professional stud barked, upset with the interruption that stopped Ms. Stephins from giving him superhead. Karen was diving head first into the multi billion dollar porn industry with a how-to video. She was taking her talents to a new level.

"What the fuck is this shit?! It better be Ed McMahon with a $50 million check or somebody getting' fucked up! Stop that camera, shit! Who da fuck is it?!" Karen wiped away the excess saliva from her lips, then snatched the cell phone from the director.

"Who da fuck is dis?" Karen was mad as fuck.

"Fuck," she added before the caller could identify themselves.

"Friday, 8 p.m., Room 227, Las Vegas Hilton, be there, Ms. Stephins." The line went dead.

"Bitch, I'll be there!" Karen left the set, headed toward New Orleans. Mr. Marcus looked on, frustrated, dick as hard as times for black folks in the 60s, because he wanted Karen to finish the job she started. Somebody could replace her on the movie set, but nobody on earth could give head like her. Nobody had a mouth like Karen *Superhead* Stephins.

Compton, California

"G-G-G..U..Not! G-U-Not!" The Game continued his smear campaign on 50 Cent and G-Unit Records. He had a sellout crowd at Compton College and thousands joined in with him on the chants. 50 Cent had used his powerful influence with Jimmy Iovine, and just as he had promised, Dr. Dre was forbidden to have any tracks on the Game's new album, *Doctor's Advocate*. His album sales were going slower than acting roles for Todd Bridges, so the Game's manager, Jimmy Henchman, suggested to him that he take his beef with G-

Unit to the streets of the West Coast. The former G-Unit artist was more than willing to comply and quickly dropped *300 Bars and Running*, a mega diss record released on an underground mix tape that attacked every artist signed to G-Unit. The battle between the Game and 50 Cent was being taken to a new level. Sales of G-Unit artists were slumping and 50 didn't like that shit one bit. Curtis Jackson was fed up with the war of words. He wasn't a studio gangster.

Later on that night:

"G-U-Not, dis bitch ass nigga!!!" The gun exploded.

"Pop, pop, pop, pop, pop, pop!" The Game got caught slippin' on Cedar Block.

"I'm hit! Blood, niggas done shot me! They got a nigga." The Game saw a blurry haze and the homies scooped him up and he was rushed to Dr. Martin Luther King Hospital on Wilmington in a red Escalade.

"Hold on, hold on, hold on, young Blood." The caravan rushed down the avenue, running red lights like a diplomatic visitation.

"Sombody get a fuckin' doctor! Get a doctor now!" Bounty Hunter yelled, carrying a bloody Game in his thick arms. The gurney rolled out and they placed him on it, then he was rolled away to intensive care.

"Muthafuck them, muthafuckas! Blood, they gone pay for dis shit! They hit my dog. They shot the wrong nigga, Blood." Bounty Hunter went outside to his Escalade and made an important phone call. The war with G-Unit was being taken to the streets.

Las Vegas Hilton, Friday, 8:00 a.m., Room 227

"Ladies, ladies! I would like to call the Panhellenic Council to order. I am very proud of each and every one of you. I have kept close observations on your progress and your personal careers. I would like to congratulate you sisters on a job well done. Let's get down to business." The telephone rang and Gladiss put the call on speakerphone.

"Evening, ladies."

"Good evening, Yerfwin," the young women answered in unison.

"We have new enemies. We must terminate 50 Cent, Eminem, Snoop Dogg, and Mase. I will be watching, good luck." The line went dead, Yerfwin was gone.

"Okay, ladies. Meagan, you are assigned to Curtis '50 Cent' Jackson. Be'oncay, you have Eminem. Karen, Snoop Dogg is yours. And Dr. Lesley, we want you to finish what you started with Mase. Keep Commander Weems updated on your progress. Remember, teamwork, teamwork, teamwork. A lot of these individuals travel in the same circles, so keep all lines of communication open. The salary is the same, $1 million each. Good luck!" Gladiss handed each assassin a thick manila folder that was loaded with information about their targets.

"Questions?" Silence, even Karen was surprisingly quiet.

"Why can't I get the white boy?" Well, that would have been too good to be true.

"Because Be'oncay has the white boy. He's taken already." Everybody erupted in laughter, a rare show of humor from Gladiss.

"Okay, ladies, same rules apply for departures. Ms. Stephins, since you didn't get the white boy of your dreams, you can be the first person to leave, after me of course." Gladiss left the room.

Ten minutes later, Karen departed for her condo in Las Vegas. Ten minutes laters, Meagan headed for the 10 Freeway for her journey home to Hollywood Hills. Then after another ten minutes, Dr. Lesley was on her way to New York. Finally, after ten minutes, Be'oncay was on her way to see Jay-Z for some lip action before she went to Detroit.

Eugene L. Weems, Timothy R. Richardson

CHAPTER 16

Compton, California

The Game had gotten word over the wire that the G-Unit camp was throwing a surprise birthday party for 50 Cent at Magic City Strip Club in Atlanta. It was VIP status, celebrity invite list type shit. He was positively sure his name wouldn't be on the guest list. Word traveled fast about the ugly breakup and how he was dropped like a bad habit from the G-Unit roster. After the shooting, the Game continued shitting on 50 Cent's name during all of his interviews and maintained the G-U-Not campaign to the streets. He had been feeling really salty about how he felt 50 Cent had treated him. The man who once was his mentor and had made him the rap star he was today was now a hated enemy.

Game didn't give a damn about the blessings he received. His feelings were hurt. He was acting out with childlike emotions that ignited deep rooted feelings of hatred toward 50 Cent. He wanted revenge that spelled DEATH and this opportunity to deaden the entire G-Unit camp had been dropped into his lap. He called a meeting with this gunmen at the studio in Compton. The main topic of conversation was the hit on G-Unit. At the end of the meting, the Game stood up and leaned forward into the ear of his main man,

119

Bounty Hunter, then he whispered, "Blood, are you sure you can get some of our niggas inside the joint with heats?" His voice was calm.

Bounty Hunter turned to face Game, "My nigga, don't trip. I gots dis. I got a cat on the payroll who works security for the place. It's not a problem. I'll have some of our niggas posted inside the spot before the doors break and we'll have no problem pushin' right inside, because my guy is going to be working security at the front door, so stop sweatin'. Just kick back and be cool, because I got everything under control."

"I hope so BH, because I need to level this nigga and his whole punk ass camp."

"Young Blood, I gots you. Have I ever let you down?" Bounty Hunter asked, raising his cell to his ear.

"Nah, and.." Bounty Hunter quickly raised his hand to cut Game short, then gave instructions to the person on the phone. He paused for a moment to listen, then snapped shut the phone with one hand and looked at Game.

"Like I done said before, I got this under control. We leave in 45 minutes." He paused dramatically. He consulted his watch. It was 2 p.m. in California. "I called in a favor from a good friend of mine. He's loanin' us the use of his private jet. It will be waiting for us at LAX Airport."

Game nodded his head in approval and watched Bounty Hunter make more calls and mouth instructions into the phone. Shortly after, Bounty Hunter rose from his chair and smiled at the Game and the rest of the gunmen.

"It's time to raise up," he said with authority, and led the way out the studio.

Atlanta, Georgia

Olvia was pleasuring herself with a manicure at the vanity table that was filled with cosmetics when she heard the hard thumps at her room door. She was in the middle of pampering herself and hated being bothered while she did her girly treatment. She wanted to ignore the knocks at the door until whoever it was that wanted her attention pounded harder with an edge of emergency.

"Wait a damn minute, I'm comin'," she shouted, setting down the fingernail file on the table and then rising from her seat. "Have patience, muthafucka," she whispered under her breath, ambling quickly across the soft, cocaine-white carpet and handmade African scatter rugs. She loved the way the plush carpet felt underneath her bare feet. "Who is it," she asked sweetly.

"Yayo, Buck, and Prodigy," Tony Yayo answered. Olivia pulled the terry cloth bathrobe closed, then tied the belt tight.

"Just a sec!" The lock clicked, and then the security chain dangled loose against the doorframe. The door was eventually opened up.

"Girl, you ain't ready yet," Prodigy frowned, "You know we have to get to the club."

"It should be something on the bar, help yourself," Olivia said, pointing over her shoulder, "Ya'll come on in. It ain't gone take me but a minute to get dressed. Is 50 ready?" No one responded.

Buck headed straight to the mini bar and Prodigy admired the exquisitely furnished hotel room. It was unlike the suite he occupied, not even close. He noticed the abstract oil painting by Boo Bung on the wall over the oyster colored couch and twin Lazy Boy chairs. An African rug shimmered on the cocaine-white carpet. Yayo closed the door behind him, then went and flopped lazily into one of the chairs. Olivia dressed quickly in form-fitting white

121

leather, a sexy pantsuit. She strolled out into the living room, waiting to hear a compliment on her outfit, but no one paid much attention.

"Y'all ready," she asked snobbishly.

"Yeah, let's get goin' because we still have to swoop up 50, Havoc, Fame, and Billy," Buck said before turning up the glass to finish his drink and heading for the door.

The limousine was waiting for them when they made it downstairs to the lobby and exited the hotel. The limousine driver held the door open as they stepped inside. Once everyone was in, he gently closed the door, then released a burst of energy as he raced around the driver's side in long sprinting stride. There wasn't a need for anyone to give him instructions because he had already been informed of the requested destinations. The driver quickly began to thread through the heavy downtown traffic. Prodigy decided to phone Havoc to let him know they were en route. By the time someone answered the phone, the limo was turning into the parking lot.

"Yo, who is this," Prodigy asked, not recognizing the voice.

"Who you trying to call?" Prodigy quickly pinpointed the voice. It was Fame.

"Yo, my nig', we right outside."

The driver jumped out when he saw 50 Cent stroll out the hotel with his crew and hurried around to open the door for them. He waited until they were safely inside before hustling back into the driver's seat. Then, in an instant, he gracefully swerved the stretch limousine out the lot and back into the thick of traffic.

The sound of thunder roared across the darkening skies. The smell of rain drifted into the open window by a gust of wind with a threatening breeze. Meagan shivered at the chill, glanced toward the open window in thought, and remembered that she had opened it earlier that day to allow some fresh air into the room.

She turned back toward the bed and began swiftly changing into the elegant two-piece pantsuit and stilettos. She fingered the blonde wig until it had a well kept look. Then she studied herself in the shattered dresser mirror before putting on a full length mink coat that was far too big, but an important piece of article was needed to complete the outfit. The disguise was mainly due to her starring role a few years back in 50 Cent's video for the hit song, *21 Questions*. She was the sexy number that was down with 50 and made him the envy of every man ever held in captivity when she blessed him with a conjugal visit. She met 50 Cent before and didn't feel any type of emotions for him. It was strictly business. He was an enemy of Gladiss and the Panhellenic Council, so now he was an enemy of Meagan's. Nothing was going to stop Meagan from killing Curtis James Jackson III.

She sat on the edge of the bed, took out the Glock .40 from the duffle bag, examined it, and screwed the Teflon silencer in place. Then she checked her backup piece, dropping the clip of the nickel and silver 9 mm to assure herself that the clip was loaded before tucking it in place at the small of her back, then slid the Glock under the mink coat. She reached over and grabbed the half glass of bourbon from the nightstand that she hadn't finished drinking the night before and necked it.

She then stood and took another glance through the mirror at her creation. It was the exact character she wanted to depict, a classy, drop-dead gorgeous, and sexy super model. Then she headed for the door and entered the coldness of the Atlanta night. She closed the door behind her carefully and turned the knob to make sure that it was locked.

"If someone really wanted to break in, they wouldn't have a problem, just a hard turn at this piece of shit ass lock and the whole thing would come right off," she whispered to herself in disgust of the loose door knob. She never expected anything more from this cheap, rundown hotel that was normally used by prostitutes to entertain their tricks. It was appropriate for her mission, almost perfect. She entered her rental and headed for the Magic City Strip Club to do the honor of blowing out the birthday boy's candles.

Game and his gunmen reached their location. Bounty Hunter, being his right-hand man, took the job of orchestrating the hit on 50 Cent and the G-Unit camp. Everything was going as planned and the timing couldn't have been more precise. The flight had gone well and cars were waiting on location for their arrival that would take them to a secure place to chill. Once they arrived at the private hideout, Game noticed that the hideout spot was nothing less than a mini mansion in a gated community. Bounty Hunter wasted no time. He laid out the plan and gave instructions to each of the shooters. He decided to plant the two most experienced shooters inside the club with heavy artillery to cover him and Game when they made their move. Everyone was briefed on their duty.

"Two men inside as plants, two outside to chop down anything that may threaten our exit, and the rest of us are gonna go in together to blow out the G-Unit birthday candles."

The gunmen examined the weapons that had been supplied to do the job. Once satisfied, they armed themselves and secured the assault rifles back inside the duffle bags. The two plants were issued security outfits that were identical to the extra security that was hired for 50's surprise party. Bounty Hunter was a self-claimed specialist in tactical operations and he lived up to that title, covering every possible angle to achieve his goal. The hunt was on.

As assumed, the backup crew drove directly to the strip club at 15 minutes to 9 o'clock to keep watch on the outside of the premises, watching who was coming and going. The driver made a left into the driveway, found a parking space in the lot, where him and his partner would be completely unobserved but had a full view of the scene. Stopping the car, he turned off the lights. His eyes darted around the dark parking lot, then focused in on the security at the club's entrance. He received a boost of confidence when he recognized one of the security guard's faces. A tall, stocky-built white man who was always down to have his palm greased with a few extra big face Franklins on the under. Everything looked good and was going as planned.

Impatience had settled in and he shifted in the driver's seat, and his hip accidently touched the duffle bag by his side. Too restless to stay in the car, the passenger door opened and he stepped out and stood in the driveway behind an SUV, smoking a cigarette. The driver glanced at his watch and saw two hours had slowly crept by. The limousine that pulled up to the entrance of the club caught his attention. He watched attentively, "Bingo," he said to himself, reaching in his pocket for his cell phone, never losing sight of his targets that were hurrying along into the club. He quickly thumbed-in a number and raised the cell to his ear. It rang a few times before someone on the other end picked up, "Hello," a voice said, so muffled, so low, he had to strain to hear it.

"Dawg, it's a touchdown," the driver said, and hung up. It was a code that him and the other party on the receiving line understood that indicated 50 Cent and G-Unit had arrived.

CHAPTER 17

Atlanta, Georgia

Magic City was in full swing when 50 Cent and the G-Unit camp strolled in. The music was thumping loud, bodies mingled and moved seductively on poles, and in the laps of customers who watched and showered the curvaceous dragons with singles. The flavorful honeys grinded, winded, and gyrated their money makers as they booty clanged to the crunk music. The strip club was a celebrity attraction and what they called Magic Monday was a house packer for high rollers, gangsters, ballers, pimps, players, and champion ho slayers, but tonight was an invite-only surprise party and the spot was packed.

50 Cent and the G-Unit camp parlayed in the VIP section. He sat with immense calmness, staring at the club activity while balancing an unlit Cuban cigar between clenched teeth. He shifted in his seat and out of habit felt for his two favorite people in the world, the twin chrome 45s he kept tucked away in his front waist belt. They remained at his fingertips, at the ready.

Olivia sipped on a glass of Hennessey while bobbing her head to Tony Yayo, who was spitting lyrics to the best of the music. Buck wasn't paying much attention to anything but the big plate of fried chicken, cornbread, rice, and collard greens he was deeply indulged in. Billie Dazenie and Prodigy was scoping out the many sexy dragons that were getting' they strip on. Fame and Havoc were busy ordering drinks form the tall, thick waitress that was jotting down their orders.

50 Cent was feeling his surprise party and was in a festive mood. He felt like the king that he knew he was, reminiscing back on his days in Jamaica Queens when he had nothing, struggling, hustling for crumbs just to stay above water. "But look at me now. I'm not hungry no more. I'm the man, the king of kings that got everything my heart desires. Cars, jewelry, any woman I want, and paper by the truck loads." A smirk lined his face. What else can I possibly ask for? I got G-Unit and my fam who's loyal and down for a nigga, and my fans. Shit, I don't need nothin' else. It gets no better than this. His smirk turned into a smile. Preme, Ja and that lame nigga who call himself the Game can keep hatin' on a nigga all they want, and while they at it, they can kiss Curtis '50 Cent' Jackson's natural black ass. Fuck them chumps! He thought and decided to enjoy his party.

"Yo, Yayo," Olivia said, "Let me hear that shit you was just spittin' again."

"Aight! Check this out, it goes like this. I like a girl with a nine to five/mind right..body tight..on the weekend like to wind and grind." Tony Yayo rapped.

"What you think about that, hot or not?" Yayo sought approval from Young Buck.

"Wack den a muthafucka," Buck cut in, "Scrap that shit for real, my nigga." Yayo shot Buck a frown and turned to Olivia for her opinion. She shook her head indicating her disapproval as well. Yayo got the message and turned his attention to the piece of paper he had been writing on and began crossing shit out.

"Hey, Fiddy! Wha's up fiddy, my man?"

A scronchy speech impaired voice echoed over the music. Everyone at the table turned toward the voice to see the face that belonged to the voice. Havoc burst in laughter, and so did Yayo, when they recognized who the short, funny looking man was who approached them.

"Yo, dawg, you have to peep this lil' nigga out. The lil' nigga is funny as hell," Tony Yayo giggled, "That's that cat they call Beetle Juice. Just trip off this nigga when he come over here," he whispered to 50 but for everyone at the table to hear.

Beetle Juice strolled up to the table and invited himself to a seat. He smiled up to 50, revealing two enormous front teeth. 50 fought back the urge to laugh at the funny looking guy who was dressed in crisp, creased army fatigues and his shaved head was a black peaked cap with the word FLY written on it. The white embroidered letters glowed in the fluorescent lights that glared over the club's ceiling and walls. Beetle Juice extended out a hand toward 50, who made no attempt to shake his hand, but offered a nod instead. Beetle Juice didn't take offense to 50 leaving him hanging. He just quickly reclaimed his hand and folded his arms, and leaned forward on the table.

"Fiddy 'ent, I'm a big fan of you. I'm a G-Unit. I'll rap on your CD. I'll blow that mother fucker up like it ain't nothin'. I'll give my friends it and shove it up they ass if they don't cop it big. I know that music shit."

Everyone at the table was dying, laughing. Beetle Juice had become their new entertainment. Buck had been eyeing a man across the room, standing in the shadows near the edge of the stage, staring at them. It was something strange about the man that Buck was trying to figure out. The actual picture of his face seemed

129

familiar to him, but he couldn't quite figure out where he had seen him before. Buck convinced himself that he was just tripping, that he couldn't possibly know the nigga, and the fool probably was just staring at the table because of the famous people sitting there. It seemed kind of strange because the nigga was acting kind of strange and it was obvious he was eyeballing them from across the room. Buck rose from the table, "I'll be right back, my niggas," he said before departing and disappearing into the crowd of the club scene. Buck had learned from the streets that nothing was a coincidence.

The Game, Bounty Hunter, and two of their gunman entered the club unnoticed. They attempted to stay in the shadows as they made their way to the VIP section. Each one of them wore black trench coats and beanies pulled over their eyes. The man who was watching 50 from across the room noticed Game and the rest of his crew enter the club scene. He closely eyed their every move without losing sight of them. He bent down and removed the AK-47 assault rifle from the duffel bag and pulled back the lever, injecting a round into the chamber. He crouched down on one knee to get in position to wait for his cue. He was ready to claim the lives of his targets without hesitation, no fear, no remorse, and no feelings whatsoever.

Olivia took a sip of her drink and hastily set down the glass on the table. She uncrossed her legs and arose from her seat. "I'm going to the ladies room," she said to anyone who was listening.

Lloyd banks nodded his head at her and turned back to the paper he was scribbling his raps on. Olivia strolled across the cluttered club, then down the dimly lit hall toward the ladies room. Out of the shadows, she felt a hand grab her arm. She quickly turned toward the hand to see the person it belonged to that was invading her space.

"Excuse me," her voice intently high pitched, clearly indicating that she didn't appreciate being touched or grabbed.

"No, excuse me, sexy." The man released her arm now that he had her attention, then stepped closer. Olivia quickly put up a hand in his chest, simultaneously stepping backwards, creating a distance between them.

"Nigga, what you call yourself doing?!" She snapped harshly.

The man smiled cunningly, "Yo, baby, I apologize, but ain't you that honey from G-U-Not, I mean G-Unit camp name Olivia? Shit, I'm one of yo' biggest fans. I love you."

Olivia relaxed her defensive stance and forced a smile to her face, "Hi," she said with a sweet voice before ambling off into the ladies room, "Damn groupies." She thought as she gazed at her beauty in the wall-sized mirror above the face bowls. The ladies room was empty, odd, she thought, as she entered the first stall to relieve herself of fluids.

The man who was no stranger to Olivia thought to himself. He knew that she was the First Lady of G-Unit and had seen her in almost every hip hop and men's magazine he read. He had been watching her closely all night, just waiting for an opportunity to slide up next to her when she was alone. He looked around the club to assure himself that nobody was watching him. Once he was content that no wandering eyes were on him, he made his move to enter the ladies room. The door to the private stall was just opening up as he stepped in. He noticed it was Olivia attempting to exit, so he pushed the door with violent force, slamming Olivia back against the stall wall, stunned. She watched as the man stepped into the stall, and with a lighting quick movement, closed the door behind him with his left foot. Fear robbed Olivia of her breath as she faced the intruder. Two distinctively separate impressions burned into her consciousness. One was the glittering stare in the stranger's eyes, the other was the gun he was pointing at her head.

Buck peeped the move that a hit on G-Unit was about to go down, and from the looks of the artillery this nigga was strapped with, he didn't come to play. With urgency in his steps, he circled behind the man who was taking aim. The man turned to take a quick glance over his shoulder when he heard a simultaneous sharp snap behind him. To his surprise, he was staring at gloved hands that held 12-inch buck knives. His eyes widened at the sharp, cruel looking blades that shimmered under the sizzle of the club's fluorescent lights. He parted his mouth in protest, realizing what the sounds were that he had heard. All of a sudden, a violent death was lingering over him. *Fuck this, I ain't goin' out like no bitch*, the man thought before attempting to turn his weapon on Buck, but he came up a day late and a dollar short. Buck had already made his move. The soft whistle of the buck knives sliced through the air and the blades penetrated through flesh effortlessly. The man's body tumbled to the floor and his head rolled off.

He had been decapitated within a few split seconds. Nobody in the club noticed the headless body jerking on the floor. Everyone was too busy partying, consuming alcohol, and indulging in the entertainment. Buck bent down to wipe the blood off his knives with the lifeless man's shirt, then swiftly folded the blades back into its cradle before sliding them back in the holsters on his waist. He snatched up the AK-47, raised up, and gazed across the room toward his crew. Buck had successfully gotten rid of one of he headaches who challenged G-Unit.

CHAPTER 18

Olivia stared, frightened at the powerful hands that once touched her skin but now held the cold steel at her head. "What do you want," she whispered within the palm of her hands that she had clenched over her mouth. She could hear the trembling of fear in her words as she attempted to ask again out of panic, "Why are you doing this? What do you want?"

The intruder stared with cold eyes, "What, you gon' give me what I want?" It was more of a statement than a question, as he lowered the gun from her head and stopped at her cleavage, "I come to take the souls of you G-Unit niggas. So what do I want before I deaden you?" His free hand slid up her thigh and lingered at the softness of her love oven.

She opened her mouth to protest, but knew it would be a waste of breath to do so. She shoved his hand away out of instinct. The man angrily shoved her. She felt her shoulders and elbows slam against the back wall for the second time. Pain shot through her body, "Please, God, please don't let this fool hurt me," Olivia prayed silently.

The man aggressively palmed her face, held it steady, and attempted to kiss her lips. She moved her head, trying to free her face from the strong grip. She knew that the man had the advantage

133

over her in size and with the weapon, but she refused to give in without putting up a fight, so she did the first thing that came to mind; she clenched down hard on the man's face with her teeth. He squealed in pain, attempting to free his lips from between Olivia's clenched teeth. The gun fell to the floor. Olivia released her deadly bite. The man stepped back and quickly felt his lip to check for blood, but that was his worst mistake. Olivia swung a mean overhand right that staggered him. He tried to shake it off and tuck his head between hard round shoulders, but he was picked off in mid air with an ear popping left hook and blood bubbled between his teeth. She stepped out to her right side and crouched down like a professional boxer and swung a deadly uppercut that lifted the man's head, then another left hook that landed cleanly on his chin.

The man fell to his knees. Olivia knew she couldn't allow the man to compose himself or he would kill her for sure, so she took advantage of the moment and kicked a field goal into his ribs as he grunted in pain. In a swift movement, she circled behind him and latched her arm around his neck. Her fist gripped her left palm and she squeezed with all her might. The man struggled to get free. He was suffocating in the death hold Olivia had on him. He shivered and the tremulous movement only caused the grip to dig in tighter around his neck. His limbs shrieked a protest. His breath became shallow and his eyes bulged. It was over. His body felt limp, but Olivia didn't loosen her choke hold until she was positive that her attacker was lifeless.

She was now well alert to the hit on her crew's life, so she stormed out of the ladies room to warn the G-Unit camp of the danger lurking around them, and to her surprise she spotted the Game and three gunmen heading directly toward the VIP section. Disturbed by their urgency, she hurried across the noisy and cluttered room, never losing sight of her crew's adversaries. Suddenly, two of the men decided to split up. "Damn," Olivia had lost sight of them, but not Game and his partner.

50 Cent and Tony Yayo were too busy bullshitting with Beetle Juice to notice the threat heading toward them.

"50, look," Olivia screamed when she saw Game brandish a double barrel shotgun.

His gunmen turned toward Olivia with their weapons drawn, but to his surprise he met a flashing barrel. Three .38 slugs introduced themselves to his chest, but Game had the drop on 50 Cent. He aimed the double barrel at his chest.

"G-U-Not, bitch," Game said with venom.

Out of the shadows, Lloyd Banks decked Game in the head with a bottle of Cristal. Flames shot from the double barrel, buck shot hit the ceiling lights. The two other men that were with Game rushed into action behind him. Game scrambled for cover into the stampeding crowd. His gunmen were now wide awake and 11 slugs from their automatic weapons were fired aimlessly into the crowd. The 50 Cent twins came to life in swift response, and a rain of rapid fire emerged from the identical twin weapons and pierced the body of one of the men, sending him to his demise. Tony Yayo's .357 roared twice, and that stopped the other attacker in his tracks.

"Ain't this a bitch," Meagan stood in the shadows watching the action take place. She was now steaming hot because her plan was interrupted by the incompetence of the wannabe gangbangers who couldn't kill shit if their life depended on it, and in this case their life did depend on it. They still didn't get their targets. Meagan wondered how in the hell Game and his crew couldn't kill any of the niggas they were here for, even though they had the element of surprise on their side. Meagan shook the thought and hustled after the G-Unit camp as they stampeded out of the club. Game had vanished within the crowd and most likely was beating feet away from the crime scene. Meagan could have cared less about Game. She had no beef with him. Her mission was to deaden 50 Cent and then collect her paper. She ambled out of the club and paused at the corner where she saw two men emerge from a car with what looked like weapons in their hands. They would have gone unnoticed to an untrained eye, but Meagan was a trained professional. She stayed in the shadows, studying the two men hustle toward the limousine that the G-Unit camp was entering.

"Well, it looks like I don't have to kill this nigga after all," Meagan said under her breath, watching the execution about to go down on the G-Unit camp.

Gunfire claimed the air and the parking lot was lit up like a torch. When it was all over, the two gunmen had ben turned into dead strangers of the night.

"What the fuck!" Meagan was in disbelief of the outcome. She watched as the gunmen emerged from behind a car with smoking guns. It was Havoc.

"Damn, damn! Damn, Damn! These G-Unit niggas must be the luckiest muthafuckas in the world or God got his hand on they ass," Meagan said to no one in particular.

Before Havoc could step into the limousine, Meagan was up on the car with her weapons aimed. Without delay, she opened fire into the car at her target until the clips of her 9 mm and Glock .40 were empty. She then vanished into the night as quickly as she appeared.

CHAPTER 19

Karen made a left at the intersection and then another left into the valet parking lot of Caesar's Palace Hotel and Casino. She got word over the wire that Snoop Dogg was on the hit list and he was laying his head at Caesar's Palace. She expected a chance of meeting him and accepted the assignment with open arms. She had plans of doing more than smokin' his ass. Karen wanted to terminate his existence by killing his mind. She didn't like niggas who claimed to be pimps, and used and abused women. Snoop Dogg was cool when he was just a gangster rapper, but when he began claiming to be a pimp and appearing in magazines with women on dog leashes, that was when he had crossed the line.

A tall, thin, young white boy with an oversized nose and blonde hair that was slicked back ran over to her car and opened her door as she came to a stop. He politely introduced himself as the casino valet and requested if he could be her parking host. He produced a big smile that showed only the top row of his teeth and part of the bottom, which he tried to hide behind his thin lips. Karen recognized a hustle and allowed the white boy to be her parking host. She gave him a hefty tip in advance, then made her way inside the casino.

She loved visiting Las Vegas, Nevada, aka Sin City, the city that never sleeps and where dreams no longer had to be a fantasy. She loved Vegas so much that she purchased a condominium there that allowed one of her closest friends to housesit for her. Her good friend, Pink, was an exotic dancer, a true hustler at heart who was down to do whatever it took to get paid. Karen smiled to herself knowing that Pink would be a major asset to accomplishing her goal of peeling Snoop Dogg for some major bread before she deaden his ass. She was planning it all in her pretty little head as she stepped into the casino.

The loud sounds of ringing bells and falling coins from the slot machines acclimated with the laughs and screams of people exited by all the never-ending entertainment that was publicized on every street corner. Las Vegas was a tourist attraction that was sure to captivate the senses. The constant flickers of flashes from tourists' cameras twinkled like stars as they took pictures of the exotic monuments of huge gold, silver and ceramic sculptures and waterfalls that decorated the barriers of the most elaborate, exquisite architectural designs of the hotels. Bands played live music as dancers shook their tail feathers, performing their routines while peddlers passed out brochures with the names and locations of underground adult entertainment nightclubs, places where patrons were sure to fulfill all their fantasies and sexual desires.

Regardless of how many times a patron visited Vegas, or even if they lived there, their eyes always seemed to witness something new and exciting. There was always so much going on. Karen's eyes tried to take in the full view of activities, but such attempt was impossible. Her mind was racing, trying to figure out how she was going to get up under Snoop Dogg. She wondered even if he would remember her from many Hollywood award shows and after-parties she attended. Well, if he didn't, she was about to display her best performance ever to entice his baby brain to follow her lead. Karen understood men well, and she knew that 90 percent of all men thought with their dicks when in the company of an attractive woman, especially one with a banging body. Ms. Stephins had the complete package, the gorgeous face and banging body. She learned years ago that what she had between her thighs was Grade A choice, a true delicacy to a man's deepest and most intimate imaginations and to the depths of their pockets. Karen was confident that she had the skills to fulfill any man's sexual desires.

She strolled through the casino with an alluring stride, as if she owned the world. As she entered the lobby of Caesar's Palace Forum Shops, the aroma from the restaurants greeted her. Hunger pains swiftly made their grand premier, causing her stomach to growl, a sound that awakened her awareness to the fact she hadn't eaten anything all day. She endured the pain, then noticed a crowd of people circled around the very person she was looking for.

"Now, how fuckin' lucky can I get! This shit is not gonna be as hard as I thought," she smiled within, "Now I got to get this nigga away from his fans and alone, so I can work my magic," she told herself as she made her way toward the crowd.

"Excuse me. Excuse me, please, coming through." Karen navigated through the crowd. The red, hot cat suit she sported showed more than enough of her gifted curves. As the many wandering eyes stared in her direction, her body soon caught the attention of the very person she was there for. Snoop Dogg couldn't help but stare below her navel at what looked like a fat camel's foot pressing against the soft elastic cloth that hugged her body. Karen noticed his stare but said nothing, because that was part of her plan. She smiled at his boldness assaulting her body with his eyes in plain view of her notice, having no regard to what she or anyone else thought.

Snoop Dogg felt his nature rising as he pictured his naked body connecting with hers. He wondered how her cries of passion sounded in the heat of some exotic gangster fucking. He wondered what type of freak she was in the bedroom. Karen broke his train of thought and teased him further by spinning around so he could view her full figure.

"Do you like what you see," she asked, not giving him the opportunity to respond before she forced herself in his arms. He held her tightly and pressed his erection up against her body, "Oh, my God, you are so hard, daddy!"

She paused to look down at the bulge in his pants, then took a deep breath before saying, "It looks like you need relaxing."

For the first time, Snoop Dogg stared down into the face of the woman who so boldly pushed up into his arms. This act wasn't unusual to him. He had millions of groupies that made the same attempt to be touched by him. To his surprise, he realized that he was holding the woman that the entire rap industry bragged about and wanted to experience, the video vixen they called Superhead.

Snoop Dogg's heart was pounding with excitement. He now had plans on knocking Superhead to make her one of the new addictions to his stable. He knew if he had her on his team he could milk major chips from the industry niggas who fantasized about Superhead's head game. Such an addiction would boost his street and celebrity status through the roof and guarantee him the Player of the Year Award at the Player's Ball. He was not about to blow this opportunity, so he smiled down at her and said, "Shorty, you want to chill with Snoop D-O-Dubble-Gee? I was on my way to holla at these clothing stores to get my shoppin' on and then shoot back to the suite to relax in a tub full of bubbles while sipping on some Grand Marnier. You know a playa has to be clean as a whistle and sharp as a razor when steppin' in new threads like I'm 'bout to get. It's all about dressin' to impress and then restin' so I can beat the best. You feel me baby," he said as he watched her feline grace.

Karen paid careful attention to his every spoken word. She stood docile, staring up at him with a pair of the most gorgeous green eyes he had ever seen on a dame, with a tranquility that was indeed rare.

They walked inside of the store. Snoop Dogg didn't catch the name before they passed through the double glass doors that automatically slid open as they approached. It was only obvious that they were in a store that catered only to men by the sight of the differently posed mannequins that were dressed with the latest and hippest threads that draped their lifeless anatomical bodies. The department store demanded respect and the demeanor of a class conscious consumer by the elaborative depiction of its elegance and extravagant atmosphere.

Snoop Dogg paused temporarily at the entrance and took a deep breath while admiring the spacious store. He felt out of place, but he knew that his style and taste were resting on the walls, racks, and mannequins that surrounded him.

"Now, this is me! This is how a playa closet should look, stocked with the best of the best," he uttered out loud to himself, forcing out any doubts that he may have had in the back of his mind.

"Excuse me, sir," a delicate, sweet voice summoned from behind that suddenly interrupted his thoughts.

He slowly moved his body to turn and get a full view of the person to whom such a lovely and seductive voice belonged. There was no doubt in his mind that the woman trying to get his attention would be sexy, he assured himself before turning around.

"Damn," he cursed as his face showed a surprising expression and then eased back to its natural appearance. He matched the smile that was being displayed before him, lowered his head down, and touched the tip of his nose quickly and tried to compose himself.

"Uh-huh, look what the good Lord done blessed me with. The Bible tells us if you ask you shall receive."

"What," Snoop Dogg snapped with a frown that immediately found its way to his mug.

"Never mind me, handsome. I was just thinking out loud to myself," the store clerk admitted, "My name is Charisma Oxford. I work here at the store. May I be of some assistance with anything, or can I show you around our lovely store?"

Snoop Dogg was at a loss for words and couldn't believe what he had expected to be a fine woman turned out to be a homosexual who nonchalantly tried to hit on him. He thought about flaring up on the fool, but took the middle course and stayed jazzy with his style. He figured the punk could be useful in some type of form or fashion, then decided to string him along and play on cupcake's sexuality.

"I'm a player by birth. I have the skills to pay the bills, the charm to captivate, to cop and lock, to get paid by a punk until he get out of pocket and I have to put his head on the chopping block," Snoop Dogg said to himself in the silence of his thoughts, seeking and searching for an answer within himself if he should waste his time trying to work this fag.

He glanced around to find Superhead, wondering where she had disappeared to, "Where this bitch is when she is needed," he mumbled underneath his breath.

Karen stood in deep silence at a nearby clothing rack with a smile on her face, observing how Snoop Dogg was going to handle the homosexual who had approached him. He caught her stare and smiled, then winked his left eye at her from the distance to inform her that he had everything under control.

"Sure, why not," he answered, "You did say your name was Charisma didn't you?"

"Yessss!"

"Cha..ris..maaa," Snoop Dogg repeated the name, slowly stretching it out, "That's a fly name, baby. It really fits you from head to toe."

Charisma tried to refrain from blushing, but he felt the tightening of his skin from the huge smile that formed on his face, exposing pearly whites. He gave a feminine wave of his hand and stepped back a few feet, and placed his left hand on his hip to get another full body glance of Snoop Dogg.

"Why, thank you, honey. I have always felt that my name fit me perfectly, if I may say so myself," he admitted, then continued, "What was it that you said your name was?"

"I never said, but you can call me anything you want. Just don't call me late for dinner." They both laughted at Snoop's humor.

"No, but seriously, I would like to know your name, honey."

"My name is Snoop Dogg, but you can call me Charm."

"I like that, Mr. Charm. Is that the charm that goes with the word lucky, or is it the charm of admiration and delight?"

"No, baby, it's greater than that. I'm the charm that it takes Charisma to have."

Charisma was wide-eyed with excitement and astonished at the reply. He hadn't anticipated such a slick tongue and subliminal poetic flirting that was being presented to him in such a unique and remarkable way that left him flabbergasted and at a loss for words.

Charisma faked a light cough that followed a low guttural sound as if he was trying to clear his throat. He tried to figure out what position he should take with Snoop Dogg.

"Are you okay, baby? Do you need little pat on the back?"

Charisma began to really cough now. He had read into every word that came out of Snoop's mouth, taking it as though each word referred to an enticing sexual hidden message. Charisma was getting all hot and bothered over his own perverted and nasty imagination.

"Un, un, unnnh," he cleared his throat before saying, "For some reason, it has gotten hot in here all of a sudden. Are you hot?" He asked as he fanned himself with his hands.

Snoop Dogg didn't respond. The question was overlooked as if it had never been asked.

"What's up, baby, I thought you wanted to help me find some fly threads to cover this gigolo figure. I'm ready to slide into somethin' my skin could appreciate being intimate with."

"Oooh, no! You didn't take my mind there."

"Take your mind where, Charisma," he asked.

"Never mind me. I'm just speaking out of turn and out loud again. But if you ask me, I don't think you should never wear any clothes. That's just my opinion, but never mind me. Let me show you this tuff cashmere suit we just got in a week ago. I'm telling you, Charm, it's sharp, baby. Believe me, I know my clothes and can dress a man with my eyes closed better than women could with they eyes open," he proclaimed proudly.

"Well, let's see what type of skills you got then. I got my dame standing over there at a full rack of clothes, fumbling around an' shit, and she haven't brought nothing over here yet for me to try on,"

Snoop said as he pointed his finger in the direction where Superhead was looking at clothes. Charisma looked at Karen and gave a wave and smiled in her direction.

"She's pretty. I've meant to ask you about her, if she was with you, 'cause I noticed you both entered the store together. Are you two a couple?"

"Check this out, baby. I'm going to just say this and then you can answer that question yourself. I just got out the pen from doing a bunch of time and this is my first day out on the scene," he lied, "I'm here tryin' to get me some threads. I haven't even snugged up under all that hot loving over there yet. I'm about my money first and then the life pleasure. I can't get at that green shit without the proper tools, which is my threads to help me turn heads. You feel me," he told the truth, "I'm a playa' and my threads is a major part of the tools to help me cop. You must have the flashies of the top up-to-date fashions. Don't forget, this is Las Vegas, baby. You can't be lacking in yo' macking if you trying to do some big money stacking. You can't half step with this pimpin' or you will not get nowhere in the game, especially out here," he said.

"You got that right, honey," Charisma agreed, "Well, let me see what I can put together for a player who's about to make his premiere on the scene. I have a very strong feeling that you going to clock a grip from exploiting someone's daughters."

"Don't forget about somebody's sons also. Don't make me out to seem prejudice because I don't discriminate against money." They both smiled at the truth.

Snoop Dogg's open honesty about himself and future plans opened the flood gates to a new friendship with Charisma. Charisma liked his company and honesty, and felt the need to become a part of Snoop's life in some way. He knew what Snoop Dogg's lifestyle would consist of in his chosen profession and he wanted to make sure that he had some proper flash pieces to start off with.

"Lowgain Pier," Charisma summoned with a clap and a wave of his hand, and a short, fat man with a receding hairline came running.

"Yes, madam, what can Lowgain Pier do for you," he asked in a Swedish accent.

Snoop Dogg stared at Charisma and the fat man called Lowgain Pier. He couldn't believe this was a real life moment, watching two mismatch, funny bunnies. One was gay and the other was a true fan, but a live cartoon character with an annoying voice.

"Pier, this is my friend Charm. I want you to take his measurements and then go get the following items and have the tailors do what they do. No exceptions. This is priority over everything else. Make sure they understand that!" Charisma snapped with authority. "Do you understand me, Pier?"

"Yes, madam, it will be done," the fat man replied and immediately began taking Snoop Dogg's measurements.

Charisma gave Pier a list of clothing items he wanted him to have Snoop Dogg try and have tailor-made. He then slid a folded piece of paper in Snoop Dogg's pocket and whispered, "Whatever you choose to do in life, be the very best at it and never get too big-headed that it would cause you to forget a friend. Call me sometime, we'll do lunch. I do enjoy your company," Charisma said, "Oh, one more thing. I picked you out a few items that I felt would look nice on you. I must be getting out of here. I have a very important dinner date to attend. You see the lady at the cash register," he pointed, "I left full instructions with her. You stay sweet and handsome, Mr. Charm," he said before ambling toward the exit door.

Charisma waived goodbye to Superhead, who was now sitting down in the chair in the waiting area and watching Pier measure

Snoop Dogg from head to toe. She waved back and gave a false smile, then watched Charisma vanish through the exit doors.

Karen had peeped the nigga's move from the start. She was willing to play along with him so she could get what she wanted, and if that meant belittling herself and respecting his fake ass pimping, then that is what she was willing to do. She reached for her purse and removed the cell phone. She stared down at the small gadget while quickly dialing in a number. She raised it to her ear and began to talk.

"Hello, Pink, what's up, girl? What you doing'?"

The woman on the other end of the line spoke softy into the phone, "Who is this?" She didn't recognize the voice.

"This is me, girl, Karen," she explained in a deep pant of breath.

"Hey, I almost didn't recognize your voice. I ain't doing much of nothing, just finishing up straightenin' up my pig pen of a room. I was about to take a long, hot bubble bath with Donnell Jones before you called."

"Donnel Jones?"

"Yeah, girl, I went and bought the new Donnell Jones CD from Larry's Sight and Sound the other day. You know I had to get it. Why, what's up, girl? You sound like you have something important on your mind. Is something wrong?" Pink asked with a concerned voice. She knew it was strange for Karen to be calling her to ask questions about what she was doing.

"No, no, nothing's wrong," Karen quickly admitted, "I was just curious. The reason I called was to see if you wanted to get some big bread with me. I have this nigga Snoop Dogg sniffing all around the pussy and I want to break this nigga off something he would never forget."

"Snoop Dogg! The rapper Snoop Dogg?" Pink wanted to confirm she heard Karen correctly.

"Yeah, that nigga."

"Hell, yeah, I'm down. Just let a bitch know what you want me to do and it's done. You know I got your back," Pink said. Karen told Pink the plan and hung up the phone.

Snoop Dogg was ready to shake the spot. He had plans on getting in this bitch's head. He was going to pop his mouthpiece with the charm of his words to get her on his team.

"Shorty, let's head up to my suite and rap a minute."

"How about you come over to my spot and we can chill there. I already called my roommate and told her I might have company coming over, so she's gonna pull another shift at the strip club to give me space."

Snoop didn't attempt to respond or show any expression of interest about this roommate of hers was. He also didn't know that Superhead lived in Las Vegas. It was all tasty with him. It didn't matter one way or another where they went to parlay. He just wanted to get Superhead alone to drop some heavy game on her mind and experience her head game that he had heard so much about, but what he didn't know was that she was the real predator that was luring in the prey for the kill.

CHAPTER 20

Karen keyed the two locks on her front door, then reached inside and flipped the light switch on the wall that dimly lit the living room. She turned around and removed some of the shopping bags from Snoop Dogg's hands and led him inside of her spacious two-bedroom flat. She sat the bags on the floor, tossed her keys and pocketbook on the breakfast bar, and slid out of her Dolce & Gabbana sandals, then ambled barefoot to retrieve the entertainment remote off the glass end table. The 60-inch TV and a red light on the house stereo came to life. Mary J. Blige's *My Life* CD began to softly play. The screen on the TV projected a realistic burning fireplace.

Snoop Dogg stood at the front door, watching her glide across the living room at an impetuous pace, trying to make the atmosphere as comfortable as possible for him. He noticed the unlit candles that sat on the end tables, then glanced at the pictures and oil paintings she had decorated the gold colored walls with.

"Fo shizzle," he said under his breath, admiring her taste. He hadn't given her much credit from the start, but from looking at how her pad was laid out, he finally gave Karen her props.

The furniture matched the walls and carpet, the gold trimming that outlined her white leather sofa and loveseat set nicely on the white and gold carpet that had an Indonesian design pattern running through it. Two huge hand-carved African wooden statues rested in

149

far corners of the living room. House plants hung in each corner, as their vines laced the edges of the ceiling and produced a rain forest look that led to a romantic hideaway.

Snoop Dogg sat the rest of the bags in a neat pile on the dinner table. He then sat at the first seat of its six chairs and began exposing gifts that Charisma had left for him with the store cashier.

"Damn, baby, that punk hooked you up," Karen said enviously, "Daddy, what you done told that punk to make him buy you all of this stuff," she asked, but wasn't expecting an answer.

"A pimp's game is not to be told but sold to an up and coming playa in the game," Snoop Dogg said with a smile as he continued to empty the rest of the bags, "Baby, go run daddy some bath water, so I can get freshin' up."

Karen didn't have to be told twice. She was in the wind like a fallen leaf. Before Snoop Dogg could raise his head up from looking into one of the bags, he heard water running at a fast speed.

"I want a lot of bubbles, you hear," he shouted.

He came across a gold box that had been wrapped with a red bow. It had a card taped to it. He decided to open the card first and read:

"A pimp needs tools to build his empire, so here is a small toolkit to get you started. I'm sure you will find a way to build a skyscraper with it. I just hope you like all your gifts, especially this one. You stay sweet. Love, your new friend, Charisma Oxford."

He tossed the card onto the dinner table, sending it flying like a Frisbee. Snoop tugged one end of the bow, allowing the silk ribbon to fall onto the floor. He wasted no time removing the lid. His eyes widended at the gold Cartier large face watch that had a diamond bezel, which sat next to a diamond link bracelet and matching ring.

"Damn, Charisma," he exclaimed to no one but himself in excitement, "Is you trying to choose on a pimp or what? This is some damn gift to be giving a new friend, but I like it in you, bitch. Let it be known then, you have no problem paying a pimp and come check this shit out," he shouted out in excitement.

She came rushing into the living room in matching panties and bra to see what it was that Snoop Dogg wanted to show her. "Damn, baby," she exclaimed in excitement with both hands now over her mouth as she stared into the box at the expensive jewelry that he held up toward her face so she could get a closer look at his gift.

"You can say that again. Damn is right. Damn, damn, damnnn! Uhhh weee! The he-bitch has really blessed a pimp. The pimp Gods was looking over a nigga. This got to be my message not to fuck with no bitches who can't meet the standards that the punk has set for a ho to be up under a pimp. Yeah, that's how I'm going to look at it and rate any ho that tries to choose up, by the punk's level of choosin' fees."

"So what are you tryin' to say, Snoop? If I can't give you more than what that faggot done gave you that you're not dealing with me?"

"For one, bitch, you not a ho. You have the potentials of being a ho, but right now you just another average simple bitch who gives up the pussy to niggas you find attractive. Or when your pussy gets to twitching for some dick, you just like all the other lame bitches giving up the pussy for free. A real ho is a topnotch bitch in my eyes. She's not giving up no ass or conversation for free, horny or not. She makes her money from the womb to the tomb, and any way else she can to get paid. Honestly speaking, you can only wish to hold such high level of a title as a ho. And as for me kicking it with you, you hit the answer on the nose."

151

Karen frowned at his answer and began prancing around in front of him in her new see-through, light purple panties and bra. Snoop wasn't paying her any attention. His eyes were glued on his new jewelry. Karen purposely bumped his head with her thigh to get his attention.

"Girl, if you don't," she interrupted before he finished his sentence.

"Excuse me, dang," she said in a playful way.

Snoop gazed up at her with eyes that offered a warning. He cast a momentary look at her sexy body and returned his stare to the jewelry.

"Nigga, if you don't get your funky ass back into that room and take off those new panties, you betta. Your ass haven't even taken a bath yet and you hoppin' around in new shit, prancin' all up around me," he snapped.

"Forget you, nigga, I don't stink! What you need to do is come and jump up and down in this hot pussy and stop acting all scared an' shit. I would think after a long day and all that game you shot to get a bitch you would be trying to live in a bitch pussy," Karen said.

"Yeah, bitch, that's what you get for thinkin'. Bitch, thinking is not in your job description. Leave the thinking up to me, and you and I both would be better off. Now go see if my bath water is ready," he replied sharply.

Karen dropped her eyes and was ashamed of her ignorance. She made no attempt to defend herself. She just turned toward the bedroom and ambled off.

"Damn, that girl is fine," Snoop admitted to himself as he walked to the back room.

Bad as he wanted to tap that ass, he knew if he was to give in she would have won and he wasn't about to compromise the potential making of a gold mine for his sexual pleasures, because that wouldn't be pimping at all. She first needed to understand her functions and understand that it was a gift just being in his immediate presence, and making love to him would be a supreme royalty, but her body was enticing and the thought of making an exception to dig it out on the spot had crossed his mind.

He didn't notice that Karen had returned and was now standing in front of him with a blue and white silk bathrobe in her hand, softly calling his name, "Snoop, your bath water is ready."

He was still in deep thought and she was the topic. Her words were falling on deaf ears. She bent down and kissed him on the side of the face to get his attention. He quickly came to.

"Did you say something, baby," he asked.

"Yes, daddy, I did. Your bath water is ready. Do you like?" She asked, holding up the silk robe that had an embroidered dragon on the back.

"For shizzle, that's fly as hell there, major fly. Where did you get that from," he asked.

"I picked it up for you at the Man's shop. I thought you might like it." She decided to play along and smiled cheerfully, "Daddy, your bath is ready."

Snoop Dogg stood up and yawned, then stretched his arms over his head real wide before strolling to the back room. He sat on the foot of the bed and bounced up and down on it a few times, then glided his palms over the silk quilt and began undressing. Karen stood in the entrance of the bathroom, leaning up against the door, watching him undress down to his blue boxers. She moved her legs from one position to the next as if she had an itch between her clefts that needed to be scratched. Snoop Dogg stood and moved to enter the bathroom, but Karen didn't move. She stood there and reached out and hugged him around the neck, pressing her body up against his. She released a light moan, then slowly kissed him. Her tongue gave chase once it was inside his mouth, trapping his, then sucking it deep in her mouth.

"Uhhhm," she moaned. The heat from her body rose up like steam. She felt like her body was on fire from the inside, too hot to be held by bare hands.

Snoop Dogg reclaimed his tongue and broke free from her hold, "Damn, girl, you must be the devil or you related to him, or somethin', cuz your ass is burnin' up. What's wrong with you?" He asked, walking past her into the bathroom.

"Nothing's wrong with me. It's been over a year since I had some, of course I'ma be hot with a fine man standing naked in my bathroom."

Snoop Dogg sighed in disbelief with his back turned toward her. Karen snapped, "What, you don't believe that I went without sex that long. What you think, I'm a ho or something?!"

Snoop turned toward her with a grin, shaking his head. He didn't bother to say what was going through his mind because he saw the expression on her face. It told him that she was lost in thought and was already checking herself mentally for her loose tongue. He took off his boxers, folded them, and placed them on the floor. He stuck his forefinger inside the tub to feel the water temperature before stepping into the huge tub that he assumed four bodies could fit comfortably. There were plenty of bubbles, and the fragrance of the soap was gentle and welcomed his body. He had forgotten how good it felt to sit in a tub of hot water, which he promised himself he would do every day before bed.

Karen stood, staring at him getting acquainted with the bubbles and thinking to herself, "How could any man resist all this pussy I have between my legs and here I am trying to give it away to a nigga who had gave his all to get me on his team. Now he's shining me off like I'm not even here just to play with some fuckin' bubbles. I'm starting to think he's not into women, especially the way he charmed that punk today, who he had tickled pink and buying him a lot of expensive shit. But damn, if he is gay it would be a waste of a handsome, sexy ass man. My heart would be broken, but here I am willing to flip through rings of fire to make him happy so I can get this nigga dick and breed before killing his ass."

Eugene L. Weems, Timothy R. Richardson

CHAPTER 21

"Karen, do you hear me talking to you," Snoop shouted to get her attention.

"I'm sorry, baby, my mind drifted somewhere else."

"Yeah, I've noticed."

"What is it, baby, that you was saying," she asked, fully alert and attentive to his words.

"I was telling you to get in the tub before the water get cold," he said.

That was all he needed to say. She practically tore off her panties and bra, then entered the tub. She paused for a second, then pushed herself in between his legs and softly kissed his lips, then his chin.

"Daddy, let me wash your back," she asked, and they switched positions.

She wrapped her legs around his waist, so her pussy rested against the small of his back. Karen held him in her arms, rubbing on his small chest, and kissed and sucked on his neck and ears. He didn't stop her touchy, feely hands and lips from feeling up his body. He just sat there, enjoying the moment, fully erect. She turned his head toward her and fed him her tongue.

"Oops, excuse me," a woman's voice took Karen and Snoop Dogg by surprise.

In the heat of the passion, they didn't have a chance to hear the front door open. Snoop Dogg turned his head toward the voice and saw a high yellow dame standing in high heels and a tight dress that showed her curvy shape. Her hair was ruby red and had long, deep waves in it. He assumed that she had to be Pink, Karen's roommate, and thought he was looking at heaven in the form of a woman.

"No, you don't' have to leave," Karen shouted out to Pink before she got out of earshot.

"My baby must have been reading my mind," Snoop thought to himself.

Pink returned to the sexy scene very interested in the activities in the tub.

"What's up, girl," Karen asked, "I thought you was at work."

"I called in so I could make sure things were right for you and your man, and damn, what a man he is," Pink said, staring deep into Snoop Dogg's eyes. She took a seat on the ledge of the tub and crossed her legs, never losing eye contact with Snoop. "I had picked up a bottle of Dom Perignon and your favorite, Perrier Jouet Brut Fleur Champagne," Pink said.

Snoop held Pink's gaze because he knew this was a bitch he had to cop and lock on, a money maker for sure if not the money printer herself. She was sexually seductive, almost a mirror image of Karen, but with a totally reverse complexion. She also had a few different facial features, but body wise they both had bodies out of this world. Her sparkling hazel eyes were captivating and seemed to keep changing colors.

"Girl, you not going to introduce me to your man," Pink asked.

"Oh, excuse me. It really slipped my mind. Daddy, this is my roommate and good friend, Pink. And Pink, this is my man, the rapper Snoop Dogg. You happy now?"

Pink didn't respond to Karen. She just kept her eyes glued on the prize. She asked, "May I get you a glass of champagne, daddy of the house?"

"Yes, baby, that would be fine as long as it comes with pink passion," he said.

Pink was overwhelmed by his deep, sexy voice, and replied," I don't mean to stare at your man with lust in my eyes, Karen, but girl he is so handsome and I envy you."

"Pink, whatever you trippin' over needs to stop. Why you sweatin' over small shit," Karen asked, "Just go get the glasses and champagne. Better yet, bring me something hard."

"Girl, I think you already have that in the bath with you," Pink pointed down at Snoop Dogg's erection.

Pink stood up and quickly walked out the bathroom. Karen asked Snoop if it was okay if her friend joined them in the tub to celebrate. She knew the answer to that question before it left her lips. Everything was going as planned.

"Daddy, is that one you can add to your stable?"

Snoop smiled because he knew that Karen was shooting to stay at the top of his list. He didn't respond to her question, but just turned around and kissed her deeply. Pink returned with three glasses between her fingers and a bottle of Perrier Jouet Brut Fleur in her right hand, and a bottle of Armadale Vodka underneath her left armpit. She set down the champagne and passed the bottle of vodka to Karen. The glassed clanged together, then fluid poured from the bottle of vodka.

"Get in, baby," Snoop announced, taking Pink by surprise.

"Are you serious?" She asked, and looked in Karen's direction.

"He said you can get in with us. I'm not trippin' if he's not. So get that shit off and get your ass in here. Help me soap my man down," Karen said, and took one long swallow, downing her drink.

Pink quickly undressed, then tied her hair into a bun and got in the tub. All three soaped each other down and drank from the bottles until they were empty. Karen and Pink took turns tongue tagging Snoop Dogg, and sucking on his lips. They rinsed off the soap from their bodies, and Karen and Pink dried him off, then themselves.

Snoop Dogg walked out the bathroom and noticed that scented candles were burning around the room and a bottle of champagne was chilling on the nightstand, next to a single crystal glass. He didn't notice the white and pink rose petals spread out on top of the bed, until Karen gently pushed him down onto its surface. He laid back and stretched out, feeling the soft silk-like texture of the rose petals become intimate with his body. Karen crawled between his legs and introduced her lips to his nut sacks. She filled her mouth with his flesh and gently massaged it with her tongue. Pink laid on her stomach on his right side and piloted his hand between her legs. He began slowly finger massaging her as they kissed.

Karen performed a supernatural move, then slid her mouth over the head of his dick. The head she was blessing him with was unbelievable. His body tensed up like a single unified muscle, then he released a thunderous moan of pleasure. Pink looked toward Karen working her mouth piece and said, "That's right, Superhead, show this nigga you gots major head game."

Snoop Dogg knows these bitches had planned on sucking and fucking the life out of him. Two against one gave them a false sense of hope that they could work it on him and get him sprung on the pussy. They thought that he would fall weak for the ass, but he knew all too well that he was the only top boss in the room. These bitches were nothing but entertainment for his dick and a piece of ass to sell to a trick, so they could pay a pimp. Pink and Superhead took turns riding him and filling their mouth's with stiff dick.

The sexual trio was sweating heavily and breathing real hard from the energy released during this fuck Olympics. Just when Pink began to feel her eyes roll into the back of her head, Snoop Dogg pushed her off of him and stood up and took full control. He made Pink and Superhead get into the sixty-nine position. He slapped Pink on the ass, her back arched in response, and she inhaled air in short breaths. He stood behind her, held her by the waist and powered into her wet, hot, juicy pussy. His strong hands tilted her head forward at a perfect angle so she could suck on Karen. He massaged her breast with one hand, then entered her soul deeply. She moaned loudly and tried to crawl away, but he held her with one hand firmly in position and fed her a strict cock diet. Pink went wild until her body locked up and she began to shiver. She had reached orgasm again, her body felt weak. Pink squirmed to the side of the bed, leaving Superhead exposed to a long, hard, and throbbing cock that she laid staring up at with wide eyes.

Karen turned around and spread her legs wide, then Snoop entered her tight pussy. She squirmed and tried to wiggle away, but he gave chase. He captured her in his clutch, pinned her down to the mat, and kept digging her out. She moaned furiously. Her breathing quickened while she held him firmly under each armpit, and with every thrust it seemed like her grip tightened around him. Karen tried to control the depth of his long, deep strokes by holding the sides of his butt. The sound of her moans and screams of pleasure only excited Snoop more.

161

"Bitch, this is what you been whining about all day, so you gettin' all of my frustration now," he said, breathing hard. Snoop Dogg raised her right leg up to his shoulder and straightened her left leg flat on the bed. He thrust toward her inner thigh of the raised leg that applied a constant pressure to her exposed clitoris and increased her stimulation.

Superhead approached a super orgasm, her pussy tightened like vice grips. She tried to catch her breath. Her nails dug deep into the bed sheets while her moans became screams and then came to an end as she arched her back deeply with her head back. She was motionless. Karen froze in a pose as Snoop Dogg gripped the pillow and dug deep, tensing his butt checks and stomach muscles with every stroke. Her hot juices flowed like a stream. He quickly pulled out of her and shot his load in the crack of her ass.

The walls of the bedroom were sweating from the bodies coming together as one and the intense sex had raised the temperature in the room to a sizzle. The flames from the bed made the candles melt away faster than they should have and caused a frost to form over the chilled bottle of Dom Perignon that sat on the night stand. Snoop Dogg was ready for round two. To his surprise, Pink was stretched out and sound asleep while Karen was still trying to compose her breathing.

"Damn, sorry ass bitches! I gots to get you hos in shape if ya'll goni' to be hoin' for me 'cause I can't have you bitches rolling over off a trick and falling asleep and shit," Snoop Dogg said, pushing Karen's right leg to the side and laying down himself. Within minutes, they were all sound asleep.

For the next few days, Snoop Dogg, Karen, and Pink stayed locked in the house, allowing their bodies to get well acquainted with each other. There was nothing but real serious, passionate, erotic, and breathtaking freaking going on. Snoop felt like he was entitled to such pleasures to satisfy his inner sexual desires. He enjoyed the sensation of soaking in a woman's fundamental nature, her vagina. But what he didn't know was that these bitches were using him and allowing his ego to grow. He heard stories about Karen, aka Superhead, but he was so arrogant and stuck in the fantasy world of being a pimp that he thought he could really tame any woman on earth. His celebrity status didn't mean shit to Superhead. In her mind, it was all about the hustle that she had going on with her crime partner. It was all about the head gamez.

Eugene L. Weems, Timothy R. Richardson

CHAPTER 22

Pink woke up Snoop Dogg from a comatose state of sleep with the aroma of fresh-baked French bread and teriyaki sirloin. She stood over him, dressed in an elegant emerald green bra and panties that were trimmed with a white heart-shaped nylon lace. She was holding a shiny silver platter elegantly at both ends by the stylish handles. She called out his name and announced that it was time to eat. Snoop slowly opened his eyes, blinked a few times to focus his vision, then used the back of his paw to wipe away the excess drool from the side of his face. He then rubbed the slimy secretion onto the pillow that had been his source of comfort for the night. Once his vision came into focus, he gazed up at Pink's shapely and hard body then thought about how good her loving was before pulling the silk sheet away from his body. He sat up and placed his back against the oak headboard of the bed for support.

Pink was astounded when she glanced down at Snoop Dogg's nude body and noticed he was still fully erect after four nights and three days of constant freaking with her and Karen.

"Good evening, handsome," she said softly," I figured you might be hungry, so I made you something to eat."

Pink sat down the silver platter on the night stand and opened a wet towel and began washing his face and hands. When she was satisfied with her sterile scrub, she picked up the tray and placed it in front of him. The strong smell of paprika had now introduced itself to Snoop's nostrils. He looked down at the large plate of food that sat on the tray next to the fresh-baked, golden brown French bread croissants. A tall glass of grape juice and fresh blueberries added a hint of class to the meal. The whole plate of food was trimmed with thin slices of fresh tomatoes and chunky strips of tender teriyaki sirloin steak in the center with melted cheddar cheese and sprinkles of paprika on top. The meal looked like she had taken her time preparing it and it had an elegant look that rivaled the finest restaurants.

The sound of Bob Marley's music came through the house speakers from the living room and it gave the house an energetic feeling. Snoop Dogg glanced up at Pink with a smile and lifted the tray off his thighs into the air and said, "Baby, come over here and feed him while I'm feedin' me." He motioned his eyes toward his erection.

Pink slid out of her panties and crawled on top of him. She guided his erection upwards and eventually concealed the entire length inside of her. She closed her eyes, then released a soft moan of pleasure, and soon after, reopened them. She spoke in a voice coated with passion as if she was inhaling deeply with every spoken word, "How..does..that..feel..daddy," she asked, sitting astride him motionless with his throbbing swipe marinating inside of her. He only smiled at her question and then sat down the tray on the inner part of his upper stomach. He then positioned himself so he could lay back on his elbows, so Pink could feel him and remain straddled on top of him.

Karen came ambling into the room and immediately noticed Pink on top of Snoop Dogg, "Damn, Pink, with yo' horny ass. What

166

you tryin' to do to the nigga, fuck the life outa him?! I know the dick is the bomb, but damn! You can't be up on him 24/7 like you doing," she said and then walked into the bathroom and began running bath water.

Pink had turned toward Karen when she came into the room, then quickly returned her attention back to feeding Snoop. She just ignored what Karen was rambling off at the mouth about and dismissed it as jealousy. Snoop eventually finished with both his meals, then motioned for Pink to get off of him. He raised up and then ambled toward the bathroom to relieve himself. He glanced at his reflection as he walked past the life-sized mirror on the wall over the double sinks. Karen looked up at him and smiled as he stood over the toilet seat taking a leak.

"Daddy, your bath water is ready whenever you ready to get in. I got you a new toothbrush right there." She pointed at the white and blue box on top of the sink countertop. It had a Crip blue toothbrush inside that could be seen through the clear plastic window of the container.

"Whenever you ready just let me know so I can bathe you," she said.

Snoop Dogg strolled over to the first sink, turned on the water, and washed his hands. He then reached for the toothbrush and liberated it from the container. He allowed the running water to flow over the head of the toothbrush bristles before squeezing toothpaste onto it and brushing his teeth. Snoop stared at his reflection in silence as he took his time scrubbing his ivories. Karen sat at the edge of the tub waiting patiently until he finished. Pink was in the bedroom cleaning up. She placed fresh linen on the bed and laid out clean clothes for Snoop at the foot of the bed. She walked into the bathroom with a new pair of black No Question boxer briefs and matching tank top in her left hand, and the silk robe Karen had bought him in her other hand.

Pink hung the robe on a hook and sat the underclothes neatly on top of the sink counter. Snoop Dogg stepped into the tub like a king, and Karen and Pink followed him. He sat there, idle, while the two lovelies bathed him thoroughly and enjoyed the scented bath beads that Karen had placed in the tub. It was a fragrance that he didn't recognize, but it was still pleasant to even his high standards.

After they bathed him, the two women dried off and lotioned his body. He put on his No Question underwear and admired the small silk-screened No Question logo that was on the shirt. Snoop stared closely at it and noticed there was a letter N and a question mark that was in the middle of the letter N.

"Fly, baby, this is real fly," he said in a whisper to himself as he rubbed his right palm over the stylish emblem and felt the smooth texture of the fabric. Karen and Pink walked out of the room, leaving him to admire his matching No Question underwear. He glanced upon the mirror and turned his head from side to side to examine the neatness of his French braids that went in a zig-zag pattern and then b-lined straight down, past his shoulders with clear transparent hair beads on each individual braid. He saw that his braids were still in acceptable neatness, to his high standards of quality, and then ambled back into the bedroom.

Karen and Pink were fully dressed, standing in front of the dresser mirror, trying on lipstick. Karen's smooth, honey brown, thick left leg was exposed through the split that went down the side of her Dolce & Gabbana white leather, long skirt that stopped right at her ankles. Her feet displayed professionally pedicured toes that peeked out of the expensive python skin sandals. She wore only a python patterned bra underneath the matching white leather jacket to the skirt. Her long hair was tucked into a neat bun that allowed her full beauty to be exposed.

Pink sported the opposite. She liked bright colors because it attracted the attention she craved for. She was dressed in a pair of red leather Gucci pants and matching jacket. Her head was covered with a red leather cowboy hat with a crocodile band. To set off her designer masterpiece, she wore crocodile boots. Her red, deep, wavy hair hung long underneath the cowboy hat with trinkets of red glitter in her hair.

They didn't notice Snoop Dogg when he re-entered the bedroom and was now standing quietly, admiring both of their sophisticated, beautiful, and hourglass shaped bodies from afar. He was impressed with himself for taming two thoroughbred winners that would soon be making their public announcement. Snoop had every intention of seeing to it that his investment was announced to the public properly and managed well. Karen fell silent when she noticed Snoop Dogg's reflection in the mirror. Pink looked up at the mirror when Karen became quiet.

"Hey, daddy, what's on the agenda today," Karen rushed over to Snoop, "I saw this sharp ass outfit that would really look nice on this body," she said before he could answer.

As she spoke the words, she was b-lining her hand down her womanly figure. Pink stood quiet, watching Karen do what she did best, which was to get a nigga sprung on the pussy and head game, then appoint them the job position as boss so she could collect a fat check. Like most females who were in the line of work of working niggas for they paper, she knew that Karen didn't give a fuck about trying to empty the nigga's pockets for chump change. The bitch always shot fire for the 40 acres and a mule of a nigga's life savings. That was one of the qualities Pink loved about Karen and she knew the bitch was now at work, stroking gently at the cow to be milked. She knew all she had to do was continue to play along and she would be awarded a nice chunk of cheese when it was all said and done. Without a doubt, she was down to walk through hell and back with her girl, Karen. Karen had been her savior when she was broke, hungry, and homeless.

"Well, let's go get that 'din," Snoop Dogg looked down at his shirt, "I have some more shopping to do anyway. I like this No Question shit."   He rubbed at the logo on his shirt again, experiencing the fine craftsmanship. "I never heard of this clothing line in Cali, but this shit is real fly. You got to swing me by the store where I can get some more of this, but first we gotta drop by my suite so I can scoop up a few ends."

That was the wrong thing to say around Karen. She knew that she had this nigga nose wide open now. In so many words, he had just told her that he had money sitting up in his hotel waiting for the taking.   Karen turned on her heels toward Pink and raised an eyebrow. That was Pink's cue. She excused herself from the room and returned after several minutes. Snoop rapped as he got dressed, "Shootin' niggas down/ slappin' bitches up/ straight cat strut with some Henny in my cup/ groove for the hell of it/ I should be the president/ a yo homie Doggy-Dogg got that medicine/ in the cabinet/ I'm the magnet of attracting the baddest bitches on the planet. Ain't that right, baby?" He looked at Karen.

"You know that's right," she agreed, just to stroke his ego. "Daddy, is it a must that we need to swing by your spot? You can put whatever you gonna get on a credit card. You do carry credit cards when you travel, don't you?"   Karen was fishing for information.

"A playa don't fuck with credit. Cash mothafuckin' money, baby. What it look like for a playa to be out in Vegas without some real paper? The place where a nigga is surrounded by millions of dollars. I wish I would! I keep a shitload of that green shit with me, just in case of emergency," Snoop Dogg bragged.

Well, nigga, let a bitch know that she's about to get broke off swell for her role playing and sexual entertainment, Karen thought. "Aight then, enough said. Let's go get what you need to get, so we can get to the mall before it gets crowded. We don't need to get bombarded by your fans again. I ain't trying to have all them muhfuckas up in your face." Karen made an attempt to sound jealous. The truth was, she wanted to get all she could out of Snoop while still remaining under the radar, before she deadened his skinny ass. Ha!

Eugene L. Weems, Timothy R. Richardson

CHAPTER 23

The three of them took a cab to Caesar's palace. Snoop Dogg led the way up to the suite. As they entered the spacious room, he ambled toward an oak desk and shuffled through the small pile of envelopes. He paused momentarily to study the content inside of several of them.

"I'll never go to this shit! Fuck Celine Dion, and what the fuck is a Blue Man Group? Y'all want 'dis shit?" He held complimentary tickets over his shoulder like they were burning his hand. The bold title read *Celine Dion: A New Day*, a show at Caesar's, and the other tickets were to the Blue Man Show at the Venetian Hotel.

"Hell, yeah, let me have 'em. I could get some money for these." Pink grabbed the tickets from his hand and already knew a few spots to dump them.

"I been wanting to see the Tournament of the Kings Jousting and Dinner Show at the Excalibur Hotel and Casino. Check that shit and see if they gave you some tickets to that show. Now, that's the bomb show. You gotta see that, Daddy," Pink said excitedly, like a kid at Disneyland.

"Fo' shizzle. We just might have to do that tonight, or before I head back to Killa Cali."

"How long are you here in Vegas," Karen asked.

"Six weeks, maybe a little longer. Shit, whenever we finish shooting my movie."

Karen's mind was now racing. This nigga never mentioned that he was in Vegas to shoot no movie. Then again, she couldn't remember ever asking him what he was doing in Las Vegas anyway. An rare question asked of anyone found in the sin city of never-ending entertainment and pleasures.

"Catch," Snoop Dogg tossed a pair of car keys to Karen, "We rollin' out in the Lamborghinis tonight. Karen, you can push my yellow Lamborghini Gallardo, and me and Pink gonna roll in my Crip blue Lamborghini Concepts. The bar is over there." He pointed across the room. "Help y'all self to a drink. I'll be right back. I just got to grab some ends and an ounce of Chronic." Snoop strolled off into the bedroom of the suite.

Karen was now steaming over the idea of Snoop Dogg choosing Pink to ride with him, and she had to ride in a car alone. She was now beginning to question her head game, and if it was all that and a bag of chips. The way she was perceiving it, was that maybe she wasn't the head specialist that she thought she was. Karen was furious at the thought and she had every intention of making Snoop Dogg pay for the disrespect. The nigga would learn the hard way about disrespecting any other woman's mind and body. She planned on teaching him a lesson.

Snoop Dogg strolled out the room with a Chronic blunt nestled between his lips and stacks of money gripped in both hands. Karen rose from her seat and walked seductively toward him. His eyes followed her, as well as Pink's. Without warning, with as much focus as she could muster, she swung a hard overhead right that introduced itself to Snoop's jaw and caused him to stumble, then fall to the floor. Money flew everywhere and the burning blunt disappeared. She had damn near sent him into a state of unconsciousness with the powerful blow. He had been taken by surprise, but somehow he found the strength to scramble back to his feet.

"Ah, cuzz, you punk bitch!" He spit out the blood that flowed from his busted grill, then stroked his hand over his jaw as if trying to rub at the grievous ache. Karen wasted no time. She leaped with a left hook, but found herself being picked off in midair with a straight right jab that shook her world. She was dazed, darkness swiftly closing in on her light. She was knocked out cold.

"Now, cuzz, that's how you check a bitch," Snoop Dogg said to his ego.

He slipped his left hand under his suit jacket and pulled out a weapon. He didn't notice Pink as she stepped around him. He pointed his weapon at the unconscious Karen. Frown lines wrinkled Snoop Dogg's forehead and his face clouded up. His mouth hung in a slack silent cry. He couldn't draw breath against the pain that suddenly screamed throughout his body. He fell to his knees and the gun fell to the floor from his hand. Pink removed the switchblade knife from his neck.

"Now, bitch ass, wannabe pimp, fake crab ass gansta rapper, you know you done fucked up royally by putting your hands on my girl. Now I'ma have to kill yo ho' ass nigga!" Pink growled.

Snoop Dogg knew he couldn't go out like this, not by the hands of a bitch. He could just see the headlines, "Snoop Dogg, the lengendary gangster/pimp was found dead in Vegas with his throat cut. He was last seen with two unidentified women." He shook the thought. He refused to be another Tupac, a gangster rapper who got murdered in Vegas. Sin city was not about to be his final resting place, he told himself. He made his move, quickly reached up, almost in slow motion, grabbed the knife handle, jerked it from his neck. He then spun toward the knife hand, sending Pink to her stomach. He swiftly straddled her from behind and took positive possession of the knife.

"Now, bitch, I'm gonna kill you, tramp!" Snoop held the knife high above his head and was about to plunge the six-inch blade deep into Pink like she was a pin cushion.

"I doubt that, nigga," Karen's voice took Snoop Dogg by surprise before his lights went out, courtesy of the Grand Marnier bottle that shattered over his head.

This time Karen didn't give him any time to regain his senses. She followed up with flurry of punches and kicks that pulverized Snoop. She had finally succeeded in what she attempted to accomplish in her first attack; she had knocked Snoop out cold. She then hustled toward the telephone and jerked the cord out of the wall and hog tied Snoop Dogg like one of Michael Vick's pit bulls. Once he was helpless, she checked to see how Pink was doing. Her crimey was finally coming back to earth and was revived to consciousness with a splash of ice cold vitamin water to her face.

"You alright? Bitch, get up!" Karen stared down into clouded eyes.

"Ye..yeah, I'm good. Where is he?" Pink asked.

"Right there, tied the hell up." Karen pointed in Snoop's direction. Pink blew out a relieved breath.

"Can you help me up?" Once Pink rose to her feet, she kicked a pointed boot that connected to Snoop Dogg's face.

"Don't kill the nigga yet, girl," Karen tugged at Pink's arm, "We need him to find out where all the money is at."

"It's in that room over there," Pink pointed with authority.

"Yeah, I know that, but do you really think he has it laying out in the open?"

"I don't think so! There has to be a safe in there somewhere." Karen was right, there was a safe in the master bedroom. They dragged Snoop Dogg into the room. Pink slapped his face until he came to.

"Nigga, what's the combo to this safe," she asked with a threatening edge.

"Bitch, fuck you! The Snoop D-O-Dubble Gee is not tellin' you bitches --"

"Oh, yeah!" Pink pulled the Springfield .45 from the small of her back and the silencer from her bra. She quickly began assembling the weapon before Snoop's bulging eyes.

"Oh, that's how we gettin' down now?" Snoop's voice quivered from the large lump that was in his throat. He realized that these bitches were dead serious about what they wanted.

"Aight..Aight! Two, One, three! That's the combination. You can have all that shit. Just don't take a nigga's chronic." Snoop Dogg tried to save face.

"That's a good pound puppy," Karen said, as she punched the code in the electronic keypad. The red light blinked, then it turned green and the safe opened like magic. Karen pulled the door open wide, "Now that's what I'm talking about!" She removed one of the tall stacks of bills and examined it closely, "Now, this is a nice come up for putting up with a sorry ass nigga's bullshit."

Karen emptied out the contents of one of Snoop's suitcases and racked the money, jewelry, and the half pound of chonic into the suitcase. She then robbed him of the jewelry he had on his body.

"Don't forget the money in the living room!" Pink wanted it all.

"Don't worry about that, I got that covered." Karen wanted it all and then some. She turned on her heels, headed for the door.

"I'll meet you back at the house. Don't forget to wipe the place down after you kill that nigga. Give me five minutes before you deaden his ass." Karen hustled out of the suite with the heavy suitcase in hand.

Pink consulted her watch, affording Karen the time she requested and then aimed her weapon at Snoop Dogg.

"Turn yo' punk ass over, nigga!" She kicked him in the ribs to give him a boost.

"You got anything on your chest you want to get off before I take your life?"

"Yeah, bitch. I'll see you in hell," Snoop barked.

"I guess I will see you, but right now I really wouldn't want to be you."

Her weapon coughed twice, striking him in the chest. Snoop turned onto his stomach and the .45 coughed once more, piercing the upper part of his back. Pink unscrewed the silencer and tucked the gun inside her beltline at the small of her back. She carefully wiped down the room before departing the hotel.

Karen was at the kitchen table counting the loot when Pink entered the house.

"You handle yo' business," Karen asked, not bothering to look up because she knew that it could only have been Pink entering the room.

"It's all to the good. The dog as been put to sleep." Karen rose from her seat.

"You done good, girl. Now, come on over here and help me count up this paper. I gotta make a phone call. Start with these stacks first," she pointed, "They haven't been counted yet."

Karen then strolled off toward her bedroom, thumbing a number into the keypad of her cell phone, then she raised it to one of her ears. A woman answered and Karen spoke. "The dog pound has been shut down," then she hung up the phone.

Eugene L. Weems, Timothy R. Richardson

CHAPTER 24

"Damn! Shit! Why I gotta get the white boy?" Be'oncay asked herself the same question for the millionth time. She had been hanging out with Karen so much that she was starting to sound just like her. The new queen of pop music, actress, clothing line owner, and cosmetics super model had a thriving career that was worth well into the hundred millions. Ms. Knolls was a megasuperstar, so why was she stuck in Detroit, hundreds of miles away from her mansion, trying to track down a nerdy white boy? She was from the south and she was used to blackness. Many of the institutions in Houston were still segregated. You had your black ghettos, the Mexican haciendas, and the white wealthy suburbs. If you were black, there were still a lot of places you could never be accepted in Houston no matter how much money you brought to the table.

Be'oncay wanted to find Eminem, smoke his white ass, and get back to her career and super lips in Brooklyn. The sooner she got this assignment over with, the sooner she could get back to her life. She really got the short end of the stick this time. It was probably due to her failed assassination attempt on Suge Knight. Gladiss seemed to hold more grudges than Kobe and Shaq. Be'oncay knew the true reason behind this undesirable assignment and it definitely had something to do with what happened in Vegas. Excuses flowed through her mind and she played the sexism card to the fullest. Why not? She had learned from the best. Nobody vocalized the injustices done to the female race better than Karen Stephins.

Be'oncay thought about the Las Vegas incident and how she managed to kill Tupac and Suge Knight escaped with a bullet graze. One out of two targets, that was 50 percent or half. If she were playing pro baseball and had a .500 batting average, she would be a cinch to make it to the Hall of Fame. If she were playing in the NBA and managed to sink half of her shot attempts, she would be greater than Michael Jordan. Men still ruled the world and she wondered what happened to all the strong female rappers of yesteryear; Salt n' Pepa, MC Lyte, Yoyo, Monie Love, Lauren Hill, Oaktown 357, and even Queen Latifah, sisters with attitudes, ladies first. That's what Be'oncay was talking about.

The new generation of female rappers were just a bunch of hos and ex-strippers with microphones, and no message to the millions of women who went to concerts and supported rap music; Lil' Kim, Trina, Foxy Brown, and Lil' Mama. Come on! Where was the sisterhood? Be'oncay wasn't a sellout-type bitch and she tripped out on bitches like Diana Ross, Halle Berry, Whoopi Goldberg, and Paula Patton. Back in the slavery days, they would have been Aunt Jemimas, falling in love with white boys and sporting them around like a new pair of shoes. Be'oncay liked her men like she liked her coffee, strong and black. She loved the black knight in shining armor, the ghetto soldiers. She loved chocolate.

"Soldiers, that sounds like a good song." Be'oncay made a mental note as she turned her car onto 8 Mile. She was going to start the process of hooking back up with her girls in Destiny's Child and do a reunion album.

She cruised from the ghetto, the mostly black end of the 8 Mile, and thought back to Eminem's movie because it didn't cover this section of the road; it only focused on the white section and what went down in the trailer parks. Eminem was a tough nut to crack. He was as white as can be on his records, and as far as his fan base was concerned, but he hung out with black people and made his money from Hip Hop music. Let there be no mistaking, he was undoubtedly in control and all of the blacks who surrounded him knew that he was the boss. To make things even more confusing, once Marshall Mathers reached a certain level of celebrity, he got himself surrounded by a bunch of yessum, master-type muthafuckas. He signed an all-black roster to this plantation, Obie Trice, then he found a group of black clowns and added himself to the mix and took his circus on the road under the disguise of a rap group called D12. Give me a break! They had the nerve to call their group a 'band' with a grown ass black man running around in a diaper. Eminem was a modern day plantation owner using black music to prosper.

Be'oncay could care less who the fuck Eminem was. She wasn't paid to think. She was paid to kill niggas! Her present job was to find this cracker and crumble him like bread crumbs. The sooner the better. She faced more problems this time around because of her celebrity. It was going to be hard to avoid the media and the tabloids. Everybody wanted to know the next move to be made by the new queen of pop music, or a photo shot of Be'oncay and Jigga. She was going to make her moves at night, and pick her moments very carefully. Be'oncay was determined to find Eminem, and when she found white chocolate, she was gonna melt his ass.

Dr. Lesley was outraged. She hated when people broke their promises. Mase was on her shit list in a major way. She could not believe that Mase had looked her dead in the eyes and flat out lied. So what if she was about to blow his head off with a .44 Magnum. A little motivation never hurt anyone. Mase making a return to the world of gangster rap was a big slap in the face to Dr. Lisa. The Harlem MC was now officially one of the many people who had made the mistake of taking her kindness for weakness. Dr. Lisa had tried the therapeutical approach of talking things over peacefully and allowing a nigga to learn from his mistakes. The doctor had done her job, so now she was going to turn things over to her Ms. Hyde side.

She did her research, followed up on her instincts, and now the hunt was on. The chrome rims of the Toyota Camry rental stopped abruptly at the curb in front of the Harlem address Lisa had memorized. A black woman driving a black Toyota Camry in a black neighborhood was the perfect disguise. Nobody would have guessed that it was a superstar known all over the world, the Michael Jordan of women's basketball. She entered the brownstone and checked her dual chrome Colt .45 firearms. One was in the small of her back and the other was tucked away in her shoulder holster. Finding the tools for murder well in place, she continued her journey to Apartment D. She reached the front door, armed with shining weapons in both hands, then, "Bam, bam, bam!" Lisa kicked in the door.

"Nobody move," she yelled, with her fingers firmly on the triggers and murder on her mind.

"What the!" There was an old, elderly black couple sitting on a worn out couch, watching the news on television.

"Lord, Lord, Lord! What you done did now, Cleatus!" Told you 'bout playin' dem numbers at the pool hall!" Grandma Hayes immediately blamed her husband of 40 years for the intrusion.

"I ain't did nothin', Mabel. Who izzit, anyway," he said, holding his hands up high, eyes big with fear of the two hand cannons held by the shapely masked woman in black.

"We ain't got nuthin'. I don't gets my check until the 3rd of the months," Ms. Hayes continued.

"Wait, I apologize, I think I made a mistake. Wrong house," Dr. Lesley said, as she lowered her weapons from their targets, "Where's Mase," she questioned the couple.

"Mase? We ain't got no Mase, or no pepper spray either. Alls we got is each other," the lady said.

"I mean Mase, the rapper, the G-Unit guy. You know, Puffy, Biggie," Lisa tried to explain.

"We don't know no Mase, no Puff Dragon, or Big Boy either," Pops responded, feeling a little relieved.

"I'm sorry, wrong house." Lisa started to leave the room.

"Hey, young lady, who gone pay for this door! We don't want no mo' trouble. Damn crackheads will rob us blind," Mr. Hayes protested.

"Oh..Oh, here." Dr. Lisa returned to the room and handed the old man a tight bankroll, $15,000 cash, "Sorry for the inconvenience." Lisa left the building.

Once in the comfort of her car, Dr. Lesley removed her mask and wondered where she had gone wrong. Mase was supposed to be in that Harlem apartment. A short, quick hit and exit was out of the question now. She was going to have to find a needle in a haystack. New York was a small barn, area wise, but it held a whole lot of hay. The Toyota Camry stopped at the Waldorf Astoria Hotel and cruised

185

to the valet parking area. Lisa grabbed her briefcase and travel bag, then exited the driver's side of her vehicle.

"Oh, my God! Oh, my God! Dr. L! Dr. L! I can't believe it. Can I have your autograph? My girls love you! Can I take a picture wit' you? I loooove you! You won me a thousand bucks in the 2008 WNBA Finals!" The white parking attendant was ecstatic, but Dr. Lesley was used to the responses by now.

A small crowd of people crowded around her, pens out. It quickly became an organized confusion. Dr. L had no choice. She had to give the fans what they wanted, so she pulled out her Sharpie and started signing autographs.

Two hours later

In the presidential suit of the Waldorf Astoria, Dr. Lesley rested her tired hands and feet. It seemed like she was never going to make it to the hotel lobby, but fortunately she was saved from the mob by hotel management. She relaxed in the ecstasy of the large hot tub as the warmth of the fragranced waters marinated her shapely body. The complex puzzle of trying to figure out the whereabouts of Mase was wearing heavily on her mind. She hated not having the answers. She had developed several theories, but they all led to dead ends.

After hours of wracking her brain and evaluating every piece of information she had on Mase, she was still dumbfounded. She finally pulled out her laptop and logged onto the internet. She did a web search at BET.com. The past few years had been so busy playing in the WNBA, performing surgeries at the three clinics, and perfecting her miracle drug that she didn't have time to stay in touch with the gossip trends of the music industry.

"Rapper, Mase, dropped from G-Unit Records citing contract obligations to Bad Boy. Mase files for bankruptcy, attorney fees to blame."

Lisa looked at the two-week-old headlines in awe, "No wonder Mase disappeared." Lisa found part of the answer. Anything about anyone could be found on the internet, but she wasn't looking for facts anymore. She was looking for a nigga!

Dr. Lesley sat back in her silk bathrobe. Her long, muscular, butter cream legs were crossed gracefully and her clearly defined cleavage played peek-a-boo through the opening of her robe. She looked like the sexiest woman in the world, even in her confused state. A tall, slender version of Stacy Dash. The doctor had been to school most of her life and she had learned two things early in her academic years, which dated all the way back to pre-school. One was that no question was a stupid question, so never hesitate to ask. The second thing she learned was that a closed mouth could never get fed knowledge. In her nude state, she began to think about the pleasures she had received to her body from the only man that could solve her problems, a master of the art of search and destroy, her mentor, the answer man.

"Where are you, Mase?" Lisa got out her cell phone and speed dialed the number.

"Hello, Weems speaking." It was the distinctive voice of Commander Eugene Weems, the answer to all her problems.

Eugene L. Weems, Timothy R. Richardson

CHAPTER 25

A Private Location Somewhere in Delaware:

Curtis James Jackson III sat in the study of his secured mansion, fortunate to be alive. Who would have thought that The Game would have the balls to retaliate against him in Atlanta? To make matters worse, that Compton buster had ruined his birthday celebration. The owner of Magic City had quickly filed a multimillion dollar lawsuit against 50 Cent for the damages that happened to his club. The crazy shit that topped things off and really fucked him up was the class action lawsuit that fools had filed against him in civil court. Twenty-five strippers who worked at the club, four waitresses, and ten bouncers filed the lawsuit for personal damages. The muthafuckas claimed injuries from chipped fingernails, skinned knees, neck pains from ducking bullets to pieces of glass fragments from shattered chandeliers getting in their eyes. They wanted $150 million for their pain and suffering! Everybody in the universe knew that 50 was rich, so the list of names joining the lawsuit grew longer by the second. Muthafuckas who were driving by the club at the time of the shooting were claiming injuries. It seemed like everybody in Atlanta wanted in on the hog killing.

"Fuck dat shit!" 50 Cent was not going to sit back idle and be a victim. He had his top lawyers on the case and was not about to let niggas beat him out of his hard earned money. There was no way that he was going to let people take away what was rightfully his, definitely not after all the pain he had been through to get to the top, taking nine bullets, growing up broke, being rejected, and spending six fucking months in boot camp back in 1994. 50 worked hard for every penny and was not about to give up his riches. He was willing to die for his shit! The thought of dying brought him back to his present predicament.

"What am I gonna do 'bout this nigga, Game," 50 thought out loud. A million and one ways of getting his payback came to mind. 50 Cent had already severed the Game's financial neck by removing Dr. Dre's songs from his album, *Doctor's Advocate*. The promotions budget was cut down to pennies and zero dollars was the budget dedicated to making videos for his singles. In spite of all these obstacles, the nigga's album still sold over 500,000 units and 50 got most of that. The hired assassin in Cali had missed his target, so the hired assassin in Cali was eliminated. Curtis Jackson didn't tolerate failure in his organization. He was disgusted with himself for underestimating Jayson Taylor and it had almost cost him his life. Niggas got desperate when their backs were against the wall.

He thought back to the dreadful night in Atlanta, and in all the action, 50 was glad about his decision to bulletproof his limo. Mobb Deep stayed around to take out what he thought was the last two fools in Game's crew, but some crazy ass female came out of nowhere, blasting with bad intentions. If it wasn't for the last minute upgrades to his ride, him and his entire crew would have been the recipients of some slow singin' and some flower bringin'.

"Who was that masked bitch?!" 50 Cent asked himself the question because he knew from past experience that the Game had no game when it came to women. The last time he checked the Black Wall Street click, he just saw a bunch of young damn thugs who were unorganized and bickering among themselves. 50 knew that whoever the masked bitch was, she definitely was a professional. The several well-placed bullet holes placed in his limo were proof positive that she wasn't bullshittin'.

The Game must have scraped up enough money to hire professional help from somewhere. The entire episode was costing 50 a lot of money and he hated paying money out without getting money in. It just wasn't good business and something had to be done. The feeling of being shot at wasn't new to 50 Cent at all. He had experienced it before, the street wars in Queens. Shootin' at muthafuckas and muthafuckas shootin' back at him, it was a daily activity in the ghetto back in his hustlin' days of robbing and dealing heroin and crack cocaine. Back then, he didn't have anything to lose and didn't give a fuck about dyin' either. Today was a different day. He had built a vast empire worth hundreds of millions and wasn't about to die before he got a chance to enjoy every penny of it. He loved his life. 50 Cent was tired of playing games with Game. He was going to use everything that he had at his disposal to find that muthafucka, and when he did, the Game was going to be over!

Manhattan, New York

Meagan was mad as fuck. She had just hung up the phone from her debriefing with Commander Weems. The powers that be in Las Vegas were very disappointed with her inability to put 50 Cent in a vault forever. She understood Mr. Weems' position because he had given her the proper tools to complete the job. He was just the messenger, not the creator of the message. 50 was now in a secured fortress somewhere in Delaware. He was virtually untouchable, out of sight, and on the defensive. Game and his amateurs had done an excellent job of fucking things up for her. Meagan was going to have to retreat back to Cali, lay low for a while, and allow things to cool off for a minute.

The activities of the other night in Atlanta made national headlines. The lawsuits against 50 Cent were all over the television and radios. The dead bodies at Magic City were stacked up higher than the sex charges against R-Kelly. The media labeled the crime scene *The Magic City Massacre*. Meagan didn't fire a single shot inside the club, but when the entire incident was over and the smoke cleared, Gladiss blamed everything on Ms. Goodwin. The truth of the matter was that Meagan hated imperfection more than anyone. She was extremely hard on herself. The failure of the mission had really upset her, but who could she complain to? It wasn't the first time that she met defeat. But Meagan had the perfect remedy for her ailments, a couple of blunts of Chronic, a tall goblet of Grand Marnier, and a long visit from her Trojan Man.

Las Vegas, Nevada

"Snoop Dogg Survives Gunshot Wounds! Rapper Upgraded to Stable Condition!" Karen couldn't believe the shit she was reading in the *Las Vegas Review Journal*, Snoop Dogg survived.

"Man! Damn! That nigga know my face! He know who I am!" Karen was on fire, and we ain't talking about in the bedroom either. She was irate about the situation. And to top things off, when the Las Vegas Metro Police questioned Snoop about the robbery, he kept his mouth shut. The D-O-Double Gee was most definitely a gangster-type nigga. No stitches for snitches in Snoop Dogg's britches. It was just an indication that the Doggfather was secretly declaring war on Karen and Pink. She had started a war with half of the city of Long Beach and almost every Crip in Southern California. Snoop still had a lot of money and that meant he had a lot of power, 500 grand wasn't shit to him.

"Damn, Damn Damn!" Karen felt like Florida on that episode of *Good Times* when James got shot. Failure had reared its ugly head at the worst time.

Her career was going well. Her book was due out and she had just inked a multimillion dollar deal with Vivid Adult Entertainment to produce and star in an X-rated how-to video of herself performing Superhead. Karen was going to have total creative control and was going to be able to choose her leading man. She had narrowed her list down to Mr. Marcus, Delbert Smith, and of course Lil' Wayne. It was going to be a tough decision, but now she wondered if she was going to live long enough to make it.

"Why, why!" Only God knew the answer to that question. It seemed like every time things seemed to be going her way something would come along and fuck things up again.

Under direct orders from Commander Weems, Karen had to clean up the situation in Las Vegas. She loved her beautiful hideaway, but her spot had been blown up like Iraq. Snoop Dogg had been to her home, so he knew where she and Pink laid their heads. It was time for a little damage control.

"Pink! Pink!"

"I'll be there in a minute, baby. I'm in the tub," Pink responded.

It wasn't a surprise to Karen. She knew where the fuck Pink was at. She was the person that told her to wash her stinky pussy from all the sobbin' and cryin' she had been doing. Karen had given her the impression that everything was cool and all was forgiven for the Snoop blunder.

"What a waste! So much beauty, so little brains," she mumbled to herself as she walked toward the bathroom to join Pink.

Once she was in the confines of the large restroom, she looked at her flawless beauty in the mirror. Karen plugged in the blow dryer. "Everything okay? Sorry for yelling at you, Pink. You know you my baby girl, right," Karen said, while she gently teased strands of her hair with her manicured fingers. She was still looking in the mirror.

"I'm sorry, baybay. I'm so, so sorry," Pink repeated for the thousandth time.

Karen tuned out her pleas. She turned on the blow dryer, then tossed it in the tub with Pink. Her victim immediately went into a spasmic state of shock. The stench of fried flesh encompassed the room and it smelled like burnt vomit.

"Sorry didn't fuck up, bitch, you did! Quit blaming it on sorry!" Karen strolled out of the room, grabbed her packed bags, and headed for New York on the first thing smoking.

CHAPTER 26

Compton, California

The rapper, Jayson Taylor, aka The Game, had emerged to make it back to his neighborhood on Cedar Block to a less than hero's welcome. Shit like that happened when you were responsible for getting damn near half the OGs from your hood smoked. Who would have thought that those G-Unit niggas would come out blastin' heats like that? The Game thought that California niggas were the only fools banging like that, but 50 and his crew turned out to be real killers. He barely escaped Atlanta by the rubber on his Chucks and now the word was out in the hood that he was a buster that ran off and left his homies for dead. Rumors spread swiftly in Compton, faster than the blue line Metro Link. The game got ran out of Atlanta by 50 and his crew, and everybody knew it. He only confirmed the stories when he returned back to Cali minus seven members of his crew. Now he had seven families of their loved ones to deal with.

To think that it all happened because of Jimmy Henchman and his effort to accept money to do songs with Fat Joe, Ja Rule, and anybody else who had a few dollars on the table. His manager was pimping him out to the music industry like a cheap male exotic dancer with a microphone. Jimmy didn't care because he was making more money than a tax collector. The Game treated the same homies that had his back and put their lives on the line for him in the beginning of his career like shit. On the other hand, he treated his newly found New York fast-talking manager like family. But when the bullets had started flying in Compton, and then later in Atlanta, Mr. Henchman was nowhere to be found. The Game was finally seeing the light; all money wasn't good money. It was time to face the reality that there was no way that he could fight a war against 50 Cent anymore. The flop of his album and the decreased popularity of his music was really putting a dent in his pockets. The Game was over.

"Hello, Dre, I need yo' help, man. Tell 50 I quit. No mo' dissin', no mo' mix tapes and shit. I wanna truce. OG, can you make it happen for me in Compton?" Believe it or not, Game showed a rare display of emotion.

"I got you, nigga. I'll see what I can do. Told you not to cross that nigga, 50. I got you covered. I'm out." The Game heard a dial tone, then hung up his cell. Jayson Taylor breathed a sigh of relief because he was confident that Dr. Dre could find a cure for the situation.

Harlem, New York

Commander Weems was a genius. He had pulled a few strings at the FBI and got the 411 on the whereabouts of Mase. Dr. Lesley had to do a double take as she parked her vehicle across from the address that Mr. Weems gave her as the place of employment for Mase. The entire trip to New York had been a wild goose chase with pages and pages of misinformation. Lisa was confused as fuck about the entire mission and this present stop on this adventure just added another crazy twist to the puzzle. Dr. Lesley entered through the glass double doors of the business. All eyes immediately focused on her. She was an international celebrity. She ignored the stares and smiles of admiration, then made her way over to the counter.

"Welcome to McDonald's, Dr. L. I'm your number one fan! May I help you? Anything you want, it's on the house!" Lisa couldn't believe the voice she was hearing. It was the distinctive mumble of Mase. He was a cashier at McDonald's!

Two hours later on a New York busy street, in traffic

"Damn!" Dr. Lesley couldn't believe the sight that she had just witnessed with her own eyes. She couldn't believe that Mase had gone out like that, ten dollars an hour at McDonald's. Just the thought of that scenario was funny to her.

Once she gathered her composure and realized that Mase didn't recognize her from their intimate encounter years ago, she took in the comedy of the situation. She pulled out her American Express Black Card and bought all the kids in McDonald's Happy Meals. Of course, a couple of the bigger kids wanted shakes, Big Macs, and Quarter Pounders and shit. It was like a festive feast. And when it was all over, there wasn't a hungry stomach within a mile's radius. The bill was over $2,000, but Dr. L didn't mind one bit. She kept a close eye on Mase and monitored his reaction to the people he served. He actually looked happy with his job. He seemed to bring smiles to everyone he came in contact with, even the children. Lisa saw a different side of him. He was still loved in Harlem World.

After things had clamed down a bit, Dr. L had a private conversation with the manager and got the information she needed on Mase. His hiring was more of a publicity ploy and business had tripled since his first day on the job. Mase had a pregnant girlfriend and had moved back to the small house in Harlem that he had purchased for his sister.

Dr. Lesley thought about her assignment and what good killing Mase would do for the children of Harlem. She then thought about her million that she received from the Panhellenic Council and the lies Mase told to convince her to spare his life. Ms. Hyde plucked a quarter from her purse and said, "Heads, he dies. Tails, he lives!" She flipped the silver coin, gracefully caught it in her palm, and then clapped it together flat between her hands like a coin sandwich. She removed a manicured hand from atop the coin. It was tails! She tossed the quarter out the window. Mase was safe for now; the rap gods were on his side.

Dr. Lisa took the time to make a psychological assessment of the situation. She thought about Mase's career with Bad Boy and how he was just a flashy dressed sidekick for Puffy. He was always a second class citizen to Biggie and his crew. She wondered how difficult it must have been for Mase to be forced to try and live up to the street-tough image created by Puffy Combs. It must have been a living hell to try to be something that he wasn't. The real Mase was nothing close to the image of a street gangster created by Bad Boy.

Today, she saw something different, a confidence and an attitude that was more positive. The smile on his face wasn't forced. It seemed real and natural. The Lord worked in mysterious ways and he was definitely with Mase this time around. Sometimes you to lose everything around you to get a clear view of yourself. Mase had finally found himself.

"Yes, Commander, the rapper Mase is dead," Dr. Lesley said into the phone, then added before she hung up, "But a black man has come back to life." Dr. L headed home to Detroit.

Detroit, Michigan

After days in Detroit, radio station visits, tours of Motown, a contract deal with Chevy, and singing the national anthem at a Detroit Pistons basketball game at the Palace, Be'oncay was tired. The daily activities were actually not the source of her frustrations. It was the late night adventures where she had to wear her disguise and creep around town like TLC. Be'oncay would go out hunting for traces of Eminem, but always came up empty. The blonde boy wonder had done an excellent job of keeping his royal whereabouts a secret from the commoners in the hood, and his employees.

He was like Robin Da Hood, using the black ghettos of Detroit to perfect his rhyme flow, stealing a flow style here, borrowing a few lyrics there, and showing that a white boy could shine in the underground battle rap club circuit. Marshall Mathers was the Larry Bird, the Osmonds, the Rocky Balboa, the John Riggins, the Elvis, and the New Kids on the Block of rap music. Finally, white folks could say that a white boy was the greatest rapper ever. The words of his rhymes were actually garbage, meaningless rhymes, dogging his mother and shit, about his whorish girlfriend, Kim. He could have written rhymes about taking a shit and white folks would have bought his albums, and probably a lot of black folks, too. America had a new great white hope.

Be'oncay didn't like his music. She believed that Jay-Z was the best rapper alive. She grew up bumpin' Scarface and the Getto Boys. She had seen too much shit happen in the south to be a blind follower to a white nigga who could be on some Jim Jones type shit. She wasn't about to fall for the worship this cracker, then sip on the Kool-Aid laced with cyanide treatment. Southern women didn't play that shit. Texas blacks were the last ones to find out that blacks were freed from slavery, and she was still mad about that shit.

Finally, she got a break and one of Eminem's flunkies was a regular at a local strip club on 8 Mile. She was there in her prescription glasses, black wig, and hoochie outfit, but no matter how hard she tried she could not disguise that phat ass. However, the costume had the desired effect and made her look like a project version of her very distant relative, with ass of course. She entered the club to a gang of stares and made sure that the Glock 9 mm was well hidden in her purse. It was Lady's Night, so admission was free. She made a move to a quiet, dark area of the club. She took a seat. In milliseconds, a long line of fools was waiting in line for a chance to ask her for a dance. They would approach her smiling, compliments flowing freely, then leave her table with frowns of disappointment. She wasn't there to dance. Her visit was strictly business.

Just when Be'oncay was about to give up hope and head back to her hotel suite, a long line of tightly clothed women formed. It rivaled her line of admirers in comparison. "Damn, who could be more popular than my look-a-like cousin?" Be'oncay muttered and stared toward the long Disneyland-like line that formed from the pool table area.

"Excuse me! Oops, excuse me. Excuse me, honey, coming through." Be'oncay cut through the maze of groupies waiting to be chosen. She eventually reached the front of the line. It was Proof, Eminem's right hand man. She looked him up and down and noticed the long diamond-studded P that hung from his neck as he shot pool with one of his bodyguards. The women fought for his attention, but the men in the room had a tension toward him that was so thick Jam Master Jay couldn't cut it with his turntables. Be'oncay made her move, because getting to Proof was going to be her road map to getting to Marshall.

"Hey, good lookin', can I get winners," Be'oncay said with a heavy Southern geechy accent, hands on her curvaceous hips. Immediately, Proof's bodyguard got on the defensive. He put up a large paw and stopped her progress.

"Hey, chill, she cool, Big Jeff. Let her through." The hand lowered like a lever. Who did this nigga think he was, a start or something?

"How about dat game, sugar?" Be'oncay said, licking her full, painted lips.

"What type of game you wanna play? Damn, you look like somebody I seen before. Let me see..." Proof looked at her body, deep in thought.

"Yeah, boss, she look like Jay-Z old lady! Yeah, that Destiny Child chick, be in dem videos," Big Jeff broke in.

"Be'oncay," she said, saving the two slow pokes the misery before their brains exploded from thinking.

"Yeah, that's who you look like, Be'oncay," Proof said in agreement, taking a closer look at her body that looked like an 8. He was already perfecting his story of how he was going to brag to his homies in D-12 about how he fucked a bitch that looked like Be'oncay Knolls.

"Yeah, I get that all the time. When everybody see me, they say I look like her," she said in response, striking a sexy pose.

"Yeah, you can get next. In fact, you can get right now! Rack them balls up, Jeff. Can't you see the lady waitin' to play a playa." Jeff jumped to action and quickly began gathering pool balls together and placing them into the triangular rack.

"Why, thanks cutie. What did you say your name was," Be'oncay said, as she extended a manicured hand.

"Proof is the name. You gotta know me. I'm in D-12, Eminem my homie. I was the star of the movie *8 Mile*." Proof looked at Be'oncay like she was from another planet. How could she be in Detroit and not know who Proof was?

"Oh, excuse me, Mr. Proof, of course I heard of Eminem. D-12, too. You just look a little different in person. I'm sorry." Be'oncay responded in her best groupie impression.

"Okay, now that you know you in the presence of a superstar, if you act right I might pick you to be in my video." Proof laid on the most commonly used pick-up line and she had heard it many times before.

"Dat would be marvelous!" She acted impressed. If only he knew.

"What you drinkin' on? Jeff, go fetch the waitress." The big flunky got ghost in the wind.

"Sex on the Beach. I like that," Be'oncay requested with emphasis on the word sex.

"Ah! Ha! That's kind of cute. Well, ain't no beaches in Detroit, but how 'bout a good fuck on Lake Michigan?" Proof was beyond the point of being shy. Besides, he had a whole club full of bitches to work with if this one wasn't down with it.

"Hold that thought, big boy." Be'oncay felt like throwin' up.

"May I take your order, please?" She was rescued by the half-dressed lady holding a platter.

"Yeh, you can do that. A bottle of Dom Perignon for me. Sex on the Beach for the lady. Oh, yeah, you can also give every single woman on this side of the club a drank on Proof. Tell 'em it's from D-12." Proof was really feeling himself.

"Wow!" Be'oncay acted impressed, even though she was used to high rollers. Shit, Jay-Z owned five clubs.

"Glack!" The balls exploded and chased each other around the table. One sunk into a pocket of the pool table, then another vanished into a side pocket, then another disappeared. Be'oncay was a sharpshooter on the pool table as well.

"You say you know Eminem ? Well, I'm a singer. Can you hook me up with him?" Another pool ball sunk into a pocket. She took aim again, tenderly stroking the long stick between her fingers.

"Yeah, I got the hookup. Is we friends? Shit, me and Em like brothers and shit, but I gotta hear you sing first. Sing something," Proof said, with his chest poked out.

"Oh, okay, later, baby, when we alone," Be'oncay said, as she made yet another shot.

"Well, if you can sing as good as you can play pool, you got it made. You in like Flint. I know music. I discovered Em, Obie Trice, and MC Breed. Real singers can do that shit accapello right there on the spot. You got a good look. I probably can manage you or somethin'. Here, take my card." This nigga was gifted with gab. He popped out a card that read, Talent Scout, Shady Records.

"Wow!" Be'oncay acted amazed. "I can really sing, sir, I do everything top notch. Game over," Be'oncay said, as she sank the eight ball in the corner pocket.

"Damn, baby, I didn't even get a shot in! Here, let me rack these shits up. Run this shit back." Proof pulled the balls out of the pockets and organized them inside the plastic triangle.

"Okay, Proof, one Sex on the Beach, one bottle of Dom Perignon on the rocks, and 87 assorted drinks. That'll be $1,273, please." The waitress handed Proof a long receipt.

"Cool. Jeff, pay the lady." Steroid boy pulled out a tall wad of C-notes and peeled off several, then tossed them to the waitress. Proof finished racking the pool balls, very disinterested in the transaction.

"Okay, I'ma shoot first dis time!" He didn't like losing to a woman.

"Go ahead, sugar, knock yourself out." Be'oncay smiled and sipped on her drink.

"Clack!"

"Damn! Shit, this table is wack. They need to level it off or something." He tried to justify his scratch shot.

"Yeah, sugar, I noticed that, too," Be'oncay said, sinking her shot with ease.

"What a pretty girl like you doing in a place like this? You wanna get to know y.."

"Hey, punk ass nigga! Yeah, you fool! I know who you is! You Proof! Went to high school wit' you. You wasn't shit then, now you a gangster?" It was a local.

"Whoa, what's the problem? I know you ain't talkin' to me, nigga." Proof approached the fool with a pool stick in his hand and a frown on his face.

"Yeah, I'm talkin' to you, nigga! I gots big problems wit' you. Did you order my girl a drink," he said, pointing toward a skinny, crossed-eyed and bucktoothed girl a few feet away.

"I don't know what you talkin' 'about, nigga! I'm shootin' pool," Proof said, gripping the pool stick. His bodyguard arrived to the scene.

"You callin' my girl a liar? You callin' my woman a liar," the goon said un-intimidated and balling up his fists.

"I don't even know you or Bucky Beaver over there! I ain't said nothin' to that skinny bitch. She chose.."

The fool hit Proof with a stiff right jab. Proof stumbled but recovered quickly, then whap, whap, whap, he started going to town on top of homeboy's head with the pool stick. Big Jeff jumped in and started stomping homeboy out. They were whoopin' his ass worse than Denzel got spanked in that movie *Glory*. The bouncers jumped in and saved homeboy from a crucifixion. One of the club security dudes grabbed Proof. The other rent-a-cop grabbed Big Jeff in a choke hold. Homeboy got up off the ground and immediately took two punches to Proof's head, whap, whap, the punches connected firmly. Proof struggled free from D-Bo's grasp and pulled out his gun, then pop, pop, pop. Proof's eyes grew as big as egg whites and he collapsed to the ground. The bouncer had shot Proof in the back three times.

"Aaah, aaah, aaah!" There was total chaos. Screams echoed throughout the club and feet beat the hardwood floor. Muthafuckas was running for cover and getting out of the way. Weaves were flying all over the place and people stampeded in all directions.

"Shit, shit, shit," Be'oncay yelled, but her words were just a whisper in the mass confusion in the club. She blended in with the outgoing flow of traffic and tried her best to get out of dodge before the Detroit Police arrived. She would have been fingered as an ideal witness, and of course her cover would have been blown. Be'oncay Knolls at a club shootout? Nigga, please. She definitely was not going out like that. Ms. Knolls reached her parked car, put the key in the ignition, and the engine came to life. She burned rubber away from the scene of the shootout.

"Detroit Rapper Proof Dead, Shootout at 8 Mile Strip Club." Be'oncay stared at the newspaper headlines in disbelief. She was so close but yet she was so far away. Her heart beat fast just thinking about the whole incident and how close she was to the action. Proof was going to be her path to Eminem, but now that path led to a dead end.

"Funeral arrangements scheduled for next week. Detroit mourns the death of a hometown rap pioneer." Be'oncays attention was distracted from the newspaper in front of her. She focused on the local news playing on the hotel television.

"Well, kiss my grits!" A light bulb went off inside her head. Maybe Proof wasn't lying about his industry connections in the Detroit music scene. "Maybe he did discover Eminim," Be'oncay announced to nobody in particular. She realized that the tragedy of Proofs death was all the bait she needed to pull Eminem out of hiding in the white suburbs. He was going to have to come back to the same ghettos he now avoided to pay his last respects to his homie. Not even Marshall Mathers could get away with missing Proofs funeral. The queen of hip hop pop grabbed her coat, because she was going out to do a little shopping for a black dress and some pumps. She had a funeral to attend and hopefully with a little luck she would get a chance to turn Slim Shady into total darkness.

CHAPTER 27

Las Vegas, Nevada

"That's the place, right there, Cuzz! That's where dem bitches live, right there!" Snoop was fresh out of the hospital, freshly bandaged up, and looking like a skinny mummy. However, the Doggfather had a newly found sense of confidence, if you could believe it, because now he had his road dogs with him and a heavy arsenal of weapons.

There was Warren G, Nate Dogg, Korrupt, Daz, Goldie Loc, Blue Boy, Sleep, and Capone. The Long Beach Gangster Crips were in full effect. The small caravan of luxury vehicles looked like a blue Christmas parade as they came to a halt in front of Karen's spot.

"Smoke dem bitches, Cuzz! They clipped me fo' half a million!" The General was speaking.

"Time to regulate!" Nate Dogg said as he tugged at his automatic, putting a hot one in the chamber. The loading of his weapon had a domino effect as the semicircle of Crips created a symphony of metallic sounds.

"Go git my money, Cuzzzz!" Snoop barked in intense pain.

BAM! BAM! The door to the house caved in. Mothafuckas entered like Marines in iraq, weapons at the ready.

"Man! Damn, Cuzz! What's dat fuckin' smell?!" Korrupt announced.

"Damn! It smell like shit in here!" Daz added.

"In here!" Nate Dogg said, breaking up the criticisms of his fellow home invaders. A congregation stormed toward the sound of Nate's voice. "Daaaamn!"

"That bitch dead as fuck, Cuzz!" Goldie Loc gave his medical opinion.

"Look at that ho'! She all fucked up!" Warren G. took a peek in the bathroom.

"Uuuuuugh! Uuuuuugh!" Sleep's stomach couldn't take the stench. He vomited streams of his gut all over the place.

"Shit! Cuzz, hold that shit in nigga! Your DNA at the scene!" Nate Dogg announced.

"Wuuuuhh! Uuuuugh!" Korrupt spilled the contents of his stomach.

"Uuuuuugh! Uuuuuugh!" Daz let loose.

"Let's get the fuck outta here! Ain't nobody in this crib alive!"

A caravan of Crips ran out of the house, gaggin' and coughin' and shit.

"Was the bitch in the tub real light skinned?" Snoop asked Nate an important question but he already knew the answer.

"I dunno, Cuzz. The bitch was fucked up. White as fuck!" Nate Dogg answered, confused, but was afraid to question Snoop.

The passenger side door of the blue Escalade opened up and Snoop snailed his way out of the vehicle. He didn't say a word. The O.G. Gangster Crip pulled out his blue bandana and put it to his grill, protected from the stench of death. The assorted rainbow from the mixtures of the little homie's vomits added a bit of spice to the pungent odor that encompassed the room.

"Shit! Damn, Cuzz! Well, well, William Tell!" Snoop antagonized a lifeless Pink. "You could have had it all but you

208

played yo' self for a funky half mil. Look at you now!" Snoop spit in the direction of the tub and the loogey performed a float atop the bacteria-coated waters of the tub. He took out a dollar bill and tossed it in the tub with the dead body. "Here go a tip for yo' services!" Snoop turned on his heels and exited the house.

"Nate! Get dat gas can out the back, Cuzz. Y'all mothafuckas got DNA all over dat bitch! Can't let niggas do shit without me. Torch dat bitch and let's go!" Snoop said, frustrated and disappointed.

"Got ya, Dogg. Daz, Korrupt, Goldie, get over here!" The captain gave orders to the foot soldiers. "Take these jugs! Spread that shit all over the inside of that crib. Y'all niggas the one that vomited. It's y'all DNA. You niggas get rid of the mess!"

A trio of Crips went inside the stink chamber and began emptying the gas cans of their contents. In a few moments they all returned to their rides, huffin' and puffin'. They were out of breath from trying to complete the assignment and hold their breath at the same time.

Snoop made one final encore visit to the site of his sexual seduction with Karen and Pink. "Burn baby, burn!" He lit his lighter, then tossed it in the house. It erupted into flames like a Jehri Curl dipped in curl activator.

Snoop Dogg sat in the passenger seat and realized that he had been played like a two dollar hooker. A pimp had just been pimped. A smile came to his face as he thought about it. Even he had to admit that Karen Stephins had mad head game. The mistake of underestimating that bitch had almost cost him his life. Snoop knew that he was going to have to kick his game up a notch if he was ever going to have any get back on Superhead. New York was her stomping grounds and the D-O double gizzle was not about to get caught up on the East Coast again. It took Johnny Cochran and Master P to get him out of that shit, and his homie, Tray Dee was still stuck somewhere in a California prison. There was no way that Snoop Dogg was going to let them mothafuckas turn him into a Coney Island hot dog. He understood that he had to elevate his game to Super Bowl-like levels to set the record straight. But first he had to do his homework and learn everything there was to know about Karen "Superhead" Stephins.

"Yo, Nate. Stop at that bookstore over there, Cuzz!" Snoop had a little researchin' to do. He knew that the best way to find out what was on a bitch's mind was to see what she was tryin' to put in yours. He entered the bookstore, anxious to make a purchase.

San Luis Obispo, California
California Men's Colony Prison (C.M.C.)

"Five thousand a hand, Blood. Can you handle dat?" Suge Knight upped the ante in the pinochle card game.

"I believe I think I can. Remember, I'm a Brando. We Italians invented gambling!" Marlon Brando's son, Ryan Brando responded with pride.

It was just another day and just another high stakes game of cards for two wealthy inmates at CMC Prison. Mr. Knight was in prison for a parole violation but he was far from being a prison inmate. For starters, he had managed to liquidate a big portion of the Death Row empire and turn it into cash money. The only thing left at Death Row records was some pieces of paper and a few paper clips. The original Damu had pulled it off again. He got away with murder. The reasons for his present stay at this California prison was due to the discovery of the vast arsenal of weapons found at his Carson, California home.

Suge was down, but definitely not out. He now had time to bick back and be bool. He caught up on the latest street rumors and saw how the commoners in the streets were living. Many things had happened since that fatal night in Las Vegas with Tupac. Suge had been kept real busy trying to hide his money and plotting his revenge. He finally had a little time to read up on the new hype and hated that Dr. Dre had taken over the West Coast rap game. Aftermath Entertainment was larger than Death Row ever was and Dre's label sold more records. The white boy was making Dre a bundle and now 50 Cent was killing the charts. Suge was jealous. He was going to take his time, pick and choose his spots, and work his way back to the top.

"That's game, nigga! 30,000 cash by Saturday. Call yo' pops." Suge got up and left the table. Mr. Knight had to be taken seriously because money was power in America and Suge had plenty of it.

New York, New York

Meagan and Karen chilled in the comforts of her penthouse. They plotted their next move against 50 Cent. The pungent-sweet aroma of Orange Haze encompassed the room as the two lovelies got blown away.

"Yeah! Girl, I'm diggin' you. I loved you in *Eve's Bayou* and *D.E.B.S.* You da bomb, baby!" Karen spread her compliments on pretty thick.

"Thanks, Kar. You doin' big thangs yourself. I read your book twice. Can't wait until your next one comes out," Meagan responded, glassy eyed from the weed.

211

"Oh shit! You can't wait? Hold up. Got somethin' for you baby." She disappeared into the rear of the roomy home, then returned. "Specially delivered to Ms. Goodwin. Signed and sealed with a kiss. It's a printer's copy. Hope you like it" Karen handed her the book.

"Wow! Thanks, Karen. I really appreciate this. If you ever need anything, let me know." Meagan was touched.

"No, I'm cool, baby. Well, maybe I do need a li'l somethin' from you."

"What is it? You name it!" Meagan said.

"Well, are you still messin' wit' Reggie Bush?" Karen was reaching.

"Yeah. Sometimes we kick it." Meagan held back details. She wasn't about to be put in one of this bitch's books.

"Oh, that's cool. I just wanted to know if he could hook me up with that Terrell Owens. The Dallas Cowboys. I need T.O. to do a little O.T. with them big ass lips. They would feel soooo sexy on my pu'nanny girl!"

Laughter filled the room. Karen managed to bring out the ghetto in everyone she met.

"Bitch. You so crazy! Ain't you fuckin' with Li'l Wayne, Ne-Yo, Ray Jay, and Mr. Marcus anyway?" Meagan responded between puffs on the blunt.

"Bitch, please! Don't hate the playa, hate the pipe laya. A car dealer can neva have too many vehicles to ride. I likes many shades of chocolate in my candy store. Know what I'm sayin?" Karen did her best pimp pose, with her manicured hand firmly on her crotch. Meagan was rolling on the floor with tears of laughter.

"Pass dat weed. Quit handcuffin' that shit!" Meagan watched as Karen took a long pull of the blunt, then held it out in her direction.

212

"I'm just fuckin' wit' you, Meagan. I used to hate all y'all prissy AKA bitches, but some of y'all cool as fuck. You all right with me, Meg." Karen got serious.

"You cool for a Delta, too. You crazy as fuck though! Here." Meagan puffed the Orange Haze, then passed a midget blunt back to Karen.

"Bitch please! You betta take that little shit to the store with you. That's too low for me. I ain't gone burn my finger tips fuckin' wit' that shit. I just got my nails done, too. Got's to keep it pimpin'. I been pimpin' since before pimpin' was pimpin' girl." Karen was on a roll.

"Fuck you bitch! Roll up. I ain't goin' to no store in that cold outside. It's colder than the devil's draw's out there," Meagan responded defiantly.

"Well, get yo' ass to work on the corner of that table! I gots plenty of that California sticky. Thanks to yo' homie, Snoop." Karen grabbed a silver box and a large box of Cuban cigars.

"What the...? You doin' too much, but I won't go there." Meagan began rolling up tight blunts of the fine herb.

"Well anyway, I gotta make a few phone calls. Kick back. Relax. I'll order us some Chinese food. We gone find that nigga 50 and touch his ass!" Karen announced with a piercing look in her eyes.

"Cool, baby girl. I got you." Meagan felt better about the situation knowing that she had capable back up. Karen was the best woman for the job. Nobody knew more about New York than Superhead. Meagan had developed a lot of respect for her over the years.

Karen laughed her way to her living room, then kicked her heels up on the table and flopped her rounded bottom in her leather recliner. She pulled out her cell and just when she was about to dial Jackie Chan's Chinese Food, "Dumm, Dumm, Dummm, dumm!" It was the ringtone to the song, *Lollipop* by Li'l Wayne. It was the distinctive sound of her Sidekick IV with an incoming call.

"Who dis?" The number was from an unidentified caller.

"Used to be my homie, now you act like you don't know me?" It was the worldly recognized voice of Snoop Dogg.

"What? What the...? How did you get my fuckin' number?" Karen's heart was beating a hundred miles and running.

"Never, never mind, bitch. Don't ever underestimate the reaches of a Mack. Just listen to me sexy." Snoop had a surprisingly calm vocal tone.

"I'm listening." She was suddenly at a loss for words, and calm.

"It was a real good job you did on dat Pink bitch. I always knew you had potentials and shit. I believed in you. You could have made a fortune workin' for me. You sold yourself short for half a mil. Pocket change. You go 'head and keep dat. Consider it a nice tip for my conjugal visit in Vegas. I'ma squash it. No harm, no foul," Snoop said, and Karen was surprisingly quiet the whole time.

"So, we cool? Just like that. Nothin' personal. I'm just barely makin' it out here." Karen tried to humble herself because she didn't want to push things too far.

"Fo' shizzle, my nizzle. You just keep yo' empire out of my empire, and we both should be able to retire. It's enough room for both of us on this blue planet. Know what I'm sayin'?" Snoop explained.

"Yeah. I'm cool. Sorry Snoop. Maybe in another life things woulda worked. You sure we cool?" She said.

"Yeah, baby girl. We's Kool and the Gang. G's up, ho's down. If a bitch can't swim, then she bound to drown. I found out the hard way. You an Olympic swimmer. Charge it to the game." He hung up the line.

"What this nigga up to now?" she asked herself. She knew that receiving a pass from Snoop was too good to be true. First of all, she had lied to him. Second of all, she had bettered his ass and ordered Pink to assassinate him and riddle him with more holes than Sponge Bob Square Pants. Last but not least, she had stolen half a million dollars from the nigga. Who was Snoop trying to fool? She knew the rules of the game. One of the pimp rules was to play to win at all times. Snoop wasn't no punk ass, new booty to the game. He was a seasoned veteran. The entire peace offering was all about some bullshit. She could read clearly between the lines. It was a coded declaration of war. She knew that she had to stay away from the West Coast as long as Snoop was alive on this planet. There was no way that she was going to disrespect the power of the Doggfather. She was going to watch her back.

"How did that nigga get my number?" She asked herself the question again. Eventually she settled down and refocused on the task that she and Meagan had at hand. She dialed the phone number and ordered Chinese food. The Orange Haze had given her the munchies like a son of a bitch.

Chino Hills, California

"Trick ass bitch!" Snoop Dogg spoke out loud, to nobody in sight. He was chilling in the study of his mansion. He had his mind on his money and his money on his mind. The Doggfather had lost the sprint but he was not going to lose the marathon.

He had finished reading Karen's book from cover to cover. Every single word, every single page, even the blank ones. He

215

looked at it and gave her literary talents a new genre. "Snitch Lit!" In his view a true pimp would never expose the game for profit and never give up names and details of tricks.

Karen was a different type of female. On the one hand, Snoop respected her hustle. The bitch was a go-getter. On the other hand, he noticed that she made a lot of mistakes and talked too much. He had never met a woman with a mouth like hers. The book as all right but what grabbed his attention the most was her acknowledgments. The people she loved and appreciated. He noticed the shoutouts to niggas. A little something for her son and her girlfriends in New York.

Then he saw the tidal wave of affection that she had for Dr. Lesley, Meagan Goodwin, and even more words for Be'oncay Knolls. Snoop had read it, and being that he was in the rap game for years, he knew the history of these bitches. They were all nobodies, then all of a sudden they blew up real big after Tupac and Biggie's death. The Doggfather didn't believe in coincidences. Something was definitely fishy and he was going to find out what it was.

He remembered back in the days of Tupac, a little before he got smoked. If his memory served him correctly, Suge was fuckin' with Karen at the Tyson fight. He remembered it vividly, because fat boy bragged to everybody about her head game. Tupac was fuckin' with Be'oncay and had even taken her to the fight that night. He had also saw Meagan with a slob nigga in the stands. "Was that a fuckin' coincidence!" Snoop questioned.

The situation was still fuzzy for the O.G. Crip, but he was going to work his theory until it was crystal clear. Too many things didn't connect correctly to each other but he knew they would eventually come together like butt cheeks. Throughout his life Snoop had learned a lot as he sat back and listened to the O.G.s that schooled him to the music and pimp game. The most important quality he learned was patience. Patience was the key. Snoop was going to kick back, do his research on all these ho's, and eventually he was going to connect the dots!

Detroit, Michigan

Proof wasn't a liar after all. He was a Detroit street legend and everybody who was anybody in Detroit was at his funeral. The mayor of Motor City, Kwame Kilpatrick, MC Breed, Joe Dumars, all the crew of D-12, Thomas Hearns and most importantly, Marshall "Eminem" Mathers. The entire state of Michigan said their farewells to a rap legend.

Fortunately for Be'oncay, Gladiss had sent her reinforcements in the form of Dr. Lisa Lesley. The assistance was a welcome breath of fresh air, even in the Detroit smog. Lisa was from the Motor City, so she knew everything about the area and the people who lived there.

Be'oncay was glad that she could finally abandon her late night antics. The costume changes and roads that led to dead ends were getting to her. Dr. L was an even bigger superstar in Detroit than her. Be'oncay welcomed the competition with open arms. Now that Eminem had come out of hiding it was going to be an easier job keeping track of him. The doctor had already debriefed her about the situation. She was going to take the lead because getting information was Lisa's specialty. All of the work was being done and Dr. Lesley could track down a mothafucka better than lojack.

After the funeral, Be'oncay headed back to her hotel room to chill and await further directions from Lisa. It was one of the rare occasions that she didn't mind playing a back-up singer. The assignment was taking longer than she expected but who could have anticipated the craziness that happened in Detroit nightlife. She couldn't wait to get her things over with and work her way back home to Texas. Life in a hotel was really cramping her style and she really missed her Jigga man. Be'oncay made a phone call for some lip service.

Dr. Lesley was happy to finally be home in Detroit. Especially after the craziness she experienced in Harlem. It felt good to be back in familiar territory although she was a bit disappointed with her superiors' reaction when they discovered that Mase was still alive. Commander Weems had managed to straighten things out with Gladiss. Eventually Lisa's decision was accepted but there was still tension. As a result of taking matters into her own hands, she was immediately reassigned to the mission on Eminem. She didn't mind the tongue lashing one bit because Mase was now helping children. He wasn't a threat anymore, and we all know how much Lisa loved the kids.

Now, Eminem was an entirely different story. Slim Shady was giving Dr. Lesley fits with his negative influences. He degraded his own mother for fun, disrespected his wife, and portrayed rebellious and very negative images to children. Lisa couldn't believe her eyes when she saw his latest ad in *Vibe* magazine for his clothing line, Shady Clothing. It was a picture of Eminem in a hospital maternity ward, with a group of babies surrounding him, holding a variety of weapons. The newborn babies brandished razor sharp knives, nunchucks, spiked brass knuckles, and their faces were concealed by Jason-like hockey masks. "Pure filth!" were Lisa's words as she looked at the gruesome images.

With Dr. L it wasn't about just black children; it was about the children of the world. She despised the way Marshall Mathers exploited those little babies for a fast buck. Where was the parents of these babies when this ad was being laid out for print? What about the advertising editors of the magazine? She could not believe that such a trifling image was being put out on the pages of a major magazine for young people to see. The thing that hurt her the most was that Marshall Mathers had grown up in Detroit. He was from Motown.

Dr. Lesley was going to make things happen and find Eminem, then crush him like a peanut. But first things first. She needed to relieve her mind of the strong desires that overwhelmed her thoughts. She craved to be in the arms of the man she had fallen in love with. Eugene Weems had become the cure for all her mental and physical illnesses and pleasures. She was now questioning herself about the possibility that Eugene Weems could be meeting her at home in Detroit. She knew he was a man of his word, but she also knew he was a very busy man. It seemed to her that important shit would always come up that required his immediate attention. She shook the negative thoughts and assured herself that he would honor their plans to spend some quality time together. She reached for her phone, then decided against calling him before deciding to entertain herself with a long hot bath. The sex was so much better that way.

Eugene L. Weems, Timothy R. Richardson

CHAPTER 28

Eugene Weems strolled into the bedroom and was welcomed by the incense that filled the air. The room was dark but the dim light that flickered from the burning candles could be seen at the entrance of the bathroom. He advanced toward the light and braced himself against the door frame, staring at Lisa in a tub of bubbles. She was laid back with her eyes closed. She looked so at peace, he thought.

She had felt his presence 'cause she opened her eyes and gazed at him. "I was wondering what was taking you so long," she said softly. "Get your sexy self in here, Eugene, and let me show you how much I missed you."

"Hold on Li'l Mama," he replied in a kid's voice. Excitement sparkled in his eyes and his nature rose to the occasion of his sexual desire. He dashed out of the room then quickly returned with a plastic bottle of apple juice and placed it on the edge of the tub.

Lisa watched as he undressed. She gasped at the sight of his muscular chest and the way the hair ran down underneath his navel and disappeared inside his pants. Feeling her breath catch in her throat, she raised up into a sitting position, exposing the upper part of her body just above her cleavage.

The moment intimacy to her wanted passion had made her vulnerable to the thug loving she'd known was about to go down once she wrapped her legs around him. The mirrors were already fogged up from the steam of the water. She hadn't taken her eyes off her prize, biting on her lip in intense excitement. As he stepped into the tub with his long erection pointed directly at her, she inhaled a deep breath and gasped.

The water swirled around them in rough ripples as he lowered himself into the tub. Dr. Lesley took him in her arms and kissed him deeply, running her fingertips lightly up and down his back. He reached for the bottle of apple juice without breaking the tongue probing of her mouth. He tilted the bottle over them, and the warm liquid streamed down their faces and onto their chests. He tilted her head back and began sucking the sweet liquid from her neck. She gave off a light moan, closing her eyes.

Eugene picked up the body wash and squeezed a dab onto the bath sponge and gently soaped up her body. They took turns washing each other. Lisa kept one hand on his erection, refusing to let go. Ms. Doctor was operating. She guided herself onto it without his approval while staring into his face to observe his facial expression.

That was all it took for the real action to begin. Water splashed out of the tub onto the floor. The wicks of the candles almost met their demise. Heavy breathing took place of light panting as the two bodies assaulted each other with pain of pleasures. They ended their cravings on the bathroom floor, soaking the black mink throw rug that was confined beneath their bodies. It was ecstasy.

They dried each other with gentle hands before heading to the bedroom. The Commander glanced at the clock on the computer screen. "The morning sure is dragging slowly," he thought. He laid back in bed, still nude, watching Lisa roll up a blunt. She laid at the foot of the bed in a seductive manner that was enticing and alluring. Her smooth, golden brown, nude body, with the exception of the tattoo she had on her neck and the small of her back, seemed to pulsate in readiness for round two. Eugene admired her loyalty, honesty and strength. He had never seen a person more driven or possessed more dynamics than her.

"You not finished rolling that blunt yet?" he asked, watching her now crawl toward him. The sexy young woman's thick thighs and round hips moved with the swiftness and elegance of a panther. It was like being in the presence of a black panther, the aristocrat of the animal kingdom, next to the lion that is so beautiful and dangerous. Lisa had the physical bearing and inner self confidence of a born aristocrat, making her potentially dangerous at any given moment. She was most definitely a do or die type woman that gave her all to her man. She straddled herself on top of him and gave a coy smirk, feeling his erection under her.

"Feels like somebody is down for seconds."

"Maybe or maybe not," he teased, reaching over to the nightstand, grabbing a lighter so he could fire up the blunt. He struck the roller and the flame came to life. He held it out toward her so she could light up. Her slender face was inches from his own and her big hazel eyes penetrating his. She took a couple of drags and then relaxed in ease, seeing Eugene's impatience and disapproval. She took another pull, holding the smoke into her mouth, then she forced her lips onto Eugene's parted lips and released the smoke into his, forcing his tongue to exchange blows with hers. She pressed her plump firm breasts against his firm chest. Eugene could feel her hardened nipples vigorously rubbing and caressing his chest. He pulled apart from her and swiftly stung the right side of her cheek with an open palm.

"Get up!" he snapped harshly. She smiled down at him with teary eyes. She had anticipated the slap when she decided to force the weed smoke in his mouth. She knew that Commander Weems didn't smoke or use any type of drugs for that matter, but she got a kick out of trying to give him a contact high. Being slapped had only succeeded in getting Ms. Hyde more sexually stimulated. She moved over and continued to stare at him as he went out of the room. Seconds later she heard the water from the sink in the bathroom.

When he returned from brushing his teeth, he noticed that Dr. Lisa had pulled back the sheets for him. She had already crawled up underneath them and was waiting on him so she could massage his back before bed.

The bedroom was dimly lit as Eugene lounged in bed thinking about his agenda for the night. He glanced over at Dr. L sleeping next to him and marveled at her gorgeous profile. The bed sheets were pulled over her shoulder, slightly underneath her chin. A smooth clean line went down from the point of her shoulder to her waist, then mounded up warmly over her hip. A strand of hair laid across her cheek. He leaned over and kissed her with gentle lips. The ringing of his cell phone interrupted his thoughts.

"Wuss up?" he answered, taking his eyes off Lisa who was now beginning to wake up. The Commander listened to the womanly voice on the other end of the line. "I'll holla back." The other party hung up on him. Eugene removed the phone from his ear and stared at it in his hand.

"Hmmmm," Lisa moaned, removing the sheets from her nude body. Eugene's reddish brown complexion glowed under the light. The acknowledgment etched in Lisa's hazel brown eyes were a combination of a smile and flirtation. The kind of intimacy that was invasive and dominating.

"What's wrong baby?" she asked, looking into his eyes. She'd seen the worry in them but his facial expression didn't give away any clues.

"Nothing Baby Girl. Nothing that I can't handle," he replied with confidence while scoping out her thick shapely figure. He leaned down and kissed her on her navel. She moaned against her will, frustrated by how this man's touch had so much control over her body.

He hoisted her powerful legs over his shoulders after submerging his anaconda into her erotic love oven. Dr. Lesley met her lover's every thrust in a rhythmic sexual dance. She cried out, grabbing onto the headboard of the bed. Feeling the warmness inside of her had only inflamed her intensity to a much higher level of lust and desire. He took control of her arms, prying them loose of the headboard and crossed her wrists behind her back. Then he pushed himself deeper into her so that his groin was pressed against hers.

He raised up from her satisfied body and said, "We betta go and take a shower because time is getting away from a nigga."

Commander Weems admired the beauty of Dr. Lisa Lesley and placed the lovely images into the archives of his mind because he had no idea if it was going to be the last time he saw her alive.

Eugene L. Weems, Timothy R. Richardson

CHAPTER 29

Meagan and Karen were in plot mode and mapping out how they were going to execute the hit on 50 Cent. They understood that his security would be thicker than government cheese. Getting next to him would be virtually impossible, but they had a job to do. They were going to make an honest attempt to see it through.

"How in the hell we gonna get within a mile of this nigga when he got a million mothafuckas protecting him?" Karen asked.

Meagan studied the blueprints of 50 Cent's mansion before answering, "If there is a will, there is a way." The often used cliché made Karen turn up her nose.

A sudden shrill sound summoned the two women to reach for their cell phones. "Girl, it's me." Meagan held up her cell and placed it to her ear. "Hello? Meagan speaking," Meagan said flirtatiously, not knowing who was on the other end of the line.

"Yes, Meagan. Are you and Karen together? She recognized the voice instantly.

"Oh. Hi, Commander Eugene. Yes, Karen is with me. She right here. Would you like to speak with her?"

"Naw. What I am about to tell you can be relayed to her by you. I just received orders from headquarters to have you two abort the mission. I repeat. Abort the mission immediately." The phone went dead.

Meagan was relieved by the recent news and was sure that Karen would be also. She felt like they had been sent on a suicide mission from the start, but didn't have the nerve to state those thoughts to the powers that be. She clearly understood the consequences and possible danger that the job entailed. There was no doubt in her mind that every job she was sent on was a gamble with death. It was a game that she was tired of playing because every gamble had a winner and a loser and Meagan Goodwin had too much to lose.

She thought back to the allegiance she had pledged with the Panhellenic Council. Loyalty and honor till death. She was committed to her obligations regardless of how she felt personally. She was going to catch the first thing smoking back to California. Meagan had a lot to think about when she got home. Her mind was still devoted to Gladiss and what she had done for her, but her heart just wasn't in it anymore.

Detroit, Michigan

It was 3:00 a.m. and Dr. Lisa called Be'oncay on her cell. She sat up sleepily and listened to her crime partner's recorded words. She closed the phone after leaving an urgent message, then crawled out of bed. She quickly dressed in the same clothes she had on the previous day. She didn't give a damn, it was only temporary, she told herself before reaching for the two semi-automatic .40 Glocks. She smoothly holstered one underneath her armpit and tucked the other firmly in her belt strap at the small of her back. Dr. Lesley had a house call to make. She hurriedly rushed from her mansion.

Lisa had gotten word from a street thug who knew where Eminem was laying his head. The thug was a very reliable source from Detroit and gave good 411 if the price was right. He had been helpful to Dr. L before on many occasions in the past so she had no doubt in his credibility.

She sat in the rental keeping surveillance of the apartment door that Eminem was believed to be holding camp. She was still anxiously awaiting Be'oncay's arrival.

"Where this bitch at!" Ms. Hyde glanced angrily into the rear view mirror, becoming heated at Be'oncay for not showing up by now. To her surprise, she saw a man emerge from a S.U.V. She ducked her face low, studying the man across the street who was standing in front of the apartment door.

He reached deep in his Starter jacket pocket and fumbled around for a moment. He pulled out a sandwich bag of lime green and a fresh pack of cigar wraps. He peeled open the zip lock and took a deep whiff of its contents. He unwrapped the thin plastic seal from around the top edge of the pack with his teeth, then liberated a cigar wrap from its peers. He lined it with the lime green substance, then gently rolled it up and sealed it with the moisture of his tongue. With cupped hands, he lit it up and then intimately inhaled his lover deeply. His lungs rejected the seduction at first, but quickly gave in to the cloudy pleasures. He stood there for a moment and looked around at nothing in particular. After a while, he stubbed out the blunt on the ground and placed it in his pocket. He then spat into the street and walked up to the apartment door.

The mystery man keyed the door and soon vanished into the darkness of the entrance. Seconds later a light lit the picture window that offered his silhouette through the curtains.

"Yeah, cracker boy. I got yo' snow flake ass now," Ms. Hyde whispered to herself, fingering a pair of leather gloves. She glanced around in hopes of finding Be'oncay on the scene before she made her move on the mark. But she was a no-show. Lisa stepped out of the car, then scampered across the street. The morning life was quiet, other than the muffled chirps of birds. As she got closer to the door she pulled down the ski mask over her face and tightly gripped the Glock .40. She reached for the door knob, assured that it was locked, but to her surprise it wasn't.

"This is gonna be the easiest mil ticket ever," she told herself, thinking about the money she was going to collect and donate to a children's charity. Ms. Hyde entered the apartment as if she had been invited, weapon ready for action. She was not there to fuck around. The doctor had plans of releasing Eminem's soul from the surgical holes she envisioned blowing through his chest.

Arrogantly she walked into the living room and to her surprise a sudden pain filled her head from the metallic bottle of Armand de Brignac Champagne that struck her jaw. She stumbled, but managed to turn toward her attacker before he could crown her with another haymaker from the golden bottle of Ace of Spades Champagne.

She hadn't anticipated the kidney shot that sent her to a knee. Her weapon had escaped from her hand. Eminem instantly hustled toward it but that was his worst mistake. Lisa leaped from the floor. The flying knee randomly found a target on its prey. Eminem grunted in pain as the sharp knee slammed into the side of his ribs, sending him staggering into the wall. She lunged at him with a snap kick and a flurry of punches that found the back of his spine. He tried protecting his head with his arms but the doctor broke down his defense with a bone crushing round house.

"Hooooold up man! What's this all about?! You want money?!" Marshall Mathers managed to find the breath to speak. He staggered on his heels and turned to face the intruder who was putting hands and feet on him, something vicious. He paused, looking up at the tall frame in front of him before the spinning back fist shattered his jaw bone. He squealed like a pig at a slaughter house, and held his jaw with cupped hands. His mouth was widened into the shape of an O, and blood flowed freely from his openings.

He realized that he was no match for the giant bitch and his death lingered in the balance. He was fighting a losing battle, so he followed his survival instincts.

With all the strength he could muster, he rushed at Lisa like a raging bull, but before he could make contact with her, he darted out to the left like a running back. He jumped out the second story window and the glass shattered. "Cccrrraaassshhh!!!"

"Son of a bitch!!!" Dr. Lisa was in disbelief. She hadn't anticipated the sudden move. How cowardly, she thought as she rushed to grab her weapon from the floor and storming out the door in pursuit. "Damn," she grunted when she found no Eminem in sight.

Dr. Lesley was back in the comforts of her multimillion dollar estate feeling very uncomfortable. The entire mission was a complete failure and now Eminem was in deep hiding. She was really beginning to doubt her killing skills after two back-to-back assignments without filling up a single body bag.

Lisa was finding it harder and harder to complete these missions. She would have much rather focused her time on more important things like the ever increasing number of surgeries she had to perform on sick children at her clinics. She also wanted to guide the Shock to another WNBA championship and she had already begun talks for an expansion team in Flint.

The other reason for her lack of motivation was that she was in the final phase of perfecting her secret miracle cure. Dr. Lesley was on the verge of changing the whole world.

The only thing that kept her in the game was her loyalty to the Panhellenic Council for helping her years ago. Money was no longer an issue because Dr. L was worth over 100 million dollars and counting. The degradation of women that once existed in rap was no longer a major source of her attention because women were the main consumers, buying the music. She no longer cared about rappers bickering back and forth on albums. The more money she made, the less rap music seemed to matter. The days of being bitter like Obama with no opportunity to live up to her true potential were far gone. She was a walking goddess and was living out her dreams.

Lisa had learned a lot about men in the past few years from her love for Commander Weems and also from her recent experiences tracking down Mase in New York. She learned that all men weren't dogs and even if they were, it was always a chance that they could change their ways. She realized that the hardships of abuse that she once suffered as a child were far behind her. She also recognized that the only way to overcome her past was to put closure to those unpleasant experiences.

It was time to move on toward the future and leave the past behind her. A little love in her life had gone a long way in making her Ms. Hyde side completely disappear. She no longer needed that defense mechanism to fight off the threats to her existence. Her back was no longer against the wall. Dr. Lesley was finally free. It felt good to spread her wings like Troop, and fly high in the sky. She was the most recognizable face and body in all of professional women's sports.

The Eminem incident had taken both a physical and mental toll on her body. Her jaw was swollen and appeared to be broken from the blow she suffered in combat from the bratty rapper. It was just further proof that her heart wasn't into the assassination thing anymore. There was no doubt in her mind that it was time to move on to bigger and better things. The loyalty she had to Gladiss and the other women in the Panhellenic Council were the only reasons that she accepted the assignment. The failed assassination was most definitely going to complicate things. Eminem was a very rich nigga and had a lot of street connections in Detroit.

Lisa was at the point where she just wanted to abandon the whole assignment and move on with her busy life. Loyalty and obligation were the only two things that kept her focused on completing the mission. Speaking of loyalty and obligation, she began to think back on the episode, then questioned herself. "Where in the hell was Be'oncay when she needed her the most?"

Downtown Detroit, Michigan

Be'oncay couldn't believe that she had almost allowed her partner to get killed. Her entire day was a complete nightmare from the start. After planning things out with Lisa, she couldn't hang out any longer. She needed to feel the sensation of Jay-Z's lips on her pussy. The mere thought of those hot pink lips pleasuring her love button to a passion-filled frenzy until her manicured toes curled made her cream in her designer panties. She wanted his sex. Which turned out to be the reason why she called Jigga for a secret booty call as soon as she found out that Lisa was assigned to team up with her on the Eminem hit. A quick nut had turned into a multi-orgasmic marathon. Apparently Jay-Z had a bit of tension he wanted to release from his body also. As bad as Be'oncay wanted to, she just couldn't abandon her lover in the heat of passion. It was just too much to ask for her to leave the warmth and tenderness of his embrace for the ice cold, bitter weather of the Detroit evening.

She did manage to escape eventually, but it appeared that she arrived at the scene a few minutes too late. By the time she arrived the police were already there. She wondered why Lisa attempted the mission without her and why she couldn't wait a few minutes longer for her arrival.

Be'oncay was beginning to question her rationale for remaining a part of these missions anyway. She had a very good life established for herself and didn't want to take a chance on messing things up. She was going to make Jay-Z marry her. The music business had been very good to her and now she was writing and producing her own music. Why would she risk it all on one turn of pitch and toss?

The Panhellenic Council had been good to her. She realized that without the money from the Tupac/Suge mission there was no way that she could have made it in music. She would forever be in debt to Gladiss and Commander Weems, but she wasn't willing to risk her lifestyle paying them back. Since the first second of this present mission Be'oncay had been experiencing doubts. Her heart just wasn't in it any longer. Too many distractions and too many hesitations. The hunger was gone because she was no longer broke and at the bottom of the pile looking up. She was on top of the game and now she was a member of the same society that the rappers she hunted and destroyed belonged to. Be'oncay Knolls was rich and famous.

She pulled out her cell phone. "Lisa? Doctor L?" Be'oncay didn't give her a chance to answer.

"Yeah...mmmf...things went...bad, B. Can't talk...jaw...hurt. Call later." Lisa talked in painful spurts.

"Hey, girl! I'm sorry sister! I'm on my way!" Be'oncay hung up the line, grabbed her coat, and sprinted out the door of her suite. Dr. Lesley was left talking to a dial tone.

Be'oncay navigated the vehicle through traffic. After several hours of arguing with Lisa she had finally persuaded her to go to the hospital. Dr. Lesley had a personal friend who was going to perform x-rays and treat the injury.

It was all out war now! There was no way that Be'oncay was going to let that cracker get away with hitting her homegirl. She felt partially responsible because she was late to the scene. She wasn't there on time to watch Lisa's back. It was her assignment from the start so she felt that Marshall Mathers was her responsibility. Tears of frustration filled her eyes because she felt bad for her friend. The swelling in Lisa's jaw was a far cry from the beauty she normally displayed on television. It made her head look like a pumpkin.

They finally reached their destination. An orderly was waiting at the curb with a wheelchair, like a relay leg in a track meet. The exchange was initiated in a flash and the tires of the wheelchair burned rubber as Lisa disappeared into the building. Be'oncay gave chase behind the rolling vehicle and made sure that Lisa's journey happened without incident. They entered the waiting elevator, made their way up to seventh floor where Doctor Johnston was anxiously awaiting their arrival.

"Over there! Take her vitals! Morphine for the pain. Move it! Move it people!" A group of RNs roamed around the room responding to his directives. There was total chaos. It seemed like a lot of people for a simple jaw injury, but the victim of this injury was not your average person. It was Dr. Lisa Lesley.

Finally, after everything had calmed down and Lisa was on bed rest, Be'oncay exhaled. From the x-rays Dr. Johnston discovered that her jaw was broken in two places. It was going to take a few weeks for the injuries to heal completely. Dr. Lesley was very fortunate because things could have been worse. She was still kind of groggy from the morphine but eventually the queen of Detroit would rise to sit on her throne again.

"Sorry girl. My bad. You okay?"

Lisa nodded in a yes motion, the wire in her mouth prevented her from speaking. She was not used to being a patient.

"O...okay. I'll call the Commander and let him know what's up. Be back in a few." Be'oncay left the room and headed for the elevator. Cell phones were not allowed to be used inside the hospital so she went outside to the patio.

"Weems speaking." It was the distinctive baritone voice of the Commander.

"Yes...yeah. Commander. I messed up bad. Lisa is in the hospital. Everything is fucked up in Detroit..."

"What?!" You could immediately detect the concern in Mr. Weems' voice.

"I'm sooo sorry! Dr. Lesley went out on her own. I was late...she got hit. I fucked up!" Be'oncay was getting hysterical.

"Wait, Be'oncay, calm down. I want you to start over from the beginning. Tell me everything you know. Step by step." Eugene Weems comforted her.

"Okay, sir. Let's see. Okay, I'll start over." Be'oncay gave a blow-by-blow of everything that happened and explained what she knew.

"Okay. Stay there by her side. Don't let her out of your sight! I'm on my way." The line went dead.

Meanwhile, at a hide-out in white suburban Detroit

"Shit! Shit! Shit!" Marshall Mathers could not believe how close he had come to getting smoked. The entire incident was just another notch in the belt of the catastrophes that had been going on this past year of his life. Shit was fucked up for Slim Shady and he was losing it. Boy, was he losing it. Mentally and physically. He had married then divorced, then remarried and redivorced his daughter's mama, Kim Mathers. He was admitted to rehab for dependency on sleeping pills and gained a hell of a lot of weight. He had ballooned to 220 pounds. He looked like an M&M almond, he had gotten so big. The straw that broke the camel's back was when his long time homie and favorite house nigga on Shady Records was murdered. More money, more problems. More fame, more pain. Eminem wasn't happy. Slim Shady wasn't even slim anymore. Living up to the responsibilities of being the greatest white rapper alive was killing him.

Lucky for him he had installed the multi-thousand dollar surveillance system in his apartment and saw the assassin posted out near his pad. Whoever she was, the bitch was definitely deadly. He had come to the realization that there was somebody else out to get him besides his mother and his ex-wife. He wondered who it was. He thought about how maybe it could have been Suge Knight, especially after the hateful comments he made about him in *XXL Magazine*. It was obvious that the former Death Row CEO was jealous of Dre and Eminem's successes. He thought about the haters that he encountered coming up through the ranks and the Detroit rappers he had stolen rhymes from.

Eminem was the Elvis of rap and had just as many problems as the Memphis Rock and Roll legend. He was the Larry Bird of the rap game. The Average White Band of the funk era. He was a white boy in a black man's game and was good at what he did.

The pressure to stay on top was overwhelming because Dr. Dre was slowly moving away from him. Dre was working with his other artist on Aftermath Records. It seemed like the further Dre moved away from Marshall's career, the faster it seemed to sink toward the gutters of the trailer park. Signing 50 Cent had turned out to be the smartest move that Em ever made. Sure, Slim Shady had made money from his own record sales, and even a few chips from his movie, *8 Mile*. Even he had to admit it; 50 Cent was his franchise player but he was outgrowing Shady Records like the Green Giant in Fruit of the Loom briefs. Curtis didn't fit on Shady Records anymore, and it was only a matter of time before 50 moved the fuck on.

"AAAAARRGH!" Eminem plucked another piece of glass from his shoulder. The fall from the window had him in pain from head to toe. He thought about his next move. How was he going to counter against an enemy when he didn't know who the enemy was? It was time to plan his escape. His long time love affair with crystal meth had enabled him to deal with the ever demanding hours of being a rap legend. He would use crystal as an upper, then use the sleeping pills as a downer. Now his life was filled with more ups and downs than a roller coaster. He was cheating life and winning the battle.

As he put the glass pipe to his lips and lavished in the sizzle of the burning dope, his body responded to the smoke session instantly. His eyes glazed over like Crispy Crème Doughnuts and the pounding of his heart increased twenty fold. He immediately knew that something was very wrong this December night. He grabbed his chest directly at the source of the sharp pain as if he were trying to reach inside and fix the problem with his bare hands. He poked at the single digit to speed dial his publicist and miraculously the call went through.

"My...heart...damn. My heart, man!" The phone fell to the floor. Eminem had suffered a heart attack!

Eugene L. Weems, Timothy R. Richardson

CHAPTER 30

Las Vegas, Nevada

"Eminem Under Doctor's Care at Detroit Hospital, Suffers From Pneumonia!"

The newspaper headline caught Gladiss by surprise. The mission in Detroit had turned out horrible. It was total chaos. The assignment in New York didn't go any better. The Panhellenic Council was a messy, chaotic and disorganized cluster fuck. Ms. Nyte didn't like what was going on a single bit. The entire project had exploded in her face.

She wondered if her present group of assassins were still right for the job at hand. Be'oncay was a very successful pop star and besides that, Jay-Z had her nose open like a 24 hour Wal-Mart. Meagan Goodwin was making millions on the stock market and totally involved in a prosperous acting career. Dr. Lesley was a worldwide superstar in athletics and her progress in treating children was recognized globally. Finally there was Ms. Karen Stephins, the new Queen of Smut and a hapless loner. She had her own individual desires at the forefront of her list of priorities. The Panhellenic Council was in chaos and clearly, the four women assassins hearts were no longer in it.

Something was going to have to be done about this situation. The girls were getting very sloppy and things were getting out of hand. Yerfwin had already voiced displeasure with the present group of failures. The failed assassination attempt on 50 Cent. Snoop Dogg was healthy again and out of the hospital running his mouth. The situation in Vegas had actually increased his street credibility. Even Mase was alive and breathing and talk of a comeback was in the making. Harlem's Finest was as unpredictable as the weather.

Gladiss was beginning to doubt her reasons for ever forming the Panhellenic Council. In her eyes, Gangster Rap was a horrible gangrene that was eating away at itself. Eventually it was going to self-destruct, killing itself. It was evident in the wars going on between East Coast and West Coast, Queens versus Brooklyn, Crips against Bloods, double platinum fighting artists who went double lead. The divisions in Gangster Rap couldn't have been more visible if they were placed there by Willie Lynch himself.

Gladiss realized that it was time to set her children free. She wondered if she should allow her angels to spread their wings. She had sat back and watched each member of the Council blossom from confused girls to strong, powerful black women. They had shared their purpose. Lisa's injuries in Detroit and Be'oncay's lack of support because of distractions had cemented her decision. The Panhellenic Council was a mess. There was only one way to clean up the scene, if only he would help her out one last time. She picked up the phone, dialed the secret number and,

"Yes. Weems speaking."

"Eugene, it's Gladiss. I need one last favor." She contacted the clean-up man!

North Las Vegas, Nevada

Commander Weems sat coldly, studying the phone in total discombobulation to what he had just agreed to do. He replayed the favor asked, and his answer over and over in his mind in attempts to make sense of his reply.

"What the hell are you doing?!" He cursed himself in disbelief. He was amazed at what his lips had so loosely uttered, the words that sealed his loyalty in an undesirable perspective. Escaping the criminal lifestyle was the very reason that drove him into the military and he had made a vow to his grandmother after her death that he would leave the unconventional lifestyle forever.

But here he was, after honoring his promise for so many years and accomplishing goals that were beyond his wildest beliefs, agreeing to reenter the doors of his past. He snatched up the receiver of the phone, then slowly fingered in each number with aggression. Nothing happened. He tried the number again, still nothing happened.

"What's the matter with this damn phone?!" He slammed the receiver hard into its cradle in disgust. He studied the numbers on the keypad and realized that he forgot to dial the area code of the number first.

"What's the area code in Compton?" he asked himself. Remembering it was 310, he typed in the area code and then the number.

This time there was an instant connection. It rung a few times before a coughing, mellow-toned man's voice answered. Commander Weems recognized his childhood friend's voice.

"Ecstasy Hayes, is that you my nig?" Commander Weems asked excitedly.

"It all depends on who's asking. If inquiring minds want to know, like the po-po, bill collectors, or my baby mama, hell naw, it ain't me!"

Commander Weems laughed because he knew that his boy was not trying to be humorous. He was dead serious. Ecstasy was a very private man. "Dawg, if you don't cut it out." Commander Weems said.

"My nigga Boo! Hell, nah, I know this ain't my nigga Boo?" Ecstasy Hayes said excitedly after recognizing the voice. They both never felt comfortable addressing each other with their birth name. Nicknames had always been appropriate between the two friends. "Man, what gives me the pleasure? It's been a long minute." Ecstasy Hayes tried to clear his throat.

"It's business and it pays a nice chunk of change. But it's not about the money, X. I owe a friend. Besides, I hear that you doing big thangs with that Orange Haze." Commander Weems stressed.

"Is that right?"

"You know that's right. Have I ever been wrong?"

"You got me on that one. What type of business we talking about, big homie?" Ecstasy asked.

"You know, the type of shit we used to do back in the days. Turning houses into parking lots. The shit I showed you," Commander Weems responded.

Ecstasy responded with a hearty laugh, reminiscing on their past adventures. He understood exactly what type of business the Commander was talking about.

"I was wondering if you was still in the construction business. I had figured you given it up ever since you decided to fly straight and join that white folks gang. I always told you that the military ain't no place for a nigga. They yell out orders from the top to use brothers as bullet catchers," X responded.

"Are you in or what?"

"Of course I am. Just let me know what's good."

"I need for you to come to my town and I'll lace you then my nig. You know where to find me."

"Aight, my nigga. I'll holla then." The phone went dead.

Compton, California

Ecstasy Hayes cruised the streets of Compton in his Phantom Rolls Royce while his mind marinated on the conversation he just had with Commander Weems. He had a lot of respect for Eugene and had met him years ago when him and Big Mike were expanding Nationwide Syndicate to Las Vegas. Eugene Weems ran the streets of Vegas and few things happened without his fingers in the pudding. Ecstasy had traveled all over the world and met people of all types of character and Weems was a top notch mothafucka. Quality recognized quality, and game recognized game. Eventually Orange Haze had made its way to Las Vegas, courtesy of Mr. Weems of course.

Ecstasy had few people that he trusted outside of the brothers he had grown up with in Compton. He had a very small circle of friends and Eugene was a member of that circle. He had taught Ecstasy the martial arts and expert marksmanship of the shooting range. The former Navy S.E.A.L. was among the top three assassins in the world and had mastered the art of making fools disappear from life existence. Nobody knew that the art of killing could be perfected, but those critics had never met Eugene Weems.

Mr. Hayes hopped on the 405 Freeway and continued his trek to his multi-million dollar mansion in the hills of Palos Verdes overlooking the ocean. He headed home to his lovely wife, Joy, and his young son, Del Hayes. He parked his Rolls in the motor port, then caught the elevator to the third floor of his home. The four story mansion was the epicenter of his billion dollar real estate business and marijuana empire. He owned properties all over the world. Ecstasy had it all. A beautiful wife, luxury vehicles, thousand of properties and over a billion dollars cash. He was on top of the world.

Don't get it twisted though. Things were not always peaches and cream for Ecstasy. He had witnessed his millionaire father murder his mother, then blow out his own brains right before his eyes. He was only 10 years old when it happened. He had grown up in a foster home in Compton, living as a peasant with no idea of the fortune awaiting him on his 18th birthday.

He had lost one of his closest friends on the way to building his empire. He still missed Reggie Robinson with a passion and thought about his fallen brother every day. The only person that knew the intimate details of his father's existence was also murdered.

Ecstasy was a mystery man and his past was a confusing puzzle. Cali Syndicate was all he had, along with his small circle of friends. So when Eugene Weems called him for his assistance in taking care of some important business, it was all good. Of course he volunteered his help because for Ecstasy, true friends were hard to find.

Las Vegas, Nevada

Commander Weems had two more pieces of artillery that he needed to secure to complete his weapon of mass destruction; his northern California comrade, Tiptoe, *The Ghost*, born Timothy Richardson, East Oakland's most ruthless assassin that its streets had produced. This nigga was a real head case who got pleasure from killing for the sport of it. But he was most definitely reliable, loyal, effective, and a professional at infiltration, the key element that made him so deadly.

Tiptoe is a nickname dubbed to him by his peers for being so quiet in his approach, appearing without a sound and leaving the same way. The added *The Ghost* title came about for two reasons. He was born with a hair disease called Alopecia, which caused him to lose all his hair as a child. He went through elementary school with no eyelashes, no eyebrows, and no hair on his head. All this in the 1970s, at a time when bald heads were far from fashionable, unless, of course, you were Telly Savales. The bald head definitely was not for kids. And since kids are cruel, the talk and disrespect began early for him. Timothy went to elementary school with a note from his parents and doctors that requested of the school district to permit him to sit in class while wearing a knitted cap. This was an effort to obscure the bald headed name-calling from beginning. Wrong! It only incited issues such as kids running by and snatching his hat as they passed, screaming rude names like Mangy Mutt or Patchez. That elicited laughs and ridicule from the girls, which was very embarrassing.

This sparked the vicious fighter and violent beginning for a kid that would grow to become a ruthless killer.

Part two of why he was called The Ghost is because of his nature of being the complete opposite of what a person would profile

247

a killer to be. You would never suspect Tiptoe, the truth lover/pimp/con man/suave businessman with so much finesse, as the methodical torturous killer who was so violently volatile that even those whom he worked with at times feared his ability to take murder to the next level.

Commander Weems reclaimed the receiver and tapped in the 415 area code, followed by the phone number. A deep ratty voice answered. There was no need for small talk. There were only a few individuals who possessed the number to Tiptoe's direct line.

"Yo, Love One, this is Eugene. I'm reuniting the team, so by the time we hang up, there should be an airplane ticket waiting for you at Oakland International Airport. I look forward to seeing you, folks." Commander Weems ended the call. Without a doubt, he knew he could depend on Tiptoe to show.

Now Danga would be an entirely different story. Commander Weems and Danga had a history that was created between the sheets and we all know if you play with a woman's emotions, you're liable to reap repercussions. The ugly break up between the two was never amended. Commander Weems knew that Danga was the type of female who held grudges, but he also knew that she loved him. He was banking on that very emotion of love to be his key to forgiveness. He knew it was going to take a little ass kissing, sweet talking, and a star role playing apology to correct the bad blood he created between him and Danga.

He reminisced back to the first time he met Danga. It was at a Las Vegas club, nothing more than a meeting ground for unchecked

248

lust for a one night stand for men. He recalled every detail of that night from the moment he gazed at his Armani watch as if pressed for time, then picked back up where he left off, scanning the room. There she was! A glowing gem that robbed him of his attention. A true dragon fire in the essence of being a drop dead gorgeous hotty with curves that sent a man's imagination and hormones running the hundred yard dash. He had found the strength and courage to make his way over to where she stood sipping on a drink. He whispered something slick into her ear as he came up behind her and put his arm around her waist.

She spun on her heels to meet the face of the voice and arm that was encroaching upon her person. Commander Weems had raised his hands in the air, taking a step back and began to explain.

"Excuse me baby, my bad. I peeped you posted from across the room, lookin' all sweet an' beautiful and thangs. So I figured I would come an' say hello and see if a light skinned brotha like myself could get the blessing of knowing the angel that stands right before my eyes, who's more beautiful than an evening sunset."

He recalled putting down the mack. Danga couldn't help but blush. She knew the bullshit he was popping off at the mouth was nothing but game, but it was so sweet and original that she began to melt from the shit. The nigga was fine and dressed to impress.

She leaned into his ear and whispered softly with a sexy voice, "Nigga, I give you your props. You are a smooth talker. I like it in you though. They call me Danga. And you?"

"Eugene Weems baby, but I go by Boo. But you can call me whatever you want. Just don't call me late for dinner."

They both shared a laugh, capturing each other's eyes, probing one another's mind. Then stood in silence holding their gaze with a steady acceptance, deliberately prolonging the moment to the admiration that flourished within them now. Danga's smile was a flirtatious one. She didn't want to admit to herself that Eugene's touch was comforting, but shivers that stormed through her body wouldn't allow her denial to overlook that it was also invasive and manipulative.

Eugene interrupted the intimate glance and undressed Danga with his eyes. He had the same kind of overwhelming physical allurement as she, but with an adventurous and threatening edge. He visualized her naked in a cheap motel double bed with black and red braided hair on the pillow. Hazel brown eyes smoldering to record his intimate touches. He remembers wanting to slide his hands up her thick, firm legs to play in the playground under the short black tight-fitting dress.

He imagined licking her there and tasting the sweetness of the chocolate and wondering if the color of her hair on her head was the same as the silky hairs between the joining of her legs. He was a potential victim of a fat ass that led to a tapered waist. To him it was the pleasurable body part that would bring the best of entertainment between the sheets. He smelled the aroma of expensive perfume, eyed the chocolate milk colored breasts that seemed to be bursting out of the red bra that she wore, with a tight black halter top. At the time she was somewhere in her early twenties, with the most full, suckable lips that he had ever seen. Commander Weems had never actually cleared his mind of Danga.

Eugene decided to make the call to Danga. It was worth giving it a try, even though he thought that she might decline his offer. She answered her private line.

"What's up, pretty face?" Commander Weems said.

"Who is this?!" Danga said nastily into the phone.

"It's me, yo' baby boy. The only man who was capable of making your fantasies a reality."

"Nigga, please. Who the hell is this? Tell me fast before I hang up in your face!"

"Chill, baby girl. This is Eugene. I just thought that I would give a queen a call to see how she was doin'."

"Oh...Eugene. I was just thinking about you the other day, wondering if trouble had caught up to you or if you was dead or alive, because you ain't called to check up on me in a while. What took you so long to get at your Baby Girl? You could have at least called to say hi, bye, or fuck you or somethin', but it's really nice to hear your voice. What's good with you?"

Commander Weems was surprised at her friendly attitude and figured she must have let bygones be bygones, but he could never be sure when he was dealing with Danga.

"I'm trying to reunite the family back together. I must admit, I got some real serious shit about to go down. I need my most important piece to complete the puzzle, which is you. Before you say anything, I want to apologize for our past misunderstandings. I do want to let you know that you always and forever will hold a special place in my heart. I thought you should know that," Commander Weems said with all honesty.

She melted from his sincerity and was now willing to assist him an any way he needed her. "Count me in. Just let me know what I got to do."

Commander Weems laced her with instructions. He now had all the elements to bring havoc to the world of Hip Hop. Fourplay Assassins were now back in business!

THE END

Eugene L. Weems, Timothy R. Richardson

THE HIT LIST

WARNING! To all you Hip Hop studio gangsters, paper copy characters, wanna be pimps, playas, champion ho' slayas, ballers, shot callers, macks and killers. The time has come to start respecting a woman's mind, body and integrity in your music, videos, interviews, and personal encounters. If you fail to take heed to this warning, you too may become a victim of the Fourplay Assissins Hit List.

If any of you chumps, squares, lames, busters, undercover rapists, gangster rappers and any other Hip Hop artist have a problem with what's been said in this book, holla at us in a real way, not on no punk ass CD; we not into poetry. Not on no gay ass video; we not into theatrics. Not in no interviews; we ain't with the he-say, she-say. Especially not with no lawsuits, because that's another form of snitchin'. Let's keep the law out of it. Express yourself like a real G. and get back at us on paper, that makes paper, that green shit that is respected by us all. If it don't make money, it don't make sense for the Fourplay Assassins to blast that ass. Beeyotch!

If you are a celebrity and have beef;
Contract:

The FOUR PLAY ASSAINS, and let them handle your lightweight.

This is Inked Out Beef Books!!!
Universal Publishing LLC.
C/O the Four Play Assassins'
PO Box 99491
Emeryville, CA 94662

Sneak Peek Preview
The Other Side
of
The Mirror

Eugene L. Weems
Timothy R. Richardson

AUTHOR'S NOTE

For argument's sake, I want you to assume that this is a work of fiction.

I want you to assume that everything herein is the product of an overactive imagination, exacerbated by long stretches of solitary confinement and everything that comes with it: sensory deprivation, arrested development, loneliness, boredom, or insanity.

Assume there's no such thing as other dimensions, time travel, or holes in the fabric of time and space; that the world you know is the only world there is.

Assume everything you learned from your parents or other family members and society is absolutely, one hundred percent true; that the way you were taught to perceive things is correct; that your religion, morals and values are right; and that those whom aren't like you or whom don't share your views are simply *wrong.*

Assume your race is superior to others; that your nation is essentially good; that those nations who don't like your nation are essentially bad; that war is necessary to protect your way of life; and that you have nothing to do with your government's policies and actions.

Assume you are living just the way you were intended to live; that you have achieved your full potential; that you are complete, happy, and content; that this is as good as it gets; and anyone who dares to envision something new or better is just pure *evil.*

By any and all means, assume that life as we know it is the only life in existence similar to ours; that there is ...

Now, navigate the depths of possibility that you are wrong about everything. Dare to dream. Dare to explore every catacomb of your imagination. Or better yet, we dare you to journey with us to places that would challenge all that we as a human race have come to accept, acknowledge, and understand as *normal*.

Allow us to introduce ***The Other Side of the Mirror.***

CHAPTER 1

George W. Bush was born with one goal in mind, to become President of the United States. It had been a long time and a vigilant journey, but finally his dream was going to become a reality. As he took a long glance at his handsome reflection and soaked in the moment of January 2001, so much had changed since his childhood days of growing up wealthy in the state of Texas and enjoying the lifestyle as the son of a wealthy oil mogul. He remembered the stories all too well of how the Bushes came to power and how his great, great-grandfather came up with the marvelous idea of importing African slaves. From cigarettes to cigars, the quality of Bush products was known throughout the world, with assets over $5 billion and products in every country.

Why would George W. Bush want to become President of the United States? It was simple, because it was what he wanted, and he usually got what he wanted. The unwavering desire to have it all served as his motivation. He once watched the Miss America pageant on his big screen plasma television, and a surprised Laura Welch from Georgia was crowned the winner. George made a few phone calls, organized a meeting, and enter the new Mrs. Laura

Bush, a perfect trophy to show off to the critics in the political realm. She was drop dead gorgeous with a runway model build and crystal clear hazel eyes. It was love at first sight, at least for a lust-filled George. Ten years, five mansions, over $3 million in jewelry, and two children later, they were a textbook couple. I can think of over a billion reasons why any man would want to be George W. Bush. He was young, wealthy, powerful, and had a beautiful wife. The final cherry on top was his landslide victory over Al Gore and Joe Lieberman to win the presidency of the United States.

George had many accomplishments, was a Rhodes Scholar, Phi Beta Kappa, Yale University, youngest Texas state senator and CEO of Bush Enterprises. Everything had come so natural and easy. Money couldn't buy everything, but it sure purchased a lot for him. He had bought his way to the top and slicked more palms than the oil used to lubricate all the cars at the Indy 500. His philosophy was, *everyone had a price; they just didn't know how much.* He was arrogant, rude, self-centered, a male chauvinist, and of course as racist as a Confederate general. He was a political fox that could out talk the most experienced politician, and everybody loved the image George W. Bush paid to create. Women adored him and men admired him from a distance. He had a lifetime commitment from his public relations firm; negative portrayals of him disappeared faster than Michael Jackson's nose. He was America's golden boy, and now the first family was going to be treated like royalty.

The soon-to-be-President of the most powerful nation in the world took one more look at himself in the full-length antique family mirror. It had been in his family for generations, passed down from his great, great-grandfather, Winston George Bush. It had been rumored to be the luck of the Bush fortune. The very same mirror was passed down to George's father from his grandfather, and now it belonged to him. It was no secret that every male Bush had spent countless hours admiring their perfection in that very same mirror. It was now his turn to hold the family treasure, and he was in his prime.

He studied his features. His eyes, nose, facial features and chiseled physique. Carefully inspecting every inch of his body for any hint of imperfection. He marveled at his flawlessness. He was the same perfectionist that would stay in his mansion for weeks as a teenager, at the sight of a pimple. Now was his time to shine.

He looked every bit the part of a man in his mid-twenties. The skin treatments had worked wonders. It was now time to meet the vast audience that awaited their new American King.

Finally, he had to perform his daily ritual of kissing his reflection in the mirror. It was the only way that he knew how to start his day. He had tricked so many people, paid his way out of so many different situations, fooled even the most astute and highest paid lawyers. He had created an image of a demi-god in the media and throughout the land, but he could not fool the mirror.

The mirror showed the truth, and George hid from the truth. He could fool his wife, his kids, his employees, his political allies, and even 90 percent of the American voting public, but he could not fool the other side of the mirror.

One additional kiss for good measure as he departed to his awaiting audience. His beautiful wife Laura was waiting with his twin daughters, Barbara and Jenna. Everything had worked out perfectly; one strong family with perfect Eurocentric genes. The epitome of excellence, a true royal family.

Thousands had gathered for the celebration as George fulfilled his dream of becoming the President of the United States. Many thoughts went through his mind as he began his acceptance speech.

After his initial thanks to his family, colleagues and numerous associates, he began to wonder if he hadn't bitten off more than he could chew. America was the most powerful nation in the world, and even George began to question his decision. So much was going to be decided by this President. Six new supreme court justices would have to be appointed, the issue of reparation for African Americans, a diminished Social Security fund, oil embargos by Iraq, communism in China, the reunification of Germany, the lack of control of the CIA and FBI, and the internal problem of the national debt. The rich wanted to stay rich; the poor wanted to be rich. So many problems and so little time to solve them.

George had his mind made up. He was going to be the greatest President ever. He was going to change the world. In spite of all his intentions to be the Kobe Bryant of the political world, he had to select a Vice President and a secretary of state out of the multitude of candidates willing to serve as his right hand.

He had selected his college roommate and trusted friend, Cheney Burrows, as Vice President and running mate. An absolute yes-man who virtually idolized George. He did not have the worry of Cheney stabbing him in the back, and he could always keep him in check.

The position of secretary of state was another story altogether different. He had to appease his African American voters, who had all but declared him the next John F. Kennedy. Mass consumers of his tobacco products, the African American women loved his young, educated white male look, almost straight out of *G.Q. Magazine*. His slick persona and hip talk had made him popular with the men. He even played the saxophone.

Although he deeply despised African American people, there was a strong push to keep them happy, so he reluctantly appointed an

African American woman as his secretary of state. It was sheer genius, as he satisfied two critics with one appointment, African American voters and women's advocates. After a nationwide search, he had found the perfect candidate, Ms. Condoleeza Kincaid, a fellow Yale Law School graduate who was a popular news anchor for WGBN in Chicago. She was also an *oreo* and married to Bill Kincaid, a white divorce lawyer. There was no secret to how she worked her way through law school and gained a reputation among the male Anglos at Yale, becoming their first African American sexual experience. The past was the past, and that was several years and several pints of tequila ago. Now Ms. Kincaid was a loving and almost committed professional wife.

All the other cabinet members would be the usual menial appointments. A Hispanic here, an Asian there, a few more women, and maybe somebody Islamic. President Bush wanted his cabinet to reflect his voting public. He was a real wolf in sheep's clothing and everyone was convinced that he was a messiah. Most of the critics loved him, and those who didn't were paid to like him a lot, the first candidate to run as an independent and win by a landslide. *A man of change* was his theme and you could hear the chants of "Bush! Bush! Bush!" from his millions of followers. At times, he would mistake the chants of "Bush" for "Lord" in his own narcissistic mind. He felt as if he were the people's Lord, a modern day savior, and they loved him.

It was a new day in the life of George Walker Bush. His dreams were finally made into reality, President of the United States of America, the most powerful country in the world, maybe even the universe.

Later on that evening, Cheney Burrows and his wife, Mary Ann were settling in for their first night at the official residence. The events of the day were still difficult for him to stomach. Butterflies still circled around mercilessly in the abyss of his soul. He was a total mess and still could not believe that he was the Vice President of the United States. He enjoyed his newly found status as the second most powerful man in the world. The aspirations that dwelled in his head were many. He was all too familiar with the trend of the Vice Presidents eventually taking the post of President, so he didn't mind playing second fiddle to Mr. George Bush. Besides, he relished the role.

Over the many years of their friendship, he was used to being second to George. If the President was Batman, it was safe to say that Cheney was Robin. There were a lot of perks playing second to a billionaire, and he graciously accepted them all. He did so with a genuine appreciation of all things granted to him by his lifelong buddy, George Bush.

They had been through so much together as roommates in college, George usually serving as the comet and Cheney the comet's tail. As youngsters, they were inseparable. Even in the many women George used like bathroom tissue, he usually got the prom queen and Cheney dated the chubby best friend. On more than one occasion, after George broke a beautiful damsel's heart, Cheney was there to gobble up the leftovers. He was not the handsome hunk that George turned out to be. In fact, he was the short and nerdy intellectual. There was not a subject in the world that escaped Cheney's knowledge. He was a walking Encyclopedia and had the IQ of a brain surgeon; the main reason that George kept him around, and everybody knew it. Cheney was not even remotely a threat to George's status and was as replaceable to him as a member of Mike

Tyson's entourage. It was the looming potential of being expendable that kept Cheney on his toes. He wanted nothing to come between he and George. It was safe to say that George was his idol. Thus, the reason for him being appointed as George's running mate and become Vice President of the United States.

Cheney had worked hard to climb the ladder of success. The wealth in his family was the result of a state lottery ticket that his dad won when he was a junior in high school. The consummate student, he was always academically blessed but financially cursed. His father was a half-decent automobile mechanic in Chicago, Illinois. His mother, a beautician at a local beauty salon. He got all of his knowledge from spending countless hours with his grandmother, who was a former college math professor and had just recently passed away. There was a rumor that the Burrows' intelligence gene skipped an entire generation, and that was the reason he was so smart.

He had scientifically created a formula that came up with the six winning numbers of the Illinois lottery at 15 years old. Even his parents doubted the validity of his formula until one day a drunken Paul Burrows gave it a try. Twenty-seven million dollars and several years later, Cheney was treated to the finest education money could buy. Rumors soon circulated about his sudden rise to family fortune in his freshman year at Yale. He was an easy target for the senior ivy leaguers to pick on, and one day George came to his rescue. They have been friends ever since that day. George was the money and the power, and Cheney was his brains, a match that was made in heaven. George did not worry about the critics because his family was wealthier than all of theirs combined. But still, the route that Bush took to fortune and fame was vastly criticized.

Cheney had made a pretty good living for himself by being George's flunky. He had a decent-sized mansion, a few luxury vehicles, millions in his bank account, and now was Vice President of the United States. He even owed George for introducing him to his beautiful and wealthy wife, Mary Ann Jennings, the darling princess of the Jennings clan, owners of a multimillion dollar chocolate company. Few children in America had not tasted the pleasures of a delightful Jennings chocolate bar.

Mary Ann was spoiled rotten as a kid, and even worse as an adult. Her brief love affair with George was short and torrid, several sexual acts in discrete locations graphically described by George to Cheney. She was far too much of a slut to have ever been considered a housewife for him, but a perfect mate for Cheney. George hooked them up about ten years ago and they have been inseparable.

The only person as bossy as George was Mary Ann. Her demands were mammoth and her mouth was as big as the Grand Canyon. She was a real slave driver and she rode Cheney relentlessly. His self-esteem was as low as a doormat. Her criticisms of his refusal to stand up to George were endless. She criticized him for leaving his secure position as a member of the House of Representatives. She criticized his decision to remain loyal to George. She criticized his hair, the clothes he wore, and his attitude. It was safe to say that he believed her family was better than Cheney's family. She had never worked an honest day in her life and she knew all about Cheney's road to family riches. She did not respect him. The only reason she married him was to keep tabs on the antics of Mr. and Mrs. Bush. It was no secret that Mary Ann was still in love with George. Cheney tolerated it all and kept his opinions to himself. Over the years, he had become the consummate sponge.

Condoleeza Kincaid lived in a world of firsts. She was the first person in her family to graduate from college, the first African American woman to graduate from Yale Law School, and now the first African American woman to serve as Secretary of State. She loved being first. She had even cum first when having sex with her mate. No words could describe the feeling that she felt about being appointed Secretary of State. She was going to be on the cover of every magazine; *Jet, Ebony, Newsweek, Time, Sisters 2 Sisters, Essence,* and even *People.* She had finally made it to the top, the third most powerful person in the United States. She loved being in the spotlight. All of her years as a token had finally paid off.

She was still in shock about her nomination endorsed by President Bush and subsequent appointment. She knew that her qualifications were more than enough of the post, but her skin color had prevented her from entering the social circles of the Yale Law School elite. Many of the white males loved having sex in secret but would never be caught fraternizing with a black girl. George had never spoken more than two words publicly to her, but she was spotted a few times leaving his off-campus home. Cheney didn't even know that she was a Yale Law School student until the graduation ceremony.

So much had changed for her over the years. She had screwed her way to the top of the news chain at WGBN in Chicago. She went from the cute, little African American weather girl in the tight miniskirt to primetime news anchor, the most popular personality on the nationwide television station, first in her timeslot. Millions of people depended on her information and her image was omnipresent on the majority of televisions in America. Condoleeza was a household name; everybody loved her.

Needless to say, her marriage to Bill Kincaid, a wealthy white lawyer from Kansas, was on the rocks. They seldom had time for each other, there was not enough time in a 24-hour day. They had no intention of having children, so sex was a thing of the past. All in all, Condoleeza loved having her white, successful *trophy* to show off among her NAACP friends in social circles. Her happiness was safely in the hands of public perception, and everybody viewed her as being happy with Bill. She could conjure up a smile almost as fast as Diana Ross. Her pearly whites graced the pages of many magazines and televisions. Condoleeza was a socializing sensation and wouldn't be caught dead without a smile on her face. Now she had the whole world as a stage, the perfect diplomat and politician for the most important position in George Bush's cabinet.

CHAPTER 2

The move to the White House was definitely a step down for President Bush and his wife, Laura. Several upgrades would have to be made for this luxurious billionaire couple. They were used to being waited-on hand and foot, usually African Americans, because in George's mind, they made the most loyal servants. Their mansion in Texas was almost twice the size of the White House, with double the staff. Some major remodeling had to be done before George would feel comfortable performing his Presidential duties. He viewed his new surroundings as being inadequate despite the numerous changes that had been made. He knew that he was going to spend as little time as possible at the White House and that Laura was already missing their Texas mansion.

His first meeting was with Vice President Cheney Burrows in the Oval Office. The newly elected President sat at his desk with the American flag on the wall behind him. It was their first meeting together and Bush beamed with a glow of confidence. His Vice President sat there with a nervous look on his face, as if they had just hijacked the White House. "I'm going to need your undying support," President Bush declared with the confidence of a championship coach.

"Whatever it takes," Cheney said in response. Bush gave him a fatherly smile of approval. They knew that Cheney was his main man. He was happy that his Vice President was at his beck and call.

So many other agencies were against him; jealousy in the Senate, opposition in the CIA, FBI and the DEA. The alphabet soup of American politics was a mixture of so many organizations with so many functions that it was impossible to pay off everyone. Vice President Burrows was going to be his political watchdog. Even President Bush knew that he was going to need help governing the most powerful country in the world. There were so many issues, so many campaign promises, and he was not going to lose his position as the new American messiah. The image of his country had taken a severe blow and the deficit was at an all-time high. All of the countries in the world were depending on him to change things around for the better. He had made bold and powerful moves as the CEO of Bush Industries, and his loyal followers expected nothing short of a miracle during his tenure as President. Now was the time for America to regain its position as a worldwide power, despite a $20 trillion deficit.

He pressed a button at the end of his desk, and seconds later, an African American uniformed servant appeared, "Yes, Mr. President?" Benson the butler inquired as humbly as possible. George ordered coffee, and within seconds the steward disappeared.

It was time for them to get reacquainted. "How's the family?," Cheney asked, as if to break the silence. He knew the answer to the question before he even had the nerve to ask. He knew all about the royal family and the immense demands of Mrs. Bush. She couldn't possibly be happy with the move to the White House and the departure from her Texas palace.

President Bush went into a long tirade about the inadequacies of the White House. Cheney listened intently to all the details and knew that he had opened the flood gates. The steward returned with a silver tray, a pot of coffee, and two cups, each imprinted with the Presidential seal. He skillfully poured the coffee, "Can I get you something else, Mr. President?"

"No, thanks," he said, and gave him a glare of discomfort. The steward took it as his cue to get lost and exited the room.

The President then continued his conversation with Cheney. He described the duties that came along with being the Vice President, how important it was for Cheney to maintain a short leash on the CIA and FBI. He demanded that his Vice President keep a watchful eye on anyone who was against his presidency. It was very important that his position be held in the highest regard. He wanted to be the best President ever, the people's messiah. For the first time, he acted as if he needed Cheney. George Bush was a master manipulator and knew exactly what he was doing. He needed the mind of Cheney working for him behind the scenes. He was the face, body and spirit, but he needed the mind of a genius to persevere.

These two men had engaged in many conversations before, but somehow this conversation was on a different level. George spoke with power and the voice of a unbridled leadership. He was powerful and very persuasive. Cheney was almost in tears. A new bond was developed, even more solid than the previous relationship the two men had shared. So much had changed in the heart of George Bush. He was fearless and charismatic. The spirit of all the Presidents in past dwelled inside of him. Cheney had a new appreciation for the spectacle that was taking place before his eyes. He liked everything about George Bush. He loved his best friend and now blindly supported him. He committed himself to his President's every effort, whim and demand. After hearing George speak as President of the United States, it was safe to say that Vice President Cheney Burrows was willing to die for his Commander in Chief.

The transition to power for Mrs. Bush was not going quite as smooth. There were too many items and not enough space for the First Lady. One of the first items to go back to their Texas mansion was George's family vanity mirror. Laura was never told the legacy of its existence, thus looked at it as a worthless piece of furniture. Every single inch of space in their master bedroom was already accounted for, mostly with her belongings. She cursed the former First Ladies of such a small area. There was no way that she was going to survive for four years in the White House, and re-election was out of the question. She commanded the movers like a drill sergeant barking orders. The White House had never seen a person who demanded more. Nothing was satisfactory. So much had to be done. She had to find tutors for the children, hire more maids and butlers, organize dinner parties, and find a beautician. Life was so much easier in Crawford and it would have been a simpler task to have George pay to have their mansion moved to Washington. It was going to take a miracle for her to adapt to life in the White House.

Secretary of State Condoleeza Kincaid made her move easily, like a thief in the night. Somehow, she had talked Bill into staying back in Chicago to take care of things. She as a free woman, ready to paint the town. Freedom she had only dreamt about was now at her fingertips. Her position as Secretary of State was going to give her the opportunity to travel the world at the expense of the government. It was heaven on earth. So many places to see, so many people to meet. She was going to be the most recognized Secretary of State, ever. She looked forward to meeting the leaders of the world on behalf of the President. She looked forward to making her boss look good and was determined not to let him down. He had made an excellent decision in appointing her. She was intelligent, beautiful, dedicated, and able to mingle with the social elite. She had a familiar face that many world leaders had seen before. The magic of television had reached even the most primitive societies. It was s dream appointment with all the trimmings. She had settled in her condo in no time at all. It was finally time to relax and celebrate a bit. She couldn't remember the last time that she had a decent orgasm, so she grabbed the thick yellow pages, looked under the long list of escort services and did a little shopping for male companionship.

Eugene L. Weems, Timothy R. Richardson

CHAPTER 3

Vice President Burrows didn't waste any time in getting to know the people under his command. He knew that his job was to play the background while the President was in the public eye. He realized that someone had to do the dirty work of maintaining democracy and recognizing any enemies to America. He was the perfect man for the job. He hated anything that was not Anglo Saxon male, and held high ranking in the Illinois Chapter of the Ku Klux Klan. He was in strong opposition of President Bush's appointment of Condoleeza Kincaid to Secretary of State, but he would never question the decision of his fearless leader. He was too much of a coward. Few people truly knew of his blatant dislike of anyone that wasn't white. He was the perfect candidate to head the branches of federal intelligence. He had made his way to the CIA Headquarters and was in a closed-door meeting with Donald Prescott, Director of the CIA.

It had already served to be an eye-opening experience for the Vice President. The public was never admitted inside of this building. Few even knew of its existence and there were no facilities for visitors. His entrance was through a long tunnel that emerged into a closed room protected by several suited guards. The entire episode seemed like a scene from a science fiction movie. Cheney immediately recognized that he oversaw a powerful tool in American government, international intelligence. He had an entire army at his beck and call. They could eliminate anyone from existence, violate the privacy of anyone in the world. It was all up to him and the President to determine who the enemies were and point a finger in their direction.

Cheney loved his position of power; Donald Prescott answered to him. He was higher on the chain of command than the director of the CIA. Director Prescott addressed him as *sir* and shared intricate details of the many secret missions going on throughout the world. Cheney had done his research and knew all too well about the exploits of the agency. The power was in his hands now and he was ready to abuse it. He and the President had came up with a list of names and organizations that they wanted fully investigated. They wanted to combat terrorism and anyone who threatened democracy. The first name on the list was Dr. David Lee Phillips, an African American lawyer who was creating a lot of noise about African Americans receiving reparations. Second was Muhammad Abdul Wail, an Arab activist from Arizona. Third was the UBN, United Blood Nation, a street gang that was more powerful than any organized criminal gang that America had seen. The list had over 40 handpicked individuals selected by the President and Vice President.

Cheney smiled as he looked down the list and quickly added Condoleeza Kincaid, Secretary of State. The future of American intelligence was in good hands. He was already giving commands and setting deadlines as if he were President. He was already abusing his power. The only person in America that he had to answer to was George Bush. He was glowing in confidence and a new sense of power that had been a stranger to him for far too long. He liked being in control. Now he knew why good Vice Presidents became decent Presidents. It was only going to be a matter of time before he had his opportunity to run the nation. He could live with his role as a follower because he knew that one day he would eventually take the lead.

After a long week on the road spent lobbying for various amendments, staffing the remaining cabinet vacancies and pledging to fulfill campaign promises, President Bush was finally back home in the White House. He exited Air Force One and entered the White House under the close protection of his Secret Service men. He arrived inside his sleeping quarters in desperate need of rest. So much was on the young President's mind. The movement for reparation spearheaded by Dr. David Lee Phillips was gaining support. It was to the point where it was moving to the forefront of issues important to the President. Even in all of his fame and fortune, he could not afford to lose the African American vote. His appointment of Condoleeza was the perfect pacifier, but now his African American supporters were hungry for real food.

Something had to be done, but there was no way that he was going to stick to his campaign promise of establishing a trillion-dollar reparations fund for the ancestors of slaves. He was not prepared to bless African American people with that much financial power. He laughed at the thought of coons running wild in society, buying up all the Cadillacs and gold chains. Chaos would rule their neighborhoods. He figured that all the money in the world couldn't turn their plight around and regretted his decision to support the reparations bill.

He noticed the lack of space in the White House sleeping quarters. Laura had brought so much junk from their Texas mansion and 80 percent of the items belonged to her. As he went through the clusterfuck, he realized that many of his belongings were missing. He wondered where they had disappeared to. He had never slept in a room so small and had never travelled without a full moving crew. He hated sleeping away from the luxuries of his mansion and especially missed his daily ritual with his family vanity mirror. It was his security blanket and his source of good fortune. He could not go for more than a week without re-energizing in front of the vanity mirror.

He went through all the items carefully this time, making sure that he did not overlook anything. He became upset when he realized that his family vanity mirror was gone from the location where he had directed it be left. "Laura," he yelled, his voice echoing throughout the White House.

A sleeping Laura was startled and feared the worst. She knew of Bush's rampages. He could become very brutal on a moment's notice. His philosophy was *spare the rod, spoil the wife and child.* On several occasions, he had become physically abusive toward her and the children. She knew from his tone that this was one of those occasions. "Yes, honey," she replied as meek as a sheep.

"Where is my mirror," George calmly asked.

Laura almost lied, but instead she opted for the truth, "I had it shipped back to Texas."

The President was overcome by a fit of anger. His eyes became red with fury from his soul. The love for his wife was immediately robbed by the hatred that filled his heart. In a chain reaction, he slapped Laura silly without hesitation. He grabbed her by the neck and choked her until she was on the verge of passing out. Then he tossed her aside like a ragdoll and stormed out of the room. Laura curled up into a ball, fearing continued assault. She was safe for the moment, as President Bush made his angered exit to Air Force One. He had one destination in mind, his Texas mansion.

Many thoughts went through his mind as his de-escalated from the incident with his wife. He wondered how a woman so beautiful could be so damn stupid. It was an obsession for him to be able to admire himself in the mirror. It was as much a part of his life as his wife and children, the sun, the sky, the moon, and even the air he breathed. To think that she shipped it back to Texas without a second thought made him so angry. He was not going to tolerate impertinence, especially from his wife and children. He was a devout Atheist and had no belief in God. In his opinion, man controlled his own destiny. He was going to realize how wrong he was.

The Vice President had an extremely busy week fulfilling his duties while the President was away playing diplomat. Somebody had to maintain the security of the country and keep tabs on the many turbulent situations emerging. Even with his genius, Cheney had trouble juggling the social, economic, political, religious, agricultural and business concerns. It was mind boggling. The past administration had not made any progress, but he was going to come up with the answers even if it killed him. He was a workaholic with one goal in mind, proving himself to President Bush.

He also did a little political positioning of his own after he realized his new sense of power. He was overseer of both the FBI and CIA. The directors of both organizations had to answer directly to him. The power of the strongest intelligence gathering forces in the world were at his disposal, unlimited power to make anyone he desired public enemy number one, and he was going to utilize every single ounce of it. Cheney was really beginning to smell himself. So much power in the hands of a once powerless man could turn out to be extremely dangerous.

He glanced over the most personal details of the lives of every single person on the list he provided to CIA Director Prescott. He knew that he had access to two very powerful tools. Information was the most important weapon in civilized society and he wanted it all. He could record all phone calls, have vehicles identified, monitor bank accounts, check employment history, have every second of your day monitored, and even have your home invaded. Just one phone call and a simple phrase, "I believe that he's a terrorist." To make matters worse, his jurisdiction was worldwide. He could not believe that so much power was granted to one man. He could make a person disappear from existence or die from a sudden heart attack. Cheney Burrows had come a long way from the scary nerd people once bullied in school. Now he was all-knowing, omniscient, with destruction at his fingertips. He was Vice President of the United States.

In the luxury of her spacious condo, Condoleeza savored her newly found freedom. She relaxed in the confines of her Jacuzzi, naked, glowing and sexually satisfied. The luxury of privacy had been a stranger to her for far too long. So much had changed in her life with her appointment. She had already scheduled her first political visit to France. It was going to be a wonderful tenure being a diplomat and having entire countries cater to her every whim. Actually, the President had not done bad in his appointment. She was an excellent speaker, sexy, and articulate. Many world leaders would love to try and seduce her into their beds. Condoleeza was going to take this opportunity to meet and greet the wealthy, and with a little luck, maybe she could find a new husband.

After all of the years of hard work, she had finally been accepted into mainstream America. So many of her African American brothers and sisters had labeled her a sellout, but now she was getting the last laugh. She had made it out of the ghetto and now rubbed elbows with the political elite while the same bitches that criticized her became dependant on the welfare system. White America loved her and had accepted her as one of their own. She was rich, sexy, and as close as possible to being white, the most politically powerful woman in the country. She had a green light to see the President with any issue that her heart desired. Victory was hers and Condoleeza was going to get as much as she could while the getting was good.

Eugene L. Weems, Timothy R. Richardson

CHAPTER 4

President Bush had finally touched down on the landing strip of his Crawford, Texas, estate, over 1400 miles from the White House, and he was glad to finally be home. His anger still boiled toward his wife and he was grateful for the distance between the two of them. Finally, he had the opportunity to spend precious time alone with his mirror, but two tall and muscular Secret Service Agents followed him like a shadow. He already had plans of forcing them to post up at the front entrance of the estate and protect him from predators.

Cheney had designed the security system himself and there was only one system like it in the world. It was owned by Ahmed Akbar, a Saudi Arabian oil billionaire, and he paid twice as much for his installation. The Gladiator Fortress was impenetrable, a complex combination of sonic traps and infrared detectors controlled from a satellite hundreds of miles overhead. No thief in the world could come within a mile's radius without being detected. George controlled the entire system from the confines of his Rolex watch. It was the ultimate in high-tech gadgets and his Texas estate was in good hands.

George was going to enjoy his time alone with his vanity mirror. He was like a compulsive gambler who had not made a wager in months. He missed the beauty and perfection of the solid gold frame and almost mystical reflection it produced. It was more than a vanity mirror to him. It was the mirror to his soul. Many times he would stare, hypnotized by the imagery displayed in the mirror. It was vivid and real, and he would talk to himself for hours and hours. He was his worst critic and had shared so many secrets with his vanity mirror. It was his best friend, his closest confidant, and soothing therapy for his fragile mind. Nothing gave him more satisfaction than being able to talk to his own image. It was how he planned his day, contemplated his future, and handled all of his insecurities. He loved his vanity mirror because he was vain.

As he made his way to the rear entrance, he saw a sight that he could not believe. He saw this vanity mirror in a large box outside, near the service entrance. He was outraged. It was like a rare and precious jewel left laying on the ground of a New York subway. Although its frame was solid gold with diamonds of all colors, the stones were so huge to the average person they might be considered to be fake. George could not believe that his wife had been so careless with such a priceless possession. She was going to pay dearly for her idiotic mishap. If she only knew the history of the mirror, she wouldn't have dared to be within a thousand feet of it, more or less, than to have it removed out the place of safety. George's ancestor had stolen the mirror from an African tribe when they invaded the tribe to collect slaves to bring to America.

He ran quickly toward the tall box and greeted it like a long-lost love. He carefully cut open the box, almost desperate to see if any harm had been done to his vanity mirror. He was amply relieved that it was still intact, as flawless as the last time he had viewed its perfection. Everything was in its proper place and it glistened in the sunlight. He quickly ordered the two Secret Service men to carefully take it upstairs to his suite. George closely supervised the move and made sure it occurred without incident. Once completed, the agents were ordered outside and George was finally alone with his vanity mirror.

Privacy at last, he had a lot of making up to do. He immediately grabbed one of his imported towels and began the process of his cleaning ritual. The thought of strangers handling his most prized possession made him sick to his stomach. He was beyond upset with Laura and was almost to the point where he wanted a divorce. Calmer heads would prevail once he realized that as a leader of America his personal life was an open book. The President of the United States of America could never divorce the First Lady, no matter how stupid she appeared. His vanity mirror shined like new money and almost met even his high standards. As he viewed his crystal clear, full body reflection, he was in love again. The gold shined like the morning sun and the image that was in the mirror was an exact replica of his perfection.

He had so much to share with his vanity mirror. His last conversation with himself was at the White House, after the inauguration. So much had changed. The metamorphosis took place almost instantly. He had changed from one of the wealthiest men in the world to the most powerful man in the world. He was officially the President of the United States. He had the power to start a world war, the power to appoint lifetime judges to the Supreme Court, to create and cancel laws that ruled the land. No single man outranked him, everyone was under him. He was the Commander in Chief, the Chief Executive Officer, and the Head of State.

George Bush loved the way he looked in his vanity mirror. The spirits of his ancestors were proud of their native son. No other Bush had reached such lofty heights, no other Bush had been so famous and noteworthy. He was immortal and would go down in history as the first Bush to become President.

He glanced at his reflection and began his conversation with the image in the mirror. He talked about the issues burdening him. His pitiful wife, spoiled children, and the incompetence that surrounded him daily. He bared his soul to his vanity mirror and it listened intently. He studied his reflection and marveled at its splendor, so handsome, so smooth, so articulate and so omnipotent. He talked on about his position of authority, how wonderful he was, and how great it was to be George Walker Bush.

As the conversation escalated beyond the level of conceit, it became therapeutic. It was an episode of intense verbal masturbation. Nobody had ever thought so much of himself. The more he talked the deeper he fell into an abyss of self-glorification. In his view, America needed him in this time of crisis. No President in history could measure up to his dashing good looks, political charm or stunning personality. He was the ideal President. The compliments flowed like a river. "I am wise, worldly and wonderful. I am here to protect and save America. I will be remembered as the messiah that saved the world. I'm great. I will create so much. Come to think of it, I am their God. I am god. I am God!"

He approached his reflection and kissed the vanity mirror. The mirror began to shake and the image of his reflection turned into a black man. It was a black version of himself. Handsome, same height, weight and physical build. George couldn't believe his eyes and was stunned beyond belief. Was it too much talk about reparations? Too many days on his feet?

He stumbled away from his vanity mirror. His mind was playing a horrible trick on him. He went over to his bar and prepared himself a tall goblet of Hennessey XO. He drank it like bottled water. Before it had reached the bottom of his throat, he poured another cup, and another, and another until, eventually, the entire contents of the bottle was gone. He wanted so desperately to remove the image he had seen. George Bush could never picture himself as a nigger. A spear chucker, a coon; not George Walker Bush. It was a brief nightmare that drove him to the point of opening yet another bottle of Hennessy XO.

He eventually drank himself to a stupor. He sat alone in the luxury of his massive bedroom on his expensive designer leather recliner. He was still in disbelief. He needed a break, but the sensation of intoxication had overwhelmed him. The horrible reflection was a distant memory as he glanced in his vanity mirror and saw the purity of a white face. He began to laugh to himself, almost hysterically, as he thought about the image of him being black. It was funny as hell, a place that he would one day call home. But for now, he sat there, calm and relieved.

Eventually, he gathered up the courage to make amends with his vanity mirror. He figured that maybe the mirror had gained a personality of its own and decided to punish him. Maybe it was his ridiculous campaign promise of supporting the reparations bill and giving a trillion dollars to African Americans for 200 years of slavery. Finally, he just realized that he had spent too many hours in his mirror adoring himself. He was pleasantly intoxicated and exhausted from all of the events of the past week. It had been one hell of a rollercoaster ride, and that was just the beginning.

He gathered himself, took a long, hot shower, and changed into his pajamas. He stumbled over to his mirror to begin his customary ritual again. He looked at the blurred image in the mirror, a fraction of the man who had just become President. He was still in love. His vanity was not permanently damaged. The self-gratifying compliments began to erupt out of his mouth again, like lava from a volcano, "I am handsome. I'm the most powerful man in the world. I can buy anything or anybody. Everyone has a price; they just don't know what it is yet. I am God. I am God. I am..."

He was close to his reflection, almost kissing his image in the mirror. The reflection changed to the black image and snatched his body through the vanity mirror. George was startled as he emerged on the other side of the mirror, as if he had been pulled through a time warp. He was magically transported to another place and time. He was no longer in the confines of the country he ruled. He was introduced to his version of hell.

He glanced around his new environment and saw a lavish master bedroom almost as wonderful as his, but slightly different. It was a room fit for royalty. Fine beautiful and exquisite furniture was in every corner. It stretched the length of a professional tennis court in both directions, east and west, north and south. In the place where he entered, behind him was a marvelous vanity mirror that rivaled his family mirror in its beauty. It was almost identical in its features. He analyzed the texture of the gold frame as it sparkled magnificently. He walked over to the solid oak dresser and noticed the spread of fine, exquisite jewelry. Rolex watches, diamond rings, emeralds, and a jewel-encrusted crown. It was like a fantasy come true. He picked up the watch to inspect its quality, an exquisite Presidential Rolex. He tried it on and it fit almost perfectly.

"Stop, thief! Security! Security!" a voice shouted that stunned George. Within seconds, two tall, black, muscle-bound men, figures worthy of being defensive linemen in the NFL, emerged through the entrance. George was instantly taken down with a banned WWE move. He had never experienced such pain and was used to being on the giving end. The restraint left him motionless and powerless. He

288

lay there in awe and wondered who in the world had the audacity to order someone to place their hands on the President of the United States. Somebody had some serious explaining to do, and fast. He looked up for an explanation and another black man stood tall and powerful over him. He was regal in his demeanor. His eyes strained but finally focused and made out the facial features. He could not believe who he saw. It was the black man that appeared in his mirror.

A powerful surge of energy went through George's body. His entire being was consumed by fire and he felt excruciating pain from the top of his head to the bottom of his feet. The princely figure was the last figure George would see, and afterwards there was darkness. The two black men handcuffed his hands and applied ankle chains to his motionless frame. They then carried his body away like weekend baggage. President Barack Obama wondered how a servant had passed several guards and made his way into his living quarters. His security minister, Solomon, had some serious explaining to do. His fortress was impenetrable, millions had been spent on his protection. The Black House had never been infiltrated.

President Barack Obama felt violated. A white man had touched his possessions and had invaded his privacy. So much had changed since the whites had been released from slavery so many years ago. Blacks had tried so many things to get rid of them, even genocide. *Those wretched whites are like roaches. They are everywhere and serve no purpose.* Something had to be done to prevent this from ever happening again, even if he had to make an example out of that intruder to prove his point. The newly elected President had a lot housecleaning to do. He was the leader of the most powerful country in the civilized world, the Republic of Acirema.

Two entire days had passed with no word from President Bush. The two Secret Service agents posted out front became worried beyond belief. Agent O'Neal finally got the nerve to enter the mansion and made his way to the door of the master bedroom. He knocked gently and first, "Mr. President?" No answer. Seconds later, "Mr. President?" Still no answer. He feared the worst. He pulled out his semiautomatic weapon and blasted the locks in an attempt to gain entrance through the steel doors. He was successful as he kicked the door from the large hinges. He was inside the master bedroom and the room appeared vacant. There were no signs of a struggle, just a neatly piled wardrobe and a Rolex watch. "Mr. President?" He called out, praying for a response, but no answer was in sight. He searched the closet, the bathroom, and even underneath the bed. He noticed no signs of forced entry. President Bush had mysteriously vanished.

Vice President Burrows was disturbed by a phone call, "Mr. Vice President, President Bush is missing," a breathless voice said.

Cheney was in shock and did not know what to do. He hoped that it was some cruel inhumane joke by the President to test his loyalty. "What do you mean, he disappeared?" The Vice President demanded an immediate explanation.

"He's gone," the voice muttered in defeat.

"Who is this? Where are you calling from? What is the meaning of this game?" Cheney was in no mood to display a sense of humor.

"Sir, this is Agent 005, Peter O'Neal. We escorted the President to his Texas estate and he is missing."

There was a brief silence. "I want your ass to meet me at the White House ASAP. I don't know what kind of games you Secret Service people are playing, but I want answers." He slammed the phone down with a hostile authority and its plastic casing cracked it in several places.

Cheney was fuming and confused. How could the leader of the most powerful country in the world just up and disappear without his personal Secret Service bodyguards knowing his whereabouts? It just didn't add up. It's unheard of. He had just met with him a few days ago. Cheney had installed the security system himself. Something had to be wrong. Somebody had made a grave mistake. How do you lose track of the President? Heads were going to roll.

Cheney quickly retrieved his cell phone and dialed the phone number to George's Texas estate. No answer.

He quickly called the private line at the White House. After several rings, Laura answered, "Yes, George," she hoped, speaking in an apologetic voice.

"Sorry, Laura, it's me Cheney." He could feel the disappointment. "Is the President available," Cheney said.

"No, he's been gone for the past two days. I believe he went to Texas," she said in response.

"Thanks. Sorry to interrupt you," Cheney said, avoiding further comment until he had a chance to get the full story from Agent O'Neal.

He exited his house and dove into the back of his Mercedes Limousine while his driver drove like a madman in the direction of the White House. A pain appeared deep in the pit of his heart for his missing friend. He cared deeply for President Bush. His love for him was borderline obsession. A million thoughts went through his mind as his vehicle surged on through the traffic. How could the President have vanished from thin air? Somebody knew all of the answers. Many scenarios circled through his recollection. Maybe it was a horrible joke, maybe the President had a mistress, maybe he was hiding somewhere within the confines of his massive Texas estate, maybe he was underneath his bed. Cheney was dumbfounded for the first time. He did not have the answer to any of the questions.

Soon he was within the gate of the White House and he cleared security. In no time at all he was in the large briefing room and several concerned faces were already there awaiting him. "What the hell is going on," he barked to a silent crowd. All eyes were on the Vice President now, making it impossible for his entrance to go unnoticed. The most powerful people in America were there and they all stood bewildered and tongue-tied. CIA Director Prescott, FBI Director Richardson, Joint Chief of Staff Admiral Striker and Secret Service Head Bob Smith, Vice President Burrows outranked them all. It was at this time he realized the magnitude of his power.

In the absence of President Bush, he was the acting Chief Executive Officer of the United States. He was all powerful and he was the HNIC (Head Nigga in Charge). He began to like being in charge. The power to intimidate powerful leaders became a welcome drug to his system. He wanted his authority to last. He rampaged on, "I want answers! All of your asses are on the line. I have never seen such incompetence." The room remained silent.

CIA Director Prescott broke the ice, "We have agents combing every inch of his Texas estate. We have questioned Mrs. Bush. Nobody knows anything."

Next, it was Secret Service Agent Smith, "My men reported the incident and we still have no leads. No signs of a struggle."

"That's ridiculous! That's absurd! Nobody just disappears into thin air," acting President Burrows said in the direction of the two men.

"That is my account of what happened, sir," Agent O'Neal said in response.

Cheney approached the agent like a raging bull and slapped him with mighty force. He then grabbed the agent by the collar and yelled, "You find George and you'd better find him soon!" Agent Smith quickly came to his deputy agent's rescue. Nobody abused CIA agents without his consent. Cheney Burrows realized the error of his ways. A leader could never be seen in public losing control of his emotions. He released the agent, gathered himself, and realized that he had an audience.

He regained control like a proven politician. "How will we explain this to the American public?" The most popular President ever was missing. He had disappeared without a trace. The tabloids and news media are going to have a field day with this. "We have to do something and do it now." The urgency of the situation had taken on a new meaning.

Cheney headed for Air Force Two with Agents O'Neal and Jones. They were headed to the Texas estate. The two agents would receive additional questions during the flight. He wanted every single detail of the President's disappearance from the two men who saw him last. Secret Service Agent Smith described Agents O'Neal and Jones as two of his best agents. Cheney had never seen such incompetence, and serious upgrades were already being thought of for the Secret Service Academy. He could not believe that the President's protection was left in the hands of such idiots. No wonder so many Presidents had been assassinated.

They touched down on the landing strip and the two agents were sweating from the vicious interrogation on the flight. Cheney was out of his seat before the jet had come to a complete stop on the Texas estate landing strip. He knew that the security system at the President's estate was impregnable. He had installed the system himself and nobody got past the Gladiator Fortress. He did not have a clue as to what was going on, but somebody was going to have to pay for this absolute travesty.

The three men stormed into the Texas mansion. There were several members of the CIA and Texas branch of the FBI already present. Cheney found the lead investigator, Paul Winston. He received a briefing on their findings and there were no new developments to report. He escorted Acting President Burrows to the master bedroom. Nothing had been touched. Cheney quickly grabbed the Rolex watch from the dresser and examined it. After a brief look, he knew that it was George's watch. It was the exact same watch that he had programmed for the security system years ago. He knew immediately that something was seriously wrong. The President loved his watch and he would not have been caught dead without it.

He scanned the room and everything was in place. No sign of a struggle or forced entry, aside from the massive door removed from the entrance. Cheney was even more confused. It was unlike George to disappear unannounced. He liked being the center of attention too much. Something had to be done fast. He quickly called CIA Director Prescott and organized another meeting with the top officials in the Executive Branch of government. He was going to need some time to figure out his plan of action. He ordered Paul Winston to have everyone removed from the mansion. He demanded that everyone be sworn to secrecy and that anyone who leaked information would face severe punishment. He spoke with bad intentions and nobody doubted the seriousness of his statement. Within minutes, the room was empty.

After a few more minutes, the entire mansion was empty. The acting President stood in the room alone, holding the diamond-studded Rolex watch of his closest friend. He was already missing him dearly. All of a sudden, he was gravitated toward the vanity mirror on the north side of the room. A strange feeling overcame his person as he glanced at his reflection in the mirror. He knew that something was wrong and he was going to figure out what it was. Nobody could disappear from the face of the earth, especially the leader of the most powerful country in the world. Nobody would be foolish enough to kidnap the President of the United States. He used every ounce of his extensive brain power but still could not rationalize what had taken place.

He glanced around the room one more time, hoping that his lost friend would appear and yell out, "Surprise!" Unfortunately, he stood alone in the utter silence. He was frustrated beyond belief and began crying tears of intense pain. For the first time, he was without his protector and ally. He felt alone for the very first time since he was a child. He could not believe how things had gone so horribly wrong. In a burst of confidence, Cheney gathered himself, looked into the mirror and said, "I am going to find you, old friend. I don't care what it takes. Even if I have to comb every inch of this planet, I promise that I will find you, George Bush, even if it kills me."

George Bush awoke in a prison cell, alone and still in shackles. After a few moments, reunited with his senses, he realized that the episode from earlier was not a dream. The pain that was still present throughout his body confirmed the reality of the entire episode. Every part of his person throbbed in agony. He had never experienced so much pain. He still did not know where he was or how he had managed to get there. Somebody had some serious explaining to do. Who was that mysterious black man? How dare they place their hands on the President of the United States. He reached for his cell phone that he kept in his coat pocket. He realized then that he was in his bathrobe. He had never seen the inside of a prison, but he knew that he was entitled to a free phone call. He would then call Cheney Burrows and settle the entire situation.

He heard the noise of heavy footsteps coming in his direction. They stopped directly in the front of the entrance of his cell. "All clear, Cell 12," said a deep soulful voice, and the door magically slid open. Two unformed black men came into the room and told George to get up on his feet.

"This way," the tall, black, muscular man said, pointing in a direction leading down a long hallway. George feared for his life, so he humbly complied. He struggled to his feet and walked painfully down the hall. He noticed several other uniformed blacks walking in the hallway. He had never seen so many black men and women in uniform.

As he walked down the hall, he glanced into the jail cells that lined the walls. He noticed that all the occupants were white inmates. Immediately, he thought he had been kidnapped by some African nation, but he did not recognize any accents. Their English diction was totally American and the atmosphere was far too advanced. He was then led through a steel sliding door into a dark room where he was pushed into a seat at a table. "Lights," one of the guards barked. The room was immediately illuminated. The two guards departed and George was left alone with handcuffs and ankle chains attached to his body. He glanced around at his new environment that seemed like some type of torture chamber or interrogation room. The walls were padded and appeared to be soundproof. He wondered who could possibly have been behind this crime, and why. He was terrified and willing to pay every penny of his $3.5 billion for his freedom.

He heard more footsteps heading toward the room and two black men in fine designer suits came walking through the door. One took a seat at the table across from George; the other remained standing. The one that was standing stared at George like he was nothing, a worthless piece of trash. The one that was seated seemed calm and collected. He smiled pleasantly and introduced himself, "I'm Special Agent McBounds, National Security of Acirema. Who are you and where are you from?"

George could not wait to identify himself, "My name is George Bush, President of the United States."

The two men burst into near hysterical laughter. George felt as if he was at the wrong end of some kind of joke. The sitting agent finally gathered himself and said, "But seriously, who are you and where are you from?"

"I'm George Bush, newly elected President of the United States."

This time, a more serious atmosphere prevailed. It was obvious that the joking mood was temporary. The atmosphere had turned serious. The standing agent said, "There is no such country. The United States? A white man never could be elected President of anything. You are insane!"

George avoided eye contact. The standing agent was all business and he did not want to argue with him. He sat in silence for a minute and then said, "My name is George Bush and I'm from the Unites States of America."

The two agents were still puzzled and gave up all hopes of an intelligent conversation. The seated agent then said, "Okay, George, what were you doing in the President's bedroom?"

George realized that he was fighting a losing battle and was not about to tell them the story of what actually happened. "I don't know," he said, and this apparently set the unidentified agent off. He approached Bush and brutally slapped him in the mouth. It was a punishing blow that made Bush see stars. Blood trickled down the side of his mouth and he felt violated.

"No more games," he yelled, "We want answers!"

Bush just sat there, shaking nervously in fear of another attack. He didn't know what they wanted to hear and he searched his mind for the right answers. He would have said just about anything to avoid being pimp slapped again. Several thoughts lingered in his mind as he thought of some type of logical solution to his problem. He wanted the whole episode to end and to go back to his life of luxury at home in Texas.

The barrage of questions from the two men continued and George finally gave up. He figured the best thing to do was to give no answer at all. He didn't want to fall victim to any more physical attacks, and his plan worked. Eventually, the two stopped. Finally, Agent McBounds said, "We are charging you with ten criminal counts and you're facing a sentence of 125 years. Do you have money for a private attorney?"

Bush was relieved; he had plenty of money. He just needed to call his wife in Washington D.C., "May I make a phone call," he asked with a new sense of confidence.

Agent McBounds un-cuffed his hands and handed him a slim cordless phone. George looked at the numbers on the keypad and they appeared foreign. He had never seen symbols like that before, nothing close to American numbers. He thumbed-in the symbols where he recalled the numbers on an American phone would be located and hoped for the best. No connection. He tried it again, but no luck. The standing agent smirked, then snatched the phone from his hands. George sat there like a school boy being disciplined. It was a living nightmare and he had never felt so hopeless.

So much had changed in such a short period of time. He went from the most powerful leader in the world to a situation of hopelessness. He had lost all of his worldly possessions and contact with everyone who had ever loved and worshipped him. His life had been perfect, and now he wondered what had caused this recent turn of events. How did he end up in such a horrible place where nobody knew of his greatness? He was a leader, a man of great wealth, and almost a God. George wanted to end it all and contemplated suicide for the first time. Any sort of afterlife would have been an improvement to his present situation, even the eternal fires of hell.

Two weeks had passed since the disappearance of President Bush and Vice President Burrows was worried beyond belief. The story that the President was sick and in bed at his Texas estate was beginning to lose its credibility. The rumors had already began to circulate, and despite his power as acting President, he still could not stop the freedom of the press. The public was tired of the picture that was being released to the media. They wanted to see a live image of the President. People in several circles around the country feared the worst. The television talk shows and tabloids added fuel to the fire with their assumptions of what happened to the President. One London tabloid had reported that he had been abducted by aliens. Another source said that he was on a secret vacation with Elvis. The stories continued to pile up like Pete Rose gaming chips, each one more sensational than the last. Vice President Burrows had to do something about the hype, and soon.

There was still no word about the President's disappearance. Just one lead had turned up and it wound up being a silly prank from a bunch of college students at University of Nevada, Las Vegas. The Vice President was desperate and had even ordered CIA Director Prescott to comb the nation for a stand-in for the President. He figured that somebody in this country of over 500 million people had to have a similar build and facial resemblance to President Bush. He could serve as a visual pacifier until the real President returned. Cheney was running out of time. Even he knew that an imitation stand-in would work for only a brief period of time. Nobody in the world could match the charisma, style and pure arrogance of George Bush. The President was one of a kind. He had to come up with a master plan that would work in the long run. He sat in the Oval Office and the genius of his mind worked overtime coming up with a solution. He was the mastermind behind Bush's rise to power and glory. He was the one who made all of the decisions for him. He was the person who had helped Bush pass every exam he had taken since he was an undergraduate. The most powerful nation in the world was about to take a serious blow to its ego. How could America ever recover from a President disappearing into thin air? What would that say about homeland security? Nobody would ever feel safe if the President came up missing. Who could be next?

Cheney Burrows tried desperately to devise a plan. His thoughts were interrupted by a ringing telephone. "Vice President Burrows," he said,

"Mr. Vice President, we found your man. He's a cowboy from Oklahoma. His name is Jim Irvin," CIA Director Prescott announced triumphantly.

"Is he a perfect physical match," the Vice President asked almost in desperation.

"As perfect as perfect can be. The two could pass as Siamese twins," Prescott replied with a wry smile in his voice.

"I want to meet him immediately," the Vice President said, and made the mood serious again.

"It's a date," the agent said.

The two conspirators hung up the phone almost simultaneously. Cheney leaned back in his leather chair, a bit more relieved after his conversation with the CIA director. He knew that he knew the President better than anyone and that if anyone could train somebody to act like Bush, he could. The second phase of the plan was already being orchestrated in his diabolic mind. In the few weeks as acting President, Cheney had grown comfortable in his new role as Commander in Chief. Besides, if something else had to take his departed friend's place, he thought it might as well be him. He rationalized his decision with all of the work that he had done in the shadows while George Bush lived in the limelight. He had his mind made up and couldn't wait to meet cowboy Jim Irvin. The nation was in total chaos and the climate was as intense as any wartime situation. In fact, the Vice President viewed the episode as an act of war, and in war there were casualties. More than a few good men gave their lives to protect America. Thousands of people have died to protect American democracy as we know it. In his eyes, what difference would it make if we lost one country boy from Oklahoma if it cured the problem in the White House?

Condoleeza Kincaid had just finished another black tie event sitting for the President. These days, her calendar was stuffed like Thanksgiving turkey. She had at least two events scheduled a day. She predicted her position as Secretary of State would keep her busy, but this was totally ridiculous. She had not talked to the President in weeks and started to worry. The questions about his health and well-being were becoming more frequent with each engagement. To make matters worse, the only person she had had talked to was the Vice President and he did not keep his dislike for her a secret. On more than one occasion she heard the "N" word come out of his lips in reference to her. The feeling was mutual. Cheney was one of the few white men that she had not slept with. She viewed him as a coward and kiss-ass to President Bush. The only reason he had made any progress was because of his relationship with Bush.

Less than a month and she was already growing tired of her post. She needed a break and the journalist in her wanted some serious answers. It was more than she had bargained for. Her dreams of worldwide vacations had been shattered. The fact that she had to deal with Cheney on a daily basis made matters worse. The media darling enjoyed being in the spotlight, but it was a little too much attention for even her. She wanted to do her job and prance happily across the globe, not tend to countless questions about the President and his secret condition. She wanted him to do the job he was elected to do. Her instincts told her that something was desperately wrong at the White House and she was going to get to the bottom of what it was. She knew that Cheney was up to something, but he would never confide in her. The George Bush that she knew would never avoid the public eye, even in terms of sickness. Something was terribly wrong in the White House and Condoleeza was determined to get to the bottom of it.

Laura Bush had not seen her husband since the day he almost strangled her to death. She was beyond the point of worry. George had disappeared before for weeks, but he would usually take time to give her a call on the telephone. He would usually phone her with some kind of ludicrous request or demand to fulfill. George loved bossing her around. She had to admit that deep inside she enjoyed being able to roam around without a leash.

In secret, she wished that he were dead so that she could enjoy his multimillion dollar estate alone. She already had her first vacation around the world planned out, but she could never let the world know her true feelings. She was being watched around the clock by the Secret Service and the CIA. The government was treating her like a common criminal. She wanted the invasion of her privacy to end. Her woman's intuition told her that there was something wrong; she just could not pinpoint what it was. Cheney Burrows spoon fed her information from time to time, but nothing concrete. She never trusted him and she didn't like his opinionated ways. She thought that maybe her husband was on some type of top secret Presidential mission or just spending time away from her to cool off after his last episode. Either way, she was enjoying her break from his constant scrutiny.

The kids were already used to their dad being gone for long periods of time. They had all but accepted their African American nanny, Mabel, was their surrogate mother. She had practically raised the two of them since birth. George spent too much time funding bribes, greasing palms, and running all of his many companies to be much of a father. Laura loved pampering herself too much and felt that she had done more than her share of work as a parent by giving birth to two children. The act of giving birth twice had almost permanently damaged her runway model physique. She thanked the devil for the miracle of modern day cosmetic surgery. She was on a first-name basis with her cosmetic surgeon and had gone through every procedure in the book.

She was in no big hurry for George to make it home. She savored the moments he spent away and loved being in control. She could be herself when she was alone but had to put up a front whenever her husband was around. Mrs. Bush longed for the day when she no longer had to play that silly game anymore. She wanted to be free. The only thing that kept her around was the promise of unlimited wealth, a little pain every now and then for a large amount of pleasure later. George often would get angry and call her a high-priced whore. She didn't mind because the wounds from the beatings and verbal abuse would all heal in time. She knew that in the long run that she would get the last laugh, all the way to the bank.

ABOUT THE AUTHORS

Timothy R. Richardson, aka *TipToe*, is a multi-talented producer and Hip Hop artist and founder of Crime Wave Clothing. He is also co-author of The *Other Side of the Mirror, Head Gamez,* and *Players Exposed.* He is from Oakland, California.

Eugene L. Weems is the bestselling author of *United We Stand* and award winning author of *Prison Secrets.* Weems is co-author of *The Other Side of the Mirror, Head Gamez, and Players Exposed* and *Bound by Loyalty.*

The former kick boxing champion is a producer, model, philanthropist, and founder of No Question Apparel and Inked Out Beef books. He is from Las Vegas, Nevada.

THE OTHER SIDE OF THE MIRROR

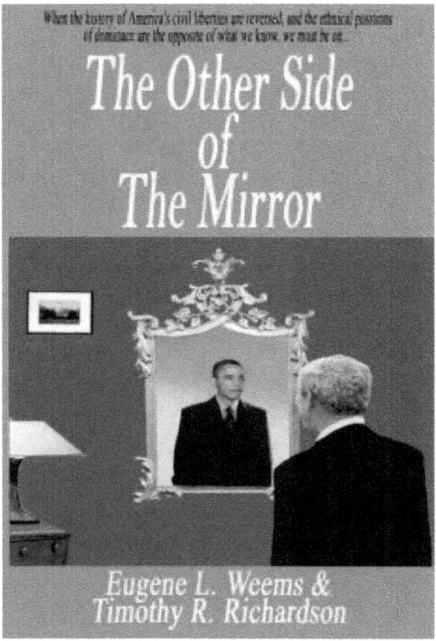

Eugene L. Weems
Timothy R. Richardson

What if Black was White and White was Black?
Could there really be an alternate universe out there?

Join this array of multi-layered characters, each with their own
secrets to protect, in their attempts to solve the mystery of the
missing President. This story of political intrigue, sexual innuendo
and blatant back-stabbing will shock, mystify and intrigue you,
with a surprise ending that will leave you breathless!

$14.95   303 pgs   6x9 Paperback   ISBN: 978-0-9840456-0-0

UNITED WE STAND

A TRIBUTE TO THE AMERICAN FALLEN HEROES OF THE WAR ON TERRORISM

By Eugene L. Weems

United We Stand is a beautiful collection of inspirational artwork and passion-filled poetry created as a living tribute to the American troops who have made the ultimate sacrifice for our country in the war against terrorism.

100% of the proceeds from this book will be contributed to provide care packages for the active duty troops who remain engaged in the war overseas and provide college scholarship trust funds for the children of our American fallen heroes.

$14.95   95 pgs   6x9 Paperback   ISBN: 978-1-4251-9130-6

Hip Hop/Music

Available Now

JACKSON RANCH RESCUE Feline Sanctuary is a nonprofit organization which aids abused, abandoned, injured and neglected felines.

We rescue animals in distress whenever an urgent call is received. Our volunteers work with feral cats to help them become familiar with humans so they can be adopted. We have had much success in this area.

Your generous support and assistance is needed. You can help by making a charitable contribution that will go toward the food, shelter and veterinary care, including spay and neuter costs, for these beautiful animals. Your contribution is tax deductible and will be gratefully received.

Contributions can be sent through PayPal using our email address: jacksonranchrescue@juno.com.

THANK YOU FOR YOUR GENEROSITY

www.ingramcontent.com/pod-product-compliance
Lightning Source LLC
Chambersburg PA
CBHW070217260626
47160CB00002B/582